Dead Man's Walk

Antony James

First published in 2017 by
The Irregular Special Press
for the Inspector Morse Society
Endeavour House
170 Woodland Road, Sawston
Cambridge, CB22 3DX, UK

Overall © The Irregular Special Press & The Inspector Morse Society, 2017
Text © remains with the author

All rights reserved

No parts of this publication may be reproduced, stored
in retrieval systems or transmitted in any form or by any
means, electronic, mechanical, photocopying, recording or
otherwise, except brief extracts for the purposes of
review, without prior permission of the publishers.

Any paperback edition of this book, whether published
simultaneously with, or subsequent to, the case bound
edition, is sold subject to the condition that it shall not by
way of trade, be lent, resold, hired out or otherwise
disposed of without the publisher's consent, in any form of
binding or cover other than that in which it was published.

This book should be regarded as a piece of fan-based fiction published on behalf of
The Inspector Morse Society to raise money for the Colin Dexter memorial fund, and
is therefore an unofficial publication not connected with the original Inspector Morse
novels of Colin Dexter as published by Pan Macmillan UK.

ISBN: 1-901091-68-6 (10 digit)
ISBN: 978-1-901091-68-7 (13 digit)

Cover Concept: Antony J. Richards

Cover Illustration: Dead Man's Walk, Oxford

Special thanks to Andy Ffrench of the *Oxford Mail* for being one of the
novel's first readers and for suggesting a number of amendments.

Also thanks to Colin Dexter who was the original inspiration for this
book and who encouraged me to write it, helped with the plotting
and various other aspects of publication.

Typeset in 12pt Palatino

For James
and in memory of
Colin

Preface

"He won't be meeting you anywhere, sir.
Chief Inspector Morse is dead."

(Final lines of chapter seventy-six in *The Remorseful Day*)

Colin Dexter's last (Detective Chief) Inspector Morse adventure was published in 1999. It brought the total number of novels to thirteen, plus a collection of short stories. It is no great spoiler to say that in that final book, *The Remorseful Day*, Endeavour Morse dies, of natural causes. The film version of that story was first shown on British television in 2000, and at the time it was thought that would be the last anybody saw, or heard, of Morse, especially when the actor who portrayed the character on television John Thaw died prematurely of cancer just two years later. However, the franchise continued, successfully with *Lewis*, and more recently the Morse prequel *Endeavour*, on television, not to mention a theatrical production (*House of Ghosts*) that has toured the United Kingdom. But for those who prefer the written word there have been no new Inspector Morse novels – at least until now.

This unofficial fan-based publication tries to redress that balance. Obviously, like *Endeavour*, it must, by necessity, also be a prequel, but one that tries to explain some of the anomalies found in the books and films. For example, when did Morse change from driving a classic Lancia to the more familiar Jaguar.

Dead Man's Walk contains all the elements that were so successfully combined in the original Colin Dexter novels: there are deaths and red herrings aplenty set against the backdrop of Oxford. There is a nasty academic (Sir Michael Chipperfield, Master of Lonsdale College) with whom Morse has to contend, there is opera, a crossword-type clue, beer in copious quantities, a new romantic interest for Morse, some well loved characters in the form of Sergeant Strange and police surgeon Max de Bryn, and even, just as in the television series, a guest appearance by a (young) person named Dexter.

The puzzle, set in early 1971, finds Morse a frustrated Detective Sergeant under the guidance of McNutt (first introduced to television viewers in *Masonic Mysteries*) solving a mystery as intriguing as any that he would later encounter. As usual, Morse is metaphorically several furlongs ahead of the field but alas on the wrong racecourse. The story concerns the apparently unconnected deaths of two men, save that they share the same name as two of the three original Oxford Martyrs. Surely their demise along Dead Man's Walk is no coincidence, nor the work of some religious maniac revelling under the name of the Oxford Ripper?

Dead Man's Walk is not only the title of this book, but is actually a path in Oxford, aptly named for it was where the Jewish dead were, in Medieval times, taken in procession from the city synagogue to the burial ground, situated where the University Botanic Gardens presently reside.

It is my sincere wish that you enjoy reading this new case for Morse as much as I did researching and writing it for you, and that I have done justice to the original brilliant creation of my friend, Colin Dexter. Part of the profits from this publication will be going to the Colin Dexter memorial fund being organised by the Inspector Morse Society (www.inspector-morse.com).

Antony James

Chapter One

"One should always look for a possible alternative and provide against it. It is the first rule of criminal investigation."

(Sherlock Holmes – *The Adventure of Black Peter*)

Sherlock Holmes did not like coincidences. Neither did Detective Sergeant Morse of the newly formed Thames Valley Police. That was just one of several things that the two detectives had in common. With a degree of self-satisfaction, Morse pondered the possibility that this too was a coincidence. Yet Morse was not in good humour of late.

It was a year into the new decade, with new currency due (if God had wanted a decimal system surely he would only have had ten disciples, Morse maintained) and new opportunities, but not it seemed for Morse considering his somewhat slow career progression within the force. He had joined seventeen summers ago and was still only a Detective Sergeant. He knew that he was better educated than most of his colleagues, (the result of time spent at St. John's College, even if he hadn't completed his studies). He was more intelligent too, certainly more so than those who sat on the top floor at Kidlington. Yet he, Morse, was never given the chance to shine in his own right, although he had already been instrumental in solving a dozen or so investigations. It seemed that the only thing of importance to those on high was the creation of new ways to hamper a case. Every week without fail, there appeared on his in-tray a new questionnaire, or some such paperwork to waste his time, supposedly aimed at improving efficiency. Why did the masters not trust to the common sense of the ordinary policemen such as Strange – and policewomen for that matter – to go about their work dutifully and be out and about preventing crime without such impedance? Instead they were being evermore confined to the police station, or the new so-called panda cars, which only served to place barriers between the police and those they served. Indeed if it had not been for Morse's faith in McNutt, his immediate superior, he would have resigned and, if ever McNutt were to move on, then Morse vowed that he would do the same.

Morse was still young … well, fairly young, having celebrated his fortieth birthday just a few months ago. He was not unattractive, but still there was no sign of romance in his life. This was not for the want of trying. He never quite understood women, nor entirely trusted them (which were often traits he shared with Holmes). His colleagues had no trouble in attracting the fairer sex, so why not he? Was he not of good character, deserving of a nice girl, gentle and kind, perhaps a little shy? His father had always told him that his time would come, but when?

In the meantime, what should he do? What would Holmes do? No doubt Holmes would resort to the locked drawer containing that seven per cent solution of cocaine to relieve the boredom. Morse was too conventional, not to say too much a coward for such action. He hated the thought of needles even more than the sight of blood. Instead he would find refuge in literature and music, the only things to bring the detective some sort of solace.

However, for the present, as he sat at his desk, there was work to be done in the form of the latest sixteen-page survey on policing methods within the division, which had been stamped with the single word 'IMPORTANT', in red, upon the first page. Surely this was not what he was destined to do for the remainder of his working life? Well, it was, at least until lunchtime, when he could escape to that nice local public house, with the equally nice barmaid with whom he would almost certainly flirt, no doubt unsuccessfully.

The morning crawled at a snail's pace. Lunchtime was all too brief and the afternoon dragged slowly but surely towards a time when he could escape back to his flat and the world of opera. It was close to five o'clock, when into the main office area breezed the Chief Superintendent.

"May I have your attention, please," he started in his schoolmasterly way that he always adopted. Everybody stopped what they were doing, which wasn't a lot at that time of day, and the room fell silent. "I have just received news from Central that Allen Jones, a.k.a. Smasher Jones, has escaped from Pentonville with just six months of his sentence remaining, and is thought to be on his way to Oxford."

There were mutterings among the detectives, until one of them ventured, "What has that got to do with us, sir?"

"Jones has family in the Oxford area, and it is thought that he will try to contact them."

"But, surely, sir, it's a uniform matter and nothing for the detective division?"

"As you know, uniform are overstretched at the moment and so have asked for our assistance over the next few days. Besides, we need plain-clothes to keep watch on the places he is most likely to frequent, without arousing suspicion. You have each been assigned your duties, which I will post on the notice board. These duties will start first thing tomorrow morning, so I suggest you all go home and make sure that you get an early night, as the next few days are going to be long ones for everybody."

With that, he turned and was gone in an instant. Morse was quite certain that the Chief Superintendent's next few days were not going to be long ones. What a waste of time and effort, he thought. He remembered the Jones case vaguely. It must have been some five years ago. Jones had been a south London bank robber of the worst kind, earning his nickname from the way in which he dealt with anybody who stood in his way. He also remembered that Jones worked alone, and that a considerable sum of money had yet to be recovered from his crime spree. Surely, thought Morse, he had no love for his relatives, and would simply collect this hidden loot and then make speed to the Continent, probably Spain, where he could not be touched by the fairly short arm of the English Law. However, the Chief Superintendent had spoken and his wish was Morse's compliance. In any case it must be better than sitting in a dingy, smoke-filled office in Kidlington, listening to the inane comments of his fellow officers all day. Maybe there would be a nice public house close to wherever he was to go on surveillance. Could it be that things were about to improve?

One by one officers crowded round the list to see their assignments. There was much excitement and some laughter. It reminded Morse of the day when the second year results were posted up at St. John's, much to his personal disappointment. This time, he thought, it must be better news.

Once everybody had disappeared, except for McNutt, who was still ensconced in his office, Morse sauntered over and perused the list, which he noted was alphabetical by surname. Despite this arrangement he still had to run his finger down the single sheet of paper until he came to his own, almost dead centre between Norris and Richards. Apparently the typist had made a mistake, or did not know her alphabet. He was wrong, it was worse news by far. He had been assigned the railway station from the arrival of the first passenger train scheduled in Oxford at just after six the following morning.

Morse heard a noise and looking around he saw McNutt heading his way. Morse could contain his frustration no longer.

"And just what am I going to do at the railway station all day?" he muttered.

'Put on some old clothes, Morse, and pretend that you are a train spotter," came the reply.

Morse let out a sigh. While he admired his superior, he did not always appreciate his sense of humour.

"Don't knock 'em, Morse. Salt of the Earth are train spotters."

"I suppose you are going to tell me that they won the war as well."

"Ay, well they certainly helped. As the bombs were falling all over the country, the railway companies had no idea where their rolling stock was located, or if indeed it was still intact. The spotters knew, though, and were happy to report every train movement to the railway managers, and hence the trains were kept going despite the best efforts of the Luftwaffe."

With that, Morse knew that he was beaten and, bowing his head in submission, returned to his desk. He packed away his things, took a photograph of Jones from the pile on the table, collected his rather grubby raincoat which was eminently suitable for the following day's task, and left for the evening bus back to his digs in Park Town. It was as if he had just drawn a bad *Community Chest* card … do not pass 'Go', do not go to the public house, do not collect £200, but go directly home, do not enjoy any opera this evening, and go straight to bed!

Chapter Two

"It was a very grand sight to see such a mass of people moving on the road from Stockton to Darlington, six hundred people were said to be in, on and about the wagons and coaches! And the engine drew not less that 90 tons ... I could tell you a great many more particulars but suppose that you are tired of it by this time."

(John Blackhouse, the world's first train spotter, on being present at the opening of the Stockton to Darlington Railway in 1825)

He had never been an early riser, particularly when forced to be up before first light, and especially for something that he saw no point in pursuing. So when the alarm clock sounded a little before 5a.m. it was a sleepy, disgruntled Morse who stretched out his left arm to stop the ringing. Alas, he was too slow, for the vibrations of the device saw it move ever further from his reach. Eventually, like a lemming, it launched itself off the side of his bedside cabinet and onto the floor. It finally slowed and stopped, but not before he heard the sound of breaking china. The timepiece had smashed the plate that he had left beside the bed, with the remnants of the previous evening's meal on it. It wasn't the best start to the new day.

No need to shave, thought Morse. It will be more authentic, and, as instructed, I will wear some old clothes instead of my usual suit and dark tie combination. Yes, that would be just fine. No need for breakfast either, not that he ever found time for sustenance on workdays, as he knew that there was an adequate café at the station.

Within fifteen minutes he was waiting at the Banbury Road bus stop for his ride to the railway station. It was only after some time that he realised that the first bus of the day along the Banbury Road from the Woodstock direction would not be for nearly an hour. He would have to walk the two miles and, to make matters worse, it looked like rain. As he set off towards the city centre the thought entered his mind that perhaps he was mean, or at least too careful with his finances. If only he had accepted that estimate from the garage, and not decided to wait until second-hand parts were available, his Lancia car would have been repaired and he would not now be getting wet. It was just that parts for foreign cars were so expensive. Again, he thought it wasn't the best start to the new day.

The first thing he did on arrival at the station was to purchase a copy of *The Times*. While on surveillance, Morse saw no reason why he should not be able to complete his daily crossword. Indeed, he felt confident that today he would be able to do it in record time, for he would not have to suffer the banal interruptions from colleagues. He made his way onto the main platform, taking note that he was in time to meet the first London train, albeit only by a few minutes. But where should he position himself? Luckily, despite there being two platforms connected by an underground passage, there was only one ticket barrier and exit, so it seemed fairly logical to find a seat somewhere close, but not too obviously so, to where the ticket collectors would be positioned.

Remembering his Conan Doyle and *The Final Problem*, he chose not the first bench, nor the second, but the third bench to present itself. The third bench would do very nicely ... not too distant, but close enough to the barrier and the underground passage, so that he could observe those coming up the steps. More importantly, he would be under cover and sheltered from the now driving rain. Morse was not a great user of the railways except for the occasional self-indulgent trip to Covent Garden, leaving as soon after work as possible and returning by the last train. Hence he was rather surprised by the number of people at this time of day. A steady stream of well-dressed businessmen bound for London lined the platform. Each had gravitated towards a specific spot where he remained fixed like a soldier on guard duty; and just like soldiers the men stayed motionless and silent, only occasionally acknowledging a fellow traveller. Each wore their uniform of dark pin-striped suit, hat, umbrella and newspaper in one hand, and most importantly a briefcase in the other. The only way to tell them apart was by their ties, which at least added a little colour to an otherwise drab spectacle.

The silence was broken by an almost inaudible station announcement informing those present that the incoming train from London would be terminating at Oxford, before forming the 06.35 to Paddington, calling at Didcot, Reading and Slough. It came as no great surprise for the captive audience to learn that, since the incoming train was running late, so the return service would also be delayed.

Minutes later, a diesel locomotive with nine coaches came into view as it made its slow approach to the terminus, first over the bridge at Osney Lane, then changing tracks onto the up line, and finally over the much larger bridge spanning the Botley Road. Even before the locomotive had come to a halt, every carriage door had swung open, with the Oxford commuters jumping from the train like paratroopers who had just been given the green light to spring into action.

There were many, and they moved so fast, that it was quite impossible to take note of them all. To make matters worse, a substantial number of the regular travellers made for the Botley Road end of the platform. But there was no way out there, so where on Earth were they all disappearing to? On further investigation, there was a gate, clearly marked as not being an exit and only for the use of employees. This was obviously well known to the regular users as a shortcut for the city centre bus stops and taxis, not to mention a way of avoiding the ticket collector.

After the hordes had gone, Morse consoled himself with the thought that Jones would almost certainly not know of this exit, and so it was probable that no harm had been done. However, from now on Morse would need to position himself between the two exits and be extra vigilant. He noted that he only had twelve minutes before the next arrival. Maybe he was not going to get the peace and quiet he desired for his crossword after all. For the third time it occurred to Morse that the day was not going well. 'Snark's Law' he thought. 'What I tell you three times is true'.

Chapter Three

"No, it's not quite so bad as that. It is the unofficial force — the
Baker Street irregulars."
As he spoke, there came a swift pattering of naked feet upon the stairs, a
clatter of high voices, and in rushed a dozen dirty and ragged little street
Arabs.

(Sherlock Holmes, *The Sign of Four*)

By 10:00a.m. the number of trains arriving and departing had settled down into a regular pattern of two trains an hour to London, one slow and one termed an express. This was much more manageable, particularly as the number of passengers had also reduced since the morning peak period for travel had passed. Those arriving presently were, in the main, either visiting academics, or day tourists to Oxford in search of a little culture – which they almost certainly would not find.

The rain had now stopped and there were even signs that the sun might break through the cloud cover. With very little to observe between trains, Morse had ample time to study the crossword, and even to visit the café where he purchased a cup of strong tea and a sausage roll. It was an unusual substitute for breakfast, but one of Morse's favourite foods, especially when on one of his opera excursions to London.

After another hour or so Morse became aware of somebody else on the platform – somebody who seemed to be watching him, albeit from a distance. It was a boy, probably no older than fourteen, dressed in scruffy clothes and holding a black book in his left hand into which he made occasional scribbles with a pencil. It was a train spotter. Morse's heart sank as he approached and looked as though he was about to strike up a conversation.

"'Ello mate. Are you a spotter too?"

"Yes," came the rather unconvincing and gruff reply.

"Been doing it long, have you?"

"Not long."

"No, I didn't think I'd seen you here before. I know most of the gang. Anyways, if you want the best spot you'll need to be over there by the running-in board," said the young lad trying to be helpful, pointing to a large sign informing arriving passengers that this was 'Oxford'.

"I am quite happy here, but thanks for the advice."

"'Ere, how many 45's have you got then?"

Morse was quite taken aback by this question, and thinking that the boy must also be a music lover – although perhaps not the type of music to which he would listen – he answered in a far more friendly manner.

"I guess I must have at least a hundred in my collection."

"What you on about, mister? In the whole of Western Region there ain't half that many 45's. Bit of a liar you are, I reckon. Let's have a look at your book then, if you got so many."

"Oh, you don't mean records then?"

"Course not! ... I mean Class 45's. Great they are, but my favourites are the 52's as they look so sad with them big windows. Wasted on freight, if you ask me. Mind you, not as sad as a Warship They're the saddest of the lot. All I seem to get are 45's and 50's. If only I lived somewhere like Didcot and not in this dump then I'd have half a chance of a 55. Reading would be even better. You can get to virtually anywhere in the country from there, and even abroad ... they've got electrics as well, but give me a Deltic any day to a 45 or one of those new electronic bolts. What's your favourite then, mister?"

Morse was quite lost for a response. It was as if he had been transported to a different planet, where letters had been supplanted by numbers to form words. He assumed, rightly, that the various numbers rattled off were classes of locomotive that one might be able to spot if one spent long enough at Oxford station. Morse sincerely hoped that he would not have the misfortune to be in a position to inform his colleagues that he had been able to see them all.

"I'm more interested on the history of the railway. Did you know that during the war that it was people like you that kept the railway going and ..."

"Well you being old would know more about that than me, wouldn't you? I'm really jealous you know ..."

"Why?"

"Well you must have got loads of steam locos before they withdrew 'em all. Catch you later, mister. Must go. The Cambrian's due in a minute, bound to be a 45."

And with that he was off, dashing towards the running-in board, leaving Morse to contemplate that there was at least one person in Oxford who thought it a dump compared to Didcot. And what was worse, that he considered Morse to be old at forty.

Chapter Four

"Depend upon it, Sir, nothing will come of them!"

(The Duke of Wellington on the arrival of the railways)

The futility of train spotting was easily exceeded by the utter boredom of surveillance. At least with the former there was always a positive result in that, by definition, if standing at the end of the platform of a mainline station one was bound to see some trains, even if the type and numbers were not those desired, but surveillance, often as not, produced nothing of use towards a case. But of what concern was this to Morse? None at all for the day had brightened up, he had finished the crossword in almost record time, and to celebrate had visited the station café once more for another cup of tea and two further sausage rolls for his lunch.

Now as the afternoon began to drag he walked up and down the main platform. The train spotting lad was on the other and Morse did not want to tempt fate by going over there and having to enter into another awkward conversation. As the boredom started to take hold he even began to read the various adverts and notices that adorned the place. The most interesting of which proclaimed that very soon the station would be subject to a major refurbishment and improvement. The existing wooden structure (in a state of advanced decay) was to be demolished and replaced with a brand new state-of-the-art pre-fabricated one.

Well, they could start by putting a few extra platforms in place for those trains terminating here thought Morse, and if they were really serious about improving the lot of passengers they could knock down the whole affair and move it somewhere closer to town. While waiting for his opera trains he had often wondered why the line from London to the south ran to a station to the north of the city, whereas surely there must have been a shorter route, and most probably a more convenient location for a station, to the south.

Having exhausted places to explore Morse sought refuge at the bookstall. There were the usual selection of newspapers and light reading, but he noted that not a single classic could be purchased. He was just about to leave when he spotted a small volume among the multitude of railway related ephemera entitled *A History of the London to Oxford Railway*. It would hopefully provide an answer to his question, and would at least give him something to read for the remainder of the day.

"That will be two-and-six, please, sir."

"How much?"

"Two-and-six."

"By God they know how to make a profit out of a hobby. I wouldn't pay that for a good book, let alone this rubbish," proffered Morse.

"Well it's up to you, sir. Do you want it, or not?"

Rather grudgingly Morse took a ten-shilling note out of his wallet and handed it over to the rather attractive cashier.

"Sorry, I didn't mean to be … well, you know …"

"That's alright, sir. I guess it will be even worse once this decimalisation comes in … everything will be rounded up so prices are bound to rise aren't they?"

Morse nodded in agreement as he took his change along with his purchase, and left for his favourite bench.

So what do you get for two-and-six thought Morse as he thumbed through the pages. Not much was the answer. A cheaply bound hardback of only sixty-four pages, with some black and white photographs of poor quality, and a text that even the boy on the opposite platform could tell was full of spelling mistakes and grammatical errors. It was the thin end of the wedge as far as Morse was concerned. It would eventually lead to the end of the English language he felt sure.

However, they say never judge a book by its cover and this was certainly the case here. Ignoring the obvious errors, the story within was full of intrigue. It seemed that an Oxford railway was first proposed in 1837. It was to have been a branch from Didcot entering Oxford along the Cowley Road and terminating to the south of the city close to Magdalen Bridge. Very sensible thought Morse. He was right, there was a better route to Oxford. He read on to see what had become of it. He should have guessed that vested interests were involved. The railway was opposed by Christ Church, which owned much of the land, and the City Corporation, who were concerned about the costs involved at having to rebuild Folly Bridge, and also afraid that if the railway came to town that it would be a success resulting in the loss of many thousands of pounds per year in road tolls. There was also the Oxford Canal Company who wanted to protect its own business, and the University who wanted to protect the morals of its students. Of course it did not help that the Chancellor of the University was none other than the Duke of Wellington, who was a long time opponent of all railways on the grounds that it would encourage the poorer classes to 'move about' as he put it.

Their combined efforts delayed the building of the Oxford railway over five years. It was rather reassuring to Morse that skulduggery was rife among the Oxford institutions even then. He read on with interest.

It seems that the University finally dropped their opposition to the new railway in return for a bizarre concession. The University was in essence to have free access to the station and be entitled to demand from any railway employee as to whether any University member was about to travel, and then be able to force the railway to decline to take that person if they so chose, even if they had already paid for their ticket. Morse smiled at the sheer power the University had over so many aspects of Oxford life.

If that was not enough the junior members of the University could only be carried to approved destinations, with Ascot not being one of them. Morse supposed that the objection here was to ensure that students would not see their tutors gambling and cavorting at the horseracing.

Almost immediately the railway was a success despite the tickets being up to three times that of the stagecoach fare. However, the time taken to London was just two hours and twenty minutes from Grandpont station. But what happened to this station? Were there any vestiges of that building still standing? That thought was quickly dismissed as Morse considered that this would be the first step to him becoming a train enthusiast.

He only glanced at the last chapter of the book, which was concerned with the various types of train tickets from Oxford. It transpired that the ticket clippers carried by the inspectors at each station were unique and making different marks on the tickets when punched. For example a 'V' shape for Oxford, a 'S' for Didcot and so on. Hence from the illustrations in the appendix anybody with sufficient interest could trace the journey of every individual from their ticket, and what was more it was evident that some very sad people actually pursued this as a hobby. It was bad enough that there were train spotters, but ticket collecting was in a whole new league of boredom as far as Morse was concerned. It was dark now with the station clock indicating that it was approaching seven-thirty. Only a few more hours to the last train, and then home to bed perchance to dream.

"'Ere, mister, I've been watching you, and I don't think you're one of us."

Morse was taken by surprise. It was his train spotting friend again.

"What makes you think that then?"

"Well for a start you've been here all day and not taken down a single number. You ain't even got a book. No, you're definitely no spotter, but I reckons you're a policeman."

"What if I am?"

"Well maybe you are looking for someone, and maybes I can help you?"

"I'm a detective sergeant, and yes I am looking for somebody."

"Got a picture then?"

Morse took the now creased photograph of Jones from his inside coat pocket and showed it to the boy.

"Important is it?"

"Every criminal case is important, boy."

"So how much does I get if I tells you about him then?"

"So have you seen this man?"

"Course I have, but how much is it worth?"

"You can have this book about the Oxford railway ... it cost me two-and-six."

"Alright, but I also wants the latest Ian Allan *British Railways Diesel Locomotives* book. It'll cost you three shillings from the bookstall."

"Fine. So when did you see this man?"

"He was over there just a an hour ago."

"Can you remember what train he got off?"

"He didn't get *off* a train, but got *on* the six-thirty to London. Don't you remember he rushed onto the platform at the last moment carrying a big suitcase just as the train was pulling out. Ah, no, you wouldn't have seen him as you were in the café at the time. He was wearing the same clothes as yesterday when he arrived from London at around the same time."

"And did he have a suitcase then?"

"No. Now, come on, mister, and get me my book ... I've more than earned it."

"So you have, but an English dictionary would do you more good." Morse paused. "A promise is a promise though ..."

Morse fumbled around in his pocket and eventually produced three shillings, which he pressed into the boy's hand.

"That's no good, mister ... I mean sergeant. The deal was that you were going to buy me the book."

"Well that's the correct money, you can go and buy it yourself."

"No I can't. She wont serve me will she?"

"And why not?"

"She'll just report me to school for playing truant all day. It ain't school holidays you know. Not much of a detective are you?"

Chapter Five

"Like two doomed ships that pass in storm
We had crossed each other's way:"

(The Ballad of Reading Gaol)

Morse knew that he must act, and act with some haste if he was to retrieve anything from the situation. Luckily for him when it really mattered he always managed to keep his composure and instinctively made the right decisions. He also recognised clues handed to him and, while sometimes he would misinterpret the obvious for something more complex, on this occasion his mind was quite clear as to where the evidence was leading.

With a speed seldom displayed he made for the ticket barrier, leaving behind his new friend, the rather disgruntled schoolboy, and exchanged some words with the ticket collector who nodded.

Next he needed to contact uniform with his findings. The public telephones in the booking hall would be the most logical option, but not for Morse. He calculated that by the time he got through to the correct person at St. Aldate's, and then spent valuable time persuading them to his point of view, it would be too late. Better then to make a visit in person, and although he was no Roger Bannister, Morse reckoned that the half-mile concerned could be covered in less than ten minutes. There if he was lucky Strange would be on desk duty. That would expedite matters greatly.

Thus it was a shabby figure that could be observed moments later leaving the station, and crossing the road to pass the old Cooper's Marmalade factory. Although it had moved out of the City several years ago, it was still allowed to produce 'Oxford' marmalade which was Morse's favourite at a weekend, especially while looking through *The Sunday Times*. He was now running along Oxpens Road, and as he did so he remembered the story of the cowman who was employed at Ox-pens farm who during Evensong at the nearby church of St. Thomas the Martyrs frequently fell asleep from weariness after his long working day, but kept the rest of the congregation awake from the odour emanating from his boots. Morse reflected that his day had been even longer than that farm worker, and was far from finished yet. Not much further to go, and just as well as he was beginning to feel breathless, and could tell that anaerobic respiration was about to take over and bring pain to his muscles.

With a single bound he made light work of the couple of steps outside the main city centre police station almost bursting into the building. It was most certainly a welcome sight to see that the ever growing frame of Strange was indeed on duty.

"What on Earth are you doing here, matey? Thought that you were on surveillance at the railway station."

"I was ... but there has been a positive sighting of Jones boarding the London bound train with a large suitcase just an hour ago."

"Right, I will get onto British Transport Police at Paddington. We may just be in time."

"I have already done that ... I spoke to the ticket collector before I left and asked him to set things in motion."

"So why are you here?"

"First because I have no faith in our transport colleagues to catch anything, and second because Paddington is not his destination. He will have got off at Reading if I'm correct."

"Is this another one of your fanciful theories, Morse?"

"I trust not. It's the suitcase. He didn't arrive with it when he was spotted yesterday evening, and now he picks an early-evening train, a time when he is most likely to be recognised. It only makes sense if he came to Oxford to retrieve his money, and is now making for the Continent via the only possible route. I asked the ticket collector and that particular train has a special connection at Reading to Weymouth, or via a further connection at Guildford to Portsmouth. He is making for a night ferry and has a choice of crossings to France, but given that Jones is no fool he will catch the boat to Jersey."

"Why Jersey?"

"First, because Jersey has fewer customs' checks, and from there he can get to France without any trouble. There is also another good reason why he needs to go to the Channel Islands."

"And what is that?"

"He needs to exchange his money before it becomes redundant when decimalisation comes in next month. That's why he needed to skip prison so close to the end of his sentence. If he waited to be released after decimalisation then all his ill gotten gains would be worthless."

"But Jersey is British ..."

"Actually it's a Bailiwick which makes all the difference in the world. Passport checks for British subjects are virtually non-existent, while the banks are most discreet towards their clients."

"All right, this is what I'll do. I will get the locals to watch the ports, and in particular the Channel Island ferries, while you go and report all this to the Chief Super in Kidlington. You can take one of the cars from the pool ... I just hope you are right."

"I am, I know it."

Morse was feeling rather pleased with himself, but was soon to learn that pride really does come before a fall.

Chapter Six

"What does Crustimoney Proseedcake mean?" said Pooh. "For I am
a Bear of Very Little Brain, and long words Bother me."

(*Winnie the Pooh*)

Oxford in the early evening is not a pretty sight. For nigh on
two hours every day the city centre, and all the surrounding roads
become blighted with fumes emanating from the endless stream of
traffic exiting the city. Should Morse push the extra button on the
dashboard to activate the blue flashing lights and siren? No, why
should he? He had done his work for the day and was in no hurry to
get to Kidlington to receive the praise he felt was coming his way.
No, keep them waiting, even if it took an hour to get to the northern
end of the Banbury Road it would be worth it. Despite there being
no radio for him to listen to the occasional sound of a horn from a
frustrated commuter sounded like music to him, such was his
present disposition.

The traffic was not quite as bad as Morse had suspected and it
only took him around twenty minutes to reach Summertown, and
another twenty before he was turning into the Kidlington
headquarters – a functional concrete building without a single
architectural feature. Indeed a building that made Slough seem

picturesque by comparison. Where was John Betjeman when this monstrosity was proposed?

Morse entered with a swagger and made his way to his desk, where waiting close by were McNutt and the Chief Superintendent in deep conversation.

"Good of you to join us at last," started McNutt. "Drop off for a quick drink en route to celebrate did you, Morse?"

"No, sir. The traffic ..."

"Thought you came by police car, not the bus."

"I did, but the traffic ..."

"Never mind," interceded the Chief Superintendent, "at least you're here now."

"Strange told us about why you think Jones is off to the Channel Islands and that does make sense, but are you sure that it was Jones?"

"Yes, sir."

"Why didn't you give chase when you spotted him?"

"I didn't catch sight of him, sir. It was somebody on the platform who reported seeing him to me."

"Well are *they* pretty sure it was Jones, Morse?"

"They seemed a reliable witness, and even said that they had seen him arrive last evening without luggage, and noticed that he was carrying a suitcase now."

"So, did you take a statement from them?"

"No, sir, there wasn't time."

"Their name?"

"No, sir."

"So did you follow any police procedure then, Morse, or just make it up as you went along?" questioned an exasperated Chief Superintendent.

"I know where I can find them again to obtain a statement, sir."

"And where might that be, then?"

"At the railway station."

"Ah, so they work at the station."

"Not exactly. They go there to observe the trains."

McNutt smiled while the more senior of the two rolled his eyes in disbelief.

"Are you telling me, Morse, that your witness is a train spotter?"

"Yes, sir."

"And just how old is this individual, Morse?"

"I would estimate they are around fourteen, sir."

"So you are committing goodness knows how many police officers on a manhunt on the word of a fourteen year old boy ... who should be at school anyway, was most likely playing truant and would say anything you wanted to hear to stop you from reporting him? I hope you didn't give him any money ..."

"Well actually I did buy him a book and ..."

"Enough, Morse. I have heard enough. Once I thought you were a promising officer, but it is all too obvious to me now that you simply can't follow the very simplest of procedures. For now just get out of my sight, and report back to the railway station tomorrow morning first thing, and this time keep you eyes open so you don't need to count on schoolboys to help you out while you were no doubt having a drink ... and, while you are at it, get this schoolboy's name along with a statement, and then take him back to school, and ..."

"You mean that you are still continuing the surveillance despite this evidence, sir?"

"You bet I am. I am not going to call off the surveillance on the so called *evidence* of some truant you paid for information ... and think yourself lucky that you're not on report."

At that moment the telephone rang in McNutt's office. It was Strange. After the briefest of exchanges McNutt returned to break the uneasy silence.

"That was city, sir. They've just found a body along Dead Man's Walk. Looks as if it may be a hit and run, sir. Pretty open and shut case by all accounts, but they want a detective there just to verify. May I suggest that you send Morse, sir. After all there is nobody else here, and there is little more damage he can do today."

"Just get out of here, Morse, and don't forget to return the pool car to St. Aldate's. You can get the bus home after you have

33

wrapped up at Dead Man's Walk … and try to remember your training and for Heaven's sake follow some sort of police procedure."

"Yes, sir," was all that Morse could muster in reply as he made for the door. However, as he passed McNutt there was at least some encouragement as he could swear that the Scot gave him a reassuring wink.

Chapter Seven

"I owe my success to having listened respectfully to the very best
advice, and then going away and doing the exact opposite."

(G. K. Chesterton)

Despite his police training nobody could ever accuse Morse of
being a fast driver. However, it took just twenty minutes for the
return to Oxford – a considerable improvement on the outward
journey. Maybe it was because Morse had been instructed to make
all haste to the crime scene, maybe it was because he was still
seething at the manner in which he had just been reprimanded by
two senior officers, but most likely because the rush hour had now
passed and the roads were considerably less congested.

There was no trouble in finding a suitable parking place in
Merton Street, right outside the Porters' Lodge of the college that
gave the street its name. A few paces and he was walking past the
college chapel (no singing this evening, alas!) and turning into
Grove Walk, a strip of land forming a border between Merton and
Corpus Christi Colleges. At the far end, in a gap, which was
originally occupied by the city wall, Morse could see the style-like
gate, a tall wrought iron affair designed to slow bicycles, and
anybody who may be a little on the large size. This obstacle was no

problem for Morse, and directly he had passed through and into Merton Field, he could see the police presence to his left, a hundred yards or so along the path known as Dead Man's Walk. There were five officers who, as far as Morse could tell, were just milling around a body that was lying prostrate across the compacted gravel. One was sitting on an adjacent bench that was set against the wall of Merton College having a cigarette. A rope cordon had already been extended across the path, and tied to the railings, which encompassed Merton Field, preserving the crime scene and making sure that no members of the public could gain access.

As Morse moved closer the picture became clearer. A few paces to the rear of the body there was an old bicycle lying on its side. If it wasn't for the dead body one would simply conclude that a middle-aged man had fallen off his bicycle. The officers acknowledged the detective's approach, with the one on the bench extinguishing his cigarette and rising to his feet rather sheepishly.

"Evening, sir."

"Where is Doctor de Bryn?"

"On his way from Abingdon, sir. Should be here soon."

"Apart from erecting the cordon, have any of you done anything?"

The tallest policeman took it upon himself to act as spokesman for the others.

"Well, sir ... we made sure that he was dead, searched the area for any clues, and asked around to see if anybody had seen anything."

"And ..."

"Nobody had, but then at this time of evening there aren't that many people around. There is a big bump on the back of the victim's neck. Could be the result of a hit and run, or maybe he just fell off his bike and hit his head on the railings. A man of that age it wouldn't take much, would it?"

"And the clues ..."

One of the other officers answered this time.

"Well, there aren't any, sir. I had a look in his pockets but he doesn't have a wallet on him, and so it looks like a mugging that has gone wrong."

In the distance from the direction of the Botanic Garden Morse could make out the familiar figure of de Bryn walking in a laboured fashion due to his heavy doctor's bag. As he came within earshot he hailed Morse.

"Hope you haven't been waiting long. I had to park by Magdalen. I wasn't told which end of Dead Man's Walk the body was."

"Well you are here now, so maybe you can give us your expert opinion as to how and when ..."

"I couldn't possibly say, Morse ... you know better than to ask such questions before I have examined the deceased in the lab, and written my report. I'll be able to tell you sometime tomorrow I expect. You are welcome to stay and observe while I make my examination ... doesn't look like there is any blood so even you should be alright, eh, Morse?"

"No, thank you, Doctor, I'll take a walk and return presently, just in case there is something of use you can communicate to me this evening. But, I'll tell you something right now, it's not an accident, nor a hit and run, but a straightforward murder."

Chapter Eight

"You see, but you do not observe."

(Sherlock Holmes, *A Scandal in Bohemia*)

O nce Morse was out of earshot the Home Office pathologist addressed the other officers with a, "Oh, just ignore him … Morse likes a touch of the dramatics now and then. I doubt if he has seen anything that you have not."

But Morse had both seen and observed, and on this occasion had already formulated a hypothesis which he would now test to form a theory.

He retraced his steps to where he had parked in Merton Street. However, just before he reached the police vehicle, he crossed the road and made for the rubbish bin attached to the wall between the real tennis court (one of only several in the country) and Logic Lane (the only such named thoroughfare in the country). He reached into the bin and after minimal effort found what he was looking for in the form of a brown leather wallet along with a bunch of keys.

He opened the wallet without the thought that he might have been wiser to handle it with more care in case any fingerprints might be obtainable. However, such was his enthusiasm that within seconds he had established the owner's name: Hugo Latimer, his occupation, philatelist, and confirmed that the probable motive for his murder was not robbery. Morse slipped the wallet and keys into his raincoat pocket and turned to make for the scene of the crime once more. He had reached Grove Walk before it struck him that it would be some little time before de Bryn would have completed his initial investigation. Time enough for a quick pint he thought, and, of course, Morse knew the exact place to find one of the finest in all of Oxford, and so he continued on past the passage leading to Dead Man's Walk, and so to Oriel Square and into Bear Lane.

There at the junction with Blue Boar Street was to be found the Bear Inn, once one of the largest establishments in Oxford on account of it being a former coaching inn. Today it was the smallest, and also the oldest, public house in the city, and most important of all they served liquid inspiration by the pint, and in his present condition that was exactly what Morse required.

Very soon he was ensconced at a table for two beside the coal fire with his back to the entrance, caressing with all due care his pint of Old Hooky, which although not the strongest bitter at 4.6% ABVA was quite sufficient at the end of what had proved an eventful day. Morse reflected that he was a 'clever bugger', at least comparatively so to his fellow officers, even if they did not recognise it. Morse was so engrossed in his own egotistical thoughts that he did not inspect any of the five thousand or so club ties that adorned the walls and ceiling of this establishment as was his usual custom when here, nor did he note the passage of time, or even the figure that had just entered the hostelry and was now standing immediately behind him.

"Thought I might find you here ... hard at work I see," came the familiar voice of de Bryn. "They should have made me a detective as I always know where to fine you, Morse."

Morse was clearly startled, and, perhaps because he had been 'found out', made an action quite uncharacteristic of him.

"I was about to get another drink, would you ... like one, Max?"

"Nothing too alcoholic for me, Morse, just a large gin and tonic, but only if you're buying?"

40

Morse made his way to the empty counter and without flinching bought the round, even remembering that it was a large measure of spirit for the police surgeon.

"So what makes you think it is murder then, Morse? There is a contusion to the back of the head which was undoubtedly the cause of death, but whether it is manslaughter or murder I couldn't possibly say, even with further investigation."

"It's murder, Max, for three reasons. First, if you are going to assault somebody and then rob them, you aren't going to do it to someone on a bicycle are you? They have the advantage over you. Too much of a chance that they would simply ride off at speed. No, you would wait, probably sitting on that bench close to the body, select your prey, somebody less fit than yourself on foot who wouldn't be able to flee, or overpower you. Then you would attract their attention with a 'have you got a light please, mate?' or something similar, and if they take the bait, and only if there are no other people around, then, and only then, would you proceed."

"A valid point, I suppose. And the next?"

"You wouldn't be able to attract the attention of somebody on a bicycle anyway ... they would be going too fast. They simply would not stop. There were no skid marks showing the bicycle had been impeded. That tells me that the cyclist stopped willingly to talk with the person who was sitting on that bench. Ergo it was somebody they knew, possibly somebody they had arranged to meet there, and somebody who was considered more than an acquaintance, or they would have just given a friendly wave as they passed."

"A little tentative, Morse, even for you. But if it was murder why did they steal his wallet?"

Morse had saved his best for last. From his raincoat pocket he took out the wallet and placed it on the table, roughly equidistant between the two drinks.

"They didn't. They took the wallet to make it look like a robbery but disposed of his as quickly as possible. As you can see no money has been removed."

"Where did you find it? The regulars searched all around the area and came up with nothing."

41

"But not in Merton Street for that was the obvious escape route. In case the victim, or perhaps another cyclist had seen what took place and was suspicious enough to follow, they could not because of that stile gate in Grove Walk. From Merton Street I suspect they simply went down Logic Lane to disappear into the usual throng in the High."

"That all seems to fit, Morse. The murder weapon, if it was murder, was something quite long and blunt, so maybe you should start your enquiries looking for somebody carrying such an unusual object in the High. However, I stress that death could equally have come during the dismount if our cyclist had fallen awkwardly against the railings for example."

"I think not. This was a premeditated murder, and as such the person had already thought of this possibility. What would be the best place to hide such a blunt instrument?"

"Among others, where it wouldn't look out of place."

"Precisely so, and Merton Fields being a sports' ground I doubt if anybody would pay much attention to somebody carrying a sports' bag with say a cricket bat sticking out of it, would they?"

"I think that they bloody well would at this time of year?

"Well a hockey stick then …"

"Better, Morse. Yes, it could have been a hockey stick, but don't jump to conclusions as the victim was not in the best of physical condition. It could equally be a man, or a woman."

De Bryn finished his drink and rose to exit. Clearly he was not going to offer Morse a reciprocal beer, at least not on this occasion. As he reached the door he turned, "I am told that you made a right cock-up of your observation at the railway station, so don't go and mess this one up as well … they'll be watching you carefully, and some will be hoping that you make a mistake."

"And who told you about the railway station?"

"McNutt. He called in at Dead Man's Walk looking for you not thirty minutes ago. I said that you were following up on a lead … which you were. By the way he says the Chief Superintendent has changed his mind and you don't have to go to the railway station tomorrow. Night, Morse."

In an instant he had disappeared through the door and into the encroaching darkness beyond, leaving Morse to ponder whether he should have a third pint, or not.

It had not been the day he had expected. It had started badly, been rather boring in the main, and when he had shown some initiative his superiors had not been appreciative, and now why was one of his closest colleagues giving him a warning? Who would be watching in the hope of his failure?

It was at times like this that Morse remembered Napoleon, and his famous quote – most likely a misquote – regarding champagne; 'in victory I deserved it, in defeat I need it'. Morse felt that champagne could easily be substituted by beer in this respect, and so took no time in downing his pint and returning to the bar to order the next, in what was to become a series of pints that evening (though he knew he would suffer for his indulgence in the morning).

Chapter Nine

"A policeman's lot is not a happy one."

(Policeman's Song, *Pirates of Penzance*)

In a policeman's work there are times of boredom as when on surveillance, periods of satisfaction following an arrest or, better still, a conviction, moments of danger mixed with excitement as a lead is acted upon, even romance on occasion (if lucky), but the duty every policeman dreads, and hopes never to encounter, is the dual task that now confronted Morse first thing the following morning – informing the bereaved, and finding somebody to formally identify a deceased.

Despite his *tête de bois*, self inflicted with the aid of a bear, Morse was at his desk rather earlier than normal. It took him no longer than a few minutes to trace Mr. Latimer, first using the new Business News Summary telephone information service to obtain his business address, and then the electoral register to ascertain his home address, which it transpired was in Headington.

The relative locations made perfect sense, since from his shop in St. Ebbes Street the most direct route home would have been via Merton Field, Dead Man's Walk, to Rose Lane, though how he ever managed to negotiate Headington Hill itself given his physique would remain a mystery to the detective. Morse assumed that he probably dismounted and walked the latter part of his journey.

Morse let out an audible sigh of relief when he noted that Latimer appeared to have lived alone in a flat: his was the only name on the electoral role at the address. That was normally an advantage as neighbours in confined residences were always prone to gossip and provide information more freely than kin. Furthermore in the absence of any relatives there was usually somebody willing to identify a body, and not being as close to the deceased as a relative were unlikely to break down and need comforting, something that Morse found difficult to supply.

Well he had better get on with it, he thought, and for once this would take precedence over the urgent paperwork awaiting him on the internal pages of that morning's *The Times*. First stop 23B Kennett Road, Headington, which Morse assumed would be designated a brown square on the Oxford Monopoly board if such a thing existed.

He wasn't far wrong for as he turned off the main London Road into the street in question he was met with a line of terraced houses in various states of repair. Number 23 was one of the better ones, making the best of the handkerchief size front garden with a variety of brightly coloured shrubs in matching brown terracotta pots. The windowsills were all painted, as was the front door. The people who lived here obviously took a pride in their home – probably not students then he thought. Morse pressed the doorbell for 23B first, expecting no answer, and after a suitable pause pushed the other button.

He was not to be disappointed. A tallish brunette, in her mid-fifties, dressed in smart, but cheap, clothes was soon standing in front of him.

"So, what are you selling?"

"Nothing, I'm afraid. My name is Morse, Detective Sergeant Morse, from the Thames Valley Police. I have some potentially bad news for you … may I come in?

The lady went ashen as she turned, leading the way to the lounge, which was located directly off the entrance hall, where Morse noted in passing another door with a lock that, no doubt, had stairs behind it and led to Hugo Latimer's flat. She sat down, and indicated that Morse should do so as well.

"What is it? Has something happened to Hugo ... I mean Mr. Latimer?

"Yes, I'm afraid so," replied Morse almost repeating himself. "A body was found along Dead Man's Walk last evening, and we have reason to believe it is that of Hugo Latimer."

Morse now realised that his earlier assumption was false as the woman burst into a fit of tears, far greater than would be exhibited by most close relatives. What could he do? He toyed with the idea of moving next to her on the settee, but thought better of it. After stammering, followed by a nervous cough and a pause, Morse's solution was to avoid any eye contact at all, instead looking at the gaudy orange patterned carpet and remaining silent until she was ready to continue.

"I thought that he must be ill ... I never heard him come home last night. Did he have a heart attack or something ... I was always telling him to lose some weight, and to cut down on the smoking and the drink too?"

"At this stage the cause of death has not been determined. All we know is that a body was found beside a bicycle along Dead Man's Walk last evening."

"I see ... I killed him ... I did it," came the revealing reply between tears. Morse paused for a moment before responding.

"You realise what you are saying?"

"Yes. It was me ... if only I hadn't have given him my bicycle he would still be alive. You see a few months ago I lost my job at Allied Electric and having no further use for my bicycle let Hugo have it. I told him that it would help keep him fit, you know, lose a few pounds. Sometimes he came home puffing fit to burst ... it must have been too much for him coming up that hill every night. He wasn't a lucky man you know, and now I have killed him."

More sobbing and tears followed.

"I must ask you some more questions. Some can wait until later when you are more … composed, but some details I will need now."

The lady nodded in assent.

"Well, what's your name?"

"French, Susan French."

"And you live here alone, apart from Mr. Latimer upstairs."

"Yes."

"And Mr. Latimer was your landlord."

"No, the other way around, I was his landlady and friend, perhaps his only friend."

Morse placed the wallet he had found the previous evening on the occasional table between them. He didn't even have to ask the question.

"That's Hugo's," she said. "I gave it to him a couple of Christmas's ago. It had a special pocket inside where he could put stamps."

"Very thoughtful. He was a stamp dealer, a philatelist, I believe."

There was another nod of the head.

"His stamps and *Dixon of Dock Green* on a Saturday night was all he lived for you know."

"I'd like to have a look at Mr. Latimer's flat."

"Yes, of course … the spare keys are on the hook in the kitchen beside the fridge. Just help yourself."

"I also need to ask if you would be willing to identify the body?"

"Of course … but not just now please … can I do it later?"

"I can send a car after lunch to collect you if you would like?"

She nodded again.

Morse rose and without haste found the key in the kitchen as directed. He compared it with the keys on the bunch he had found the previous evening and confirmed that one of them was an exact match, while another he noted fitted the front door of the house. He proceeded upstairs. At this stage of the investigation just a quick inspection to ascertain whether there was anything suspicious would suffice; any sign of a struggle for instance. The flat, however, was immaculate in every respect. Morse had no appetite to stay any longer than was necessary and so after a few minutes he returned to the lounge to bid farewell to Ms. French, informing her that nobody including herself should be allowed to go upstairs just in case the police needed to make a forensic search.

Chapter Ten

"Any idiot can face a crisis – it's day to day living that
wears you out."

(Anton Chekhov)

He had hardly set foot across the threshold at Kidlington
before Morse heard the unmistakeable Scottish accent of McNutt
calling him to his office. It was not a friendly summons, so Morse
assumed that there must be some new crisis, or that he was about to
get a further dressing down.

"No need to sit yourself down, Morse. I haven't called you to
blather. First you muck up the surveillance at the station yesterday,
and now de Bryn tells me you think this cyclist's death is murder.
What in God's name makes you think that ... there simply isn't any
evidence?"

"Well, sir, it seems to me ..."

"Don't even bother, Morse. I've enough on my plate with the
Jones case. It might surprise you that in this instance I think you're
correct. You may be hopeless at following orders, but your instincts
have never yet let you down, and that is what makes you a good
detective. You should never have been sent to the railway station – a
waste of your talents. If you tell me that you are sure that it might be
murder, then that is good enough for me."

"Thank you, sir."

"Don't interrupt, Morse. The trouble is I don't have the manpower to do a full investigation. However, you have made yourself so unpopular with upstairs that I dare not put you back on surveillance. Hence you may continue with the Latimer affair, but the only help I can give you is Strange. Not ideal I know, but a couple of days out from behind the desk at St Aldate's will do him, or at least his waistline, good and, more to the point, he is one of the few in Oxford who likes you."

"It is murder, I will stake my career on it, sir".

"You already have, Morse. Now tell me what you intend to do next."

"First Mr. Latimer's neighbour is coming in to identify the body this afternoon, though there is little doubt that it is him. Then I need to search his shop, and home, to try and work out a motive. I will also inform the press and put out a general call for information in the hope that somebody saw something last evening along Dead Man's Walk. At this stage Mr. Latimer just seems to be a pretty ordinary person in every respect."

"Fine, but no forensics unless you discover any sort of a motive. For now it is to be treated as a hit and run only."

Morse stood fixed to the spot in astonishment at this comment. On the one hand McNutt was trusting him and giving him a free reign, while at the same time ensuring that there was very little he could actually do. It was, at least, marginally better than standing in the cold all day at the railway station, and he had been given a chance to prove himself, so on balance Morse reckoned that his lot had improved.

"Well don't just stand there, man, on your way."

Chapter Eleven

"Life is rather like a tin of sardines – we're all of us looking for the key."

(Alan Bennett)

$\mathbf{B}$ack in Oxford once more Morse arrived in St. Ebbes Street to find that Strange was already standing outside the stamp shop.

St. Ebbes Street runs south from Queen Street intersecting with Bonn Square, a major shopping area, and then into Turn Again Lane where it becomes Littlegate Street. In times past it was called Little Bailey since in the 17th century it ran at a right angle to the Great Bailey (long since demolished, along with the rest of the area which was presently making way for a new shopping centre, imaginatively to be known as the Westgate). At number twenty-six was the only business of any size, Cape's the department store, which was known to stock all manner of goods that could not be found anywhere else in Oxford. Morse could remember seeing photographs from the 1920s when they had a donkey walking the streets of the city with a large placard on its back proclaiming 'I am NOT going to Cape's sale but then I'm an ass'.

Today the store was far from the hive of activity it once was, and appeared rather run down. The sort of place one's auntie or uncle might visit, spend an hour or two browsing, only to buy an out of fashion tie for a couple of bob to give as a birthday present to their young nephew. Indeed Morse wondered how in these days of the new big multiples, such as Marks & Spencer who sold the latest fashions, it could possibly survive, especially since many of the staff lived-in on the upper floors.

It is true to say that once the main store in a thoroughfare becomes a sight of faded grandeur, that is then reflected on the whole road, and Latimer's shop wasn't even close to Cape's being at the Littlegate end of the street. The wrong end of town, and the wrong end of the street for any passing trade. Morse's first impression said it all really. No wonder Morse had no recollection of ever having seen the shop; though to be fair he had never been a stamp collector, even as a boy. But there it was for all to see; big glass window displaying various items for sale, a single half glass door, neither of which had any security bars or shutters, above which was a small pub-like sign swinging and creaking in the breeze. It bore the image of a stamp and the words 'Latimer Philatelist' embedded in the design. Not just any stamp mind you, but a penny black, the world's first adhesive postage stamp, familiar even to Morse.

"There you are, Morse. Got lost did you, or did you pop off for a quick one on the way?"

"Neither. I parked the car at St. Aldate's and walked up."

"Well you could have bloody well told me what you were doing. We could have walked up together, or you could have given me a lift. I've been standing outside here, freezing my you know whats off, for the last half an hour. Thanks a lot, matey."

"Sorry, but McNutt thought that the walk would do you good, what with your weight and lack of exercise."

"Bloody cheek. Let's get inside and into the warm. Got the keys have you?"

"I am pretty sure that one of the keys I found last night will open the door, but there may be an alarm of course."

"I had a good look through the window while I was waiting for you and couldn't see any sign of a control box or an alarm box outside either. I would say that we are pretty safe to enter. Anyway if an alarm does go off we can always call the police."

Strange smiled while Morse fiddled with the six keys on the key ring, two of which he had already identified as being those to Latimer's flat in Headington. There was a small circular hole half way up the door, and as suspected there was a Banham key that fitted it perfectly. Morse never really understood why anybody paid the extra expense of having a Banham lock fitted when the keys to them were universal, and in the possession of even the most inept of burglars. He selected the larger of the two mortice type keys, and it too fitted the lower lock perfectly. Within seconds they were inside. No bell rang out.

Strange coughed as the odour of stale tobacco greeted his arrival. The culprit was clear to see for there on the counter was an ashtray with numerous cigarettes. So Latimer had not taken Ms. French's advice and cut down on the smoking.

Without really knowing what they were looking for both men started independent searches of the shop. It was a mess with piles of papers stacked haphazardly in every conceivable part. Morse thought this odd as presumably stamp collecting was all about order, arranging stamps in sets, neatly upon the pages of the album, but here everything was in disarray. However, on further inspection he discovered that there was a sort of order in the chaos. First to attract his attention was a big wooden box filled with packets of stamps all priced at a shilling. These were generally large affairs, coloured brightly and sorted into themes such as birds, cats, dogs, cars, trains and so forth. Then at the other side of the shop was another such box with packets of stamps, but this time priced at two shillings, and all sorted by country.

Along one wall were shelves piled high with album leaves with all manner of stamps, each page being individually priced from a few shillings up to around a pound. On the main counter there were two devices comprising pages protected by plastic, which could be flipped over like a book. These had individual stamps, and sometimes sets, but all at higher prices starting at a single pound upwards with the most expensive being priced at five pounds. Under the plate glass that covered the counter were smaller versions of the plastic protected pages. These had just three display lines. All had single stamps in with nothing priced below twenty pounds. Beneath the counter Morse spied a shelf upon which was a half empty bottle of Talisker, one of the finest malt whiskies, with another full bottle behind, next to which was a used spirit glass. Latimer had not taken Ms. French's advice on alcoholic intake either.

Looking to the remaining side wall there were stands with tweezers, packets of stamp hinges, new albums etc. all priced accordingly, while on the back wall behind the counter were a line of stamp albums, or more correctly stock books, each with a label on the spine giving an indication as to what was inside. Surely thought Morse this is where the most valuable stamps would be kept.

Morse took one down at random and laid it on the counter. The sticker proclaimed 'line engraved/surface printed'. Inside each page consisted of ten lines, with each line having the same type of stamp on it. The stamps were identified by a piece of paper, each of which had the letters 'SG' followed by a number.

"Did you every collect, Strange."

"No, I had better things to do as a young man," came the reply with a wink of the eye.

"Me, too."

It didn't take Morse long to realise that the 'SG' in question referred to Stanley Gibbons known as the father of stamp collecting and that the digits were the unique reference number assigned to every stamp listed in the Stanley Gibbons catalogue. Borrowing one of these catalogues from the accessories side of the shop, and in anticipation of finding something of real worth, Morse looked up the value of a small brown halfpenny stamp, SG48 and plate five – whatever that meant – in used condition which indicated that it had a postmark and had been sent through the post. It was worth less than a shilling. Morse noted, though, that SG 48 and plate nine of the same stamp was priced at several pounds, but the line allocated to that item was empty. Morse continued to search and discovered that every time he came across a more expensive stamp in the catalogue there were none in the stock book.

Morse concluded that Mr. Latimer's business was not ever going to be that successful, and it certainly did not provide a motive for murder. He was just an ordinary man, who smoked too much, drank too much, and made just enough money out of philately to pay his rent in Headington. Morse thought that he would have liked him, based mainly on his taste for malt whisky, albeit of a variety too peaty for his pallet.

Just then the door opened. A fresh-faced young man in his twenties wearing a brown overcoat stood before them.

"I'm sorry," began Strange, "but this shop is closed until further notice."

"Oh, is something wrong? I just came in to pick up a supplement that I ordered a week ago. They should be in now from Vera Trinders."

"Mr. Latimer met with an accident last evening, and will not be back for some time," said Morse diplomatically. "And your name is …"

"Claridge, Andrew Claridge. Oh, dear I really wanted those pages so I could mount my stamps this evening. I've been looking forward to it all week."

"Well then, these would appear to be for you, Mr. Claridge," replied Morse reaching under the counter to where he had found the whisky, and producing a packet of album pages upon the first of which a note had been attached, 'Windsor Album, Great Britain Supplement, 1970' and in pencil handwritten beneath 'Mr. Claridge, 12/- to pay'.

"Yes, that's it."

Morse took the green one pound note being proffered, and from his own pocket found the eight shillings in change that he handed over to the customer.

"I hope you don't need a receipt."

Mr. Claridge shook his head and turned to leave.

"Before you go, can you tell me something about Mr. Latimer?"

Claridge nodded. "Of course … I've been coming here for a good many years now. He is an absolute gentleman. He is one of the few who is happy to talk to you about stamps, without ever

57

expecting you to buy anything. He knows a great deal, especially about British stamps on which I should think he is a world authority by now – got a good collection himself I'm told. A lonely man I would say, certainly he has never mentioned any family, no wife or even a girlfriend. Think he lives up Headington Hill way. Likes a drink or two, though, and always happy to shut up shop early, and go down the pub with a customer. Mentioned a little while back that he might be retiring soon, but as stamps were his life I doubt it, as he wouldn't know what to do with himself. Practically runs the local stamp club. Apart from that there is nothing I can tell you about him."

"Well thank you, that is helpful. Just in case we need to ask you any more background questions I'll need your contact information."

Mr. Claridge was happy to comply, and having given his details to Strange departed the shop with a cheery, 'good day'.

It wasn't hard for Morse to find the till, being the drawer beneath the shop counter next to the whisky shelf. It did have a lock, though, but as Morse suspected the small desk-like key on Latimer's key ring soon opened it without any difficulty. Inside there were not even any partitions for the money, just a few notes and coins in no order to which Morse added the pound, not forgetting to take his eight shillings in change.

"Anything strike you as odd about this shop?"

"Only that it stinks of whisky and old fags, and isn't much warmer in here than outside."

"We have been here for over an hour and it's not exactly Piccadilly Circus is it? Just one customer spending a few shillings, and look in here," said Morse pointing into the cash drawer.

"Not exactly a fortune."

"Twenty-three pounds, eight shillings and six pence to be precise. So, it's now Wednesday morning and I presume this is the entire takings for the week thus far. Hardly enough to live on.

"You're wrong, it is Wednesday afternoon and my lunchtime."

Morse looked at his watch.

"I must dash. I have to be at the mortuary in under thirty minutes for the identification." Then another thought struck him.

"This final key is a Chubb so there must be a safe here somewhere."

"What about there," replied Strange pointing to the cupboard below the cash drawer.

"*Quaerite et invenietis*," came the reply as Morse opened the door to reveal a small safe inside. However, the elation of being correct soon passed as the two men noted that, although obviously an old model, it could not be opened by a key alone as it also had a dial requiring a combination to which they were not privy. Whatever was inside would have to remain undiscovered for the moment.

"We will have to get somebody in to drill it out, unless we can find the four numbers which opens this type of safe," commented Strange.

"Looks like somebody has already tried judging by the scratch marks next to the combination dial – recent too. We can get a locksmith in later perhaps, but for now I must be away. I will catch up with you at St. Aldate's after the formal examination. Maybe you could do some digging and find out something about that stamp club Mr. Claridge mentioned."

In seconds Morse was gone, leaving Strange to lock up and fix a note on the window to the effect that the shop would be closed until further notice.

Chapter Twelve

"The printing press is the greatest weapon in the
armoury of the modern commander."

(T. E. Lawrence)

It had always seemed to Morse that the more one had to achieve in a day the less time that was allotted to the tasks, and today was no exception. Within moments of leaving Latimer's stamp shop and heading down towards St. Aldate's and on to Floyd's Row he saw somebody he recognised. Indeed somebody he needed to speak with about the case. A quick look at his watch persuaded him that there was just enough time.

The person in question was Tim Coghlan, an investigative journalist at the *Oxford Mail*, and one of the few that Morse trusted, to a limited extent, for he had learnt, from experience, to be careful in all matters relating to the press. Presently, however, he was in need of his assistance in publicising the murder of Latimer and calling for any witnesses to come forward.

He crossed the road to intercept Coghlan.

"Morse, what a pleasant surprise, old chap. What brings you here? I thought that your domain was up at Kidlington these days."

"I'm here on a case. A case in which you may be able to help."

"Well now, you know that the *Oxford Mail* is always willing to help the Thames Valley Police. What's the story?"

"Nothing yet. I just need you to run a piece asking for witnesses to what looks like a hit and run along Dead Man's Walk last evening. A middle-aged man was found there having been knocked off his bicycle."

"Come on, Morse, there's more to it than that otherwise you would not be on the case would you? What's the person's name?"

"I will let you know later today after the body has been identified."

"Doesn't sound much like a story so far. But I assume that the dead man is Latimer, and that there is at least something suspicious about the death?"

"What makes you think that?"

"Well, I am not blind, my good fellow. I just saw you come out of Latimer's shop, and your colleague, Sergeant Strange, is still inside putting a note on the window."

"Well now you know as much as I do, but please don't publish anything until I tell you, as I said the body has not been formally identified yet, and de Bryn hasn't determined the cause of death ... it may not amount to anything at all."

"You have my word, as ever, Morse."

"And are you just shopping, or are you working too?"

"Like you, nothing much, but as they say from little acorns ..."

"Touché."

"If you must know I am following some leads about this Westgate development. It seems to be in all sorts of trouble, perhaps by design. The building is well behind schedule and there are rumours that it is all going to be delayed by months, or even years?"

"That will be costing the construction company a pretty penny. Let me guess ... you think somebody is trying to bankrupt them on purpose."

"The other way around actually. The contract is so tight that the only persons who will lose money are the owners of the site."

"And just who are they?"

"You and me ... it is all City of Oxford property."

"So it's some sort of scam which will inevitably be costing us money on the rates."

"Not half as much as it is costing the local shops. You can't have failed to notice that the whole area has gone down and is practically devoid of shoppers even before the foundation stone has been laid. Many a business is feeling the effects, and any further delay will make matters worse. It is even said that Cape's won't be around much longer, and is on the brink of going under. If that happens it will be the end for this part of town for a decade at least."

"I don't quite follow."

"All I know is that somebody is approaching those businesses that are most likely to fail in the interim, and offering them a way out. That is to say that they will buy their freehold, but at a price far below the market value, and making it known that should Cape's close that the property values will plummet even further."

"That is interesting. I wonder if Latimer had been approached with such an offer, and if so what his response might have been."

"Even more interesting is that there is a new planning application being made for a second phase to the Westgate development and that the head of the planning committee has just been made a non-executive director of the construction company. It transpires that the very same councillor is also a director of the property company trying to buy up the street. It all has a certain whiff about it don't you think?"

"It does give one something to ponder, but if anybody can get to the bottom of it I am sure you can. I will get Strange to give you a telephone call later today with the full details on the other matter."

With that Morse was on his way having just formulated a motive for Latimer's murder in his mind.

Chapter Thirteen

"I would rather die a meaningful death than to live a meaningless life."

(Corazon Aquino)

Morse entered Floyd's Row just in time to see Ms. French get out of the police car that had been sent to fetch her, and be ushered by the constable into the Cotswold stone clad mortuary. Despite the beauty of the edifice there was something about the building that was not welcoming, even if one did not know what might lie (literally) inside. It always seemed to Morse a cold and soulless place.

Within seconds he was at Ms. French's side and having explained in a rather awkward manner what she was about to experience, he led the way to the observation room. When the curtain was opened, her response was immediate, and left nobody in any doubt as to her grief at seeing the body of Hugo Latimer. Formal identification made, Morse tried his best to console her, but there was little he could do or say that would help. In the end he was only too pleased for the constable's assistance. He took her away for a 'nice cup of tea' in the adjoining room.

"What's the good of a cup of tea at a time like this?" she retorted.

.

"None at all Miss, but then again it certainly won't do you any harm either," came the reply with the glimmer of a smile.

Meanwhile Morse made his excuses and left the two together while he went in search of Max.

"You were wrong, Morse"

"What do you mean?"

"He wasn't murdered."

"How do you know?"

"Well, unlike you, dear boy, I don't just jump to conclusions and then retreat to the nearest public house. I went back and visited the scene of death. No doubt you noticed the wooden bench close by ..."

"Yes, of course I did ... you're not going to tell me that he fell off his bicycle, knocked his head on the bench and that is what killed him?"

"That is exactly what I am going to say. The wooden armrest is consistent with the shape of the bruise on his neck."

"But what would cause him to fall off his bicycle in such a fashion? Did he have a puncture, was he distracted, was somebody chasing him, was he pushed ..."

"You failed to notice the obvious, Morse. There was a ruddy great pothole close to that bench. He simply came a cropper, lost his balance and fell against the bench. A million to one chance, but there it is, and that is what will be in my report."

"Would a hockey stick or the like also be consistent with the bruising?"

"Yes, it could, but why are you looking for alternatives when there is a perfectly good explanation. Do you not believe in Occam's razor?"

"Because if it were an accident, Max, why was his wallet taken?"

"Perhaps somebody witnessed the accident, realised that he was dead, and decided on the spur of the moment to steal his wallet. They ran off with it and then thought the better of their actions, disposing of the wallet in the nearest waste bin. It certainly wasn't worth committing murder for, was it?"

"And the keys ... why take the keys? Surely you would only take those if you knew what they fitted, and hence, whoever it was, must have known Latimer."

"I had forgotten about them. Fine, my report will say that death was most probably accidental, caused by a blow to the back of the head, most likely from the bench, but that there are other objects that could also account for the markings observed. I bet you a pint, though, that it isn't murder."

"Thank you for the benefit of the doubt. I hope you will not be counting on a pint from me anytime soon."

"I couldn't possibly say, Morse."

Chapter Fourteen

"The most interesting thing about a postage stamp is the persistence
with which it sticks to its job."

(Napoleon Hill)

Back at St. Aldate's it took no time for Morse to appraise
Strange of the formal identification, and the fact that de Bryn's
professional opinion was that Hugo Latimer's death was accidental.
Morse also made a telephone call to the *Oxford Mail* to inform
Coghlan that the body was, as suspected, that of the stamp dealer,
and that any information that the public could provide about the
incident the previous evening at Dead Man's Walk would be treated
in the strictest confidence, stressing that at the moment there was
nothing suspicious about the death. Strange had been busy too, for
not only had be managed to get lunch from the canteen – the last
rather dried up portion of toad in the hole – but he had also made
enquiries about the local philatelic society.

"Sounds just up your street ... I found them in the local directory
and gave them a ring for you. The club has been going for years and
is run by a Captain David Boyd, retired. He is happy to speak with
you at anytime, but in essence confirmed exactly what we already
know ..."

"And what exactly do we already know? Nothing."

"Well we know that Latimer was a leading light in the stamp collecting community for many years, and we know that he was well liked too … so not much to go on as a motive for murder."

"He sounds too good to be true, and in my experience anybody that good, generally isn't. I think that I had better go and see Captain Boyd and find out more before I am taken off this case altogether."

"They meet on Thursday nights."

"Who?"

"The Oxford and District Philatelic Society … so you can catch up with them all tomorrow night at St. James church hall in Cowley, along Beauchamp Lane. They start at seven-thirty and are expecting a packed audience to hear a talk on postal history by some expert on the subject. Captain Boyd says that you may even recognise some of the attendees."

"And how might that be then? All the people I know are living."

"The Chief Superintendent is a member and might well be there."

"I will look forward to that cheery prospect as much as I do a visit to the dentist. Meanwhile we need to take a look in Latimer's shop again, and I have an idea concerning the safe combination. Come along, Strange, it will not take long. I promise you will be back in time for your tea."

It was already getting dark as the two policemen opened up Latimer's business premises for the second time that day, and turned on the lights.

"If I recall we agreed that this type of combination safe needs a sequence of four numbers along with four, three, two and one rotations of the dial, the first being clockwise in the direction of the arrow inscribed on the dial."

"Plus the key, which we already have of course."

"Well isn't it obvious what those four numbers are going to be? The clue is outside and clear for all to see, and known to every schoolboy in the land I shouldn't wonder. Even I as a non-collector know of it …"

"It's not a game, matey, just tell me what the ruddy numbers are, and let's get on with it."

"Have a little patience and let me at least have a pyrrhic triumph. Latimer would want four numbers that he could easily remember, so what better than those most associated with stamps, and in particular with the one on his shop sign."

"The penny black."

"Yes, the world's first adhesive postage stamp which came into existence on the 6th May 1840."

"Six, five, eighteen, forty ... well its worth a try."

Indeed it was. Morse rotated the dial saying aloud the numbers and rotations as he executed them, while Strange inserted the key. To Morse's great delight after the final anti-clockwise rotation from the number forty, the dial went stiff. Then there was an audible click after which the safe handle could be depressed. Very slowly Morse eased open the door with the full expectation of seeing the interior full of gold bars, diamonds, the lost treasures of Tutankhamun ... well something of value and a motive for murder at the very least."

"Not much is it, Morse?"

The two men stared at the empty box, save for twenty little white booklets, probably no larger than eight by six inches.

"But this is what we have and by virtue of the fact that they are in this safe, ergo they must be valuable."

Morse removed one for closer examination. Each had a printed front page with the words 'Oxford and District Philatelic Society' at the top. Underneath there were boxes with printed headings for 'Date', 'Owner' (Hugo Latimer), 'Packet Number', 'Type' (mixed) and then three columns for 'Name' (some unrecognisable initials), 'Number' (twenty-three) and 'Amount' (ten pounds, fifteen shillings and six pence).

He flicked through the inside pages and viewed the collection of multicoloured stamps stuck to each page. To him they looked no more valuable than those that were all around him in packets costing a few shillings. Indeed if further proof were needed the prices below each stamp were marked in pennies up to shillings, and Morse saw no reason to suspect that their value was anything but as indicated.

Every now again there appeared the undecipherable initials from the front cover. Morse soon worked out for himself that this was to signify where a stamp had been removed. To test his theory he counted the number of appearances of the initials and verified that the mystery customer had taken twenty-three items, which added up to the ten pounds, fifteen shillings and six pence as indicated on the cover. Surely this was not the full story? Why would Latimer put something of such little value in his safe? It made no sense to Morse at the moment, but he intended to ponder this problem at leisure, and most likely at leisure in a public house.

"Well you have got your pyrrhic victory, Morse. Sorry it wasn't what you wanted but there it is. Time for me to get back to the station and finish up before clocking off, unless you got any other wild goose chases for us to go on?"

"No, Strange. Thank you for your help today. Let's see what turns up overnight and start again. You be on your way. I will remain here for a little while, and close up when I go. See you in the morning."

Strange didn't hang about for Morse to change his mind and was gone in an instant. Morse stayed on for some time looking through each of the booklets in turn, but without making any progress. In the end he admitted defeat, at least for now, replacing all but three of the booklets in the safe, before locking up and leaving for the comforts of the closest public house. Here he contemplated the day's events. It had started so well, full of expectations of a murder enquiry in which he could make his name, but now it seemed no more sinister than a middle-aged man falling off his bicycle. But why were the keys taken? Now that was a mystery still to be explained.

At a little before seven Morse left the Royal Blenheim thinking that nothing further could dampen his spirits. He was wrong for as he entered Bonn Square he caught sight of a news vendor, and more crucially that evening's headlines that were displayed for all to see on the newspaper stand piled high with copies of the *Oxford Mail*.

'Stamp Man Murdered – Police Stuck For Clues'

Morse realised that somebody would be having his guts for garters in the morning.

Chapter Fifteen

"It is always darkest just before the Day dawneth."

(Thomas Fuller, *A Pisgah-Sight Of Palestine And The Confines Thereof.*)

He had always been a light sleeper, but for Morse that night was one of the most restless since he had joined the Thames Valley Police, for he had retired in the certain knowledge that his masters would be giving him a verbal thrashing in the morning. His case for murder in the Latimer death had no foundation, he had been (unfairly) criticised for his actions in the Jones case, and then there was his involvement with the press. The parting comment from de Bryn in The Bear to the effect that some people were out to get him and would like to see him fail kept going over and over in his mind as he tossed and turned in his single bed way into the early hours. This was surely their chance for within a forty-eight hour period he had probably ended his detective career.

And so it came, almost biblically to pass, that a very silent and resigned Morse entered Kidlington police station a little before eight-thirty in the morning, in the hope that he wouldn't be noticed. Fat chance.

"Chief Superintendent wants to see you in his office as soon as you arrive," came the cheery greeting from the desk sergeant.

Morse acknowledged the instruction with a wave of his arm, and a partial smile, but continued to his desk. Strangely for that time of day most of his colleagues were also at their desks, but not one of them made eye contact with him, or said a single word. It was as if they already knew what was about to happen, and were silent out of respect for they knew he would be thrown to the lions and become the newly departed.

Having hung up his coat and deposited his leather satchel beside his desk he did not take the lift, but instead made his way slowly via the back staircase to the third floor. He wanted at all costs to avoid the prospect of being trapped in the lift with a colleague and forced to converse. He paused by the fire exit door before continuing. If anybody had been close enough they may have heard Morse utter 'Well now, Khaleel' under his breath. Morse had always been a fan of General Gordon, and for that matter Charlton Heston too. He then proceeded with some confidence and knocked on the Chief Superintendent's office door.

"Enter."

"You wanted to see me, sir."

Morse noted that McNutt was also present.

"Do you have any idea why I asked to see you first thing?"

"I think so, sir. The *Oxford Mail* last night …"

"Oh, that … don't concern yourself with *that*, man. Strange has already told us that you stressed it wasn't a murder investigation."

"Aye, the relationship with the press is not a symbiotic one. They are parasites by nature, but we have to use them to get what we want. You will learn that with experience," said McNutt. "Don't look so glum man, we didn't have you come up here to tear you off a strip when congratulations are in order. Thanks to you Jones is back in custody, along with most of the missing money from his life of crime."

McNutt paused for effect before continuing.

"They caught him late last night getting off the St. Malo ferry from Jersey with a large suitcase of money … all in French francs."

"Yes, you were right, Morse, but how did you know he would make for the Channel Islands?" asked the Chief Superintendent.

"Well, sir, it seemed to me that Jones is an intelligent man, and having served most of his sentence was more than capable of finishing off his time in prison, so there must have been a very pressing reason for his escape. I remembered that he was never very close to his family, not married and had no girlfriend so it was unlikely that he would jeopardise his release by doing something so stupid on their account. Hence I didn't think he would come to Oxford at all, but would try to get out of the country as fast as possible. Maybe he had received threats while inside. Unlikely as given his nickname of 'smasher' he is more than capable of looking after himself inside. Then when I remembered that there was a considerable sum of money still unaccounted for the reason became obvious.

After next month when we turn decimal he will not simply be able to dig up his ill-gotten gains and trot along to the nearest bank to exchange his old notes for new ones as in Aladdin. An amount of that size could not be laundered either, at least not without considerable expense. It therefore seemed obvious to me that Jones had broken out with the express intent of retrieving the money, exchanging it, and fleeing the country."

"Go on ... how did you know it was the Channel Islands, and not a private boat direct to France for instance?"

"When the boy at the station told me that he had seen him depart with a suitcase that immediately told me that I was right, and that his purpose here was to retrieve the money. If he'd come here for any other reason he would have travelled light so as not to draw attention to himself by dragging a heavy suitcase around with him. The suitcase just had to be for the money. Finally when I learnt which train he chose to take from Oxford, not a fast train which would have given him least contact with anybody, and so minimise the risk of being spotted, but a slow one, and at a peak time full of people this had to be because it was the only option for him. It had to be the case that he wasn't making for London, but was going to change trains to a connecting service en route.

The ticket collector verified where the train stopped, and further that there was indeed a connecting service from Reading via Guildford to Weymouth and the night ferry to St. Helier."

McNutt interrupted.

"And the Channel Islands being a bailiwick are not subject to certain mainland laws, especially when it comes to banking. No questions asked, just like the bloody Swiss, and we all know how hard it is to get anything out of them when asked."

"Harder than a drink out of a Scotsman, eh, McNutt?"

The three men smiled.

"Added to that the Channel Islands are very much a stepping stone to France, with fewer checks from customs on passengers arriving and departing."

"Except this time they caught the bastard thanks to the tip off from Morse. Well done again, lad, you saved a lot of extra overtime. Just to tie things up you had better get down to the railway station and get a statement from that boy. You have good reason to be very thankful to him, as without his keen observation this may have been a very different talk. Isn't that so, McNutt."

McNutt nodded in assent.

"And what about the Latimer case, sir?"

"By rights I should close that case, and simply send everything off to the coroner's court, and they in turn will doubtless come back with an accidental death verdict. McNutt though tells me that you are keen on the idea of it still being murder, and have some lines of enquiry that you would like to pursue. Is that correct?"

"Yes, sir. There are one or two open ends concerning his shop and the contents of his safe that don't quite add up."

"Don't bore me with the details, Morse. Get out there and create some havoc, man. I still don't feel inclined to commit extra manpower, but I am told that you and Strange worked well enough together yesterday, so you can have him until the end of the week, after which McNutt will review your findings. Don't let this go to your head now, Morse, and remember what they say ..."

"Pride goes before a fall ... yes, sir, I will remember that in everything I do."

Morse left the office as if a humble supplicant, in much in the same manner the Lord Chancellor retreats after having delivered the Queen's speech in its silk bag to Her Majesty at the state opening of parliament. As he did so he reflected that he had actually just been commended, not for his detective work, but more for the fact that he had saved the force lots of overtime money. It seemed to Morse that the higher up in rank you became, the less crime actually mattered.

This time Morse took the lift back to his office. As he entered, the noisy room fell silent, and Morse felt the gaze of every member of staff fall on him. Then he heard a hand clap. It was followed by others, slow and rhythmic at first, but rising to full applause as every officer rose to their feet to acknowledge the man who had solved the Jones case.

"Your round at lunch. Morse," came a shout from the far side of the room.

"Mine's a large malt," came another from behind.

Morse didn't have to turn around to know that McNutt was standing immediately behind him.

"Come along now, back to work. We all know that there's as much chance of Morse here buying a round, as Aberdeen winning the cup."

Chapter Sixteen

"A man's grammar, like Caesar's wife, should not only be pure, but above suspicion of impurity."

(Edgar Allan Poe)

Following his meeting in the Chief Superintendent's office Morse was in a generous mood, albeit not generous enough to take up the suggestion that he should buy everybody a drink at lunchtime. To alleviate this potential embarrassment Morse decided that it would be best if he was somewhere else for the rest of the morning. Well, he had been instructed, to obtain a statement from the boy at the railway station, so that is exactly what he would do, and put on the back burner his investigation into the Latimer affair.

He made one stop on his way into Oxford city centre. He parked the police pool car outside No. 50 Broad Street (despite the restrictions), and swiftly entered the largest and in his opinion best bookshop in the world. Benjamin Henry Blackwell, who had founded 'the literary man's public house' in 1879, dealing at first mainly in second-hand books, had given his name to an Oxford institution that would surely stand the test of time as well as any Oxford college. Of course it was his son Basil, known as the gaffer, who had developed the business and gone into publishing with his *Oxford Poetry* series being produced annually since 1919. Morse had all but the first five editions, and treasured every one of them.

Blackwell's also had a secret for behind its exterior façade which Morse admired was something straight out of the James Bond film – *You Only Live Twice*. In that film the villain was eventually tracked down to the inside of an extinct volcano from where Ernst Stavro Blofeld hoped to execute his plan to take over the world. Morse did not much care for the James Bond films or the books for that matter, and certainly had no interest in modern architecture. However, he had to respect Pinewood Studios for constructing what was the largest set ever made for a feature film, just as he now stood in wonder at the enormous terraced chamber that Blackwell's had built under the south-east corner of Trinity College. Something a little more useful, and permanent, than a film set in his opinion.

It had been completed in 1966 and named the Norrington Room, after the then President of Trinity. Morse remembered that it was in the *Guinness Book of Records* as having the largest display of books for sale in a single room anywhere in the world, with over three miles of shelving. He had spent many a happy Saturday morning there, just browsing the shelves in search of literary inspiration, and what was more, the knowledgeable staff put no pressure on customers to actually purchase anything. To Morse it was the best combined library and reading room since Alexandria. But today he was no here to browse as he knew exactly what he was looking for, and where to find it. *First Aid in English* by Angus Maciver was the current object of his desire.

Morse purchased the book, returned to the car, thankful that there was no parking ticket affixed to the windscreen, and drove the half-mile to the railway station. He had no trouble in finding the boy he had come to interview for he was standing by the running in board at the London end of the station.

"Oh, it's you again Mr. Policeman. Do you want some more help then?"

"As a matter of fact I do. I need you to make a formal statement regarding the other day."

"Not bleedin' likely. If my father finds out I was 'ere, it will be the belt for me. Besides he always says not to help the police."

"There is no need for anybody else to know that you are here, and I won't be reporting you to school either. All you have to do is write down what you told me about the man with the suitcase the day before yesterday."

"I'm not going down any bleedin' police station, and you're not going to put any cuffs on me either."

"Correct on both accounts. You can make the statement here and I will help you. Why don't we go into the café? I'll buy you a milkshake, while you record what you saw."

"Chocolate?"

"Chocolate."

"Alright then Mr. Policeman I will do as you say, but it had better be a large milkshake."

Morse led the way with the boy in tow. The café was virtually empty at this time of day so they had no trouble in finding a table that afforded some privacy. He thought the boy akin to one of Sherlock Holmes's Baker Street Irregulars, very bright but almost certainly illiterate. Morse paid for the refreshments. He returned to the table and opened his satchel to search for the necessary form for the lad to complete, but as he did so he also took out the three stamp booklets he had kept from Latimer's shop and placed them on the table.

"Don't tell me you collect stamps as well?" said the boy.

"Do you know what these are then?"

"Course I do. They're approval packets aren't they? Used to collect myself until I got interested in trains."

"Well then have a look at them, and tell me if you think that there is anything odd about them."

The boy thumbed the pages, pausing at some longer than others.

"Looks alright to me ... bit overpriced mind, which probably explains why only one person has bought anything out of all three. Must be a mug punter."

It was something that Morse hadn't noticed and more importantly it was something that gave him a new line of enquiry.

"Tell me boy, what are you going to do with your life? You can't be a train spotter forever, and you are bound to get caught for playing truant sooner or later."

"I wants to be a writer ... like that Agatha Christie woman, and write murder mystery books. Me dad lets me listen to her stories on the radio when they are on. Brilliant she is, especially the ones with the pirate in, you know the foreigner who uses his little grey cells ... he's funny and don't speak right."

Morse sipped his tea, smiled inwardly, and made no comment at the description of Poirot, but simply continued to watch the boy scribble his statement.

"The railway one's the best."

"*Murder on the Orient Express?*"

"Na, that was too obvious. *The ABC Murders* where the murderer uses the railway timetable is the one I mean."

The lad finished writing and passed the piece of paper across the table.

"Here you are then. Will that do?"

Morse glanced at the page. It was much as he had suspected. His use of English was appalling, and his grammar even worse. However, it did cover the basics in what might be termed a unique style.

"It will do, but you will never make an author unless you can master the English language. To that end, and I am sure you will not thank me now, I bought you this book. If you read it when you are a little older then, just maybe then, you will be able to create something worthwhile out of your life."

The boy looked at the volume with disappointment.

"I preferred the other book you bought me. It at least had pictures in it, but thanks all the same. Before you go I don't know your name Mr. Policeman."

"It's Morse, just Morse ... Detective Sergeant Morse."

"Well it has been a pleasure to help you out Detective Sergeant Morse, but I got to say you are a pretty lousy policeman."

"And you're a lousy writer ..." Morse paused to ascertain the boy's name from his formal statement, "I very much doubt that I will ever see your name in print ... Master Dexter."

Chapter Seventeen

"The real voyage of discovery consists not in seeking new
landscapes, but in having new eyes."

(Marcel Proust)

From the railway station the next port of call was St. Aldate's
to pick up Strange, and then onto Latimer's abode in Headington.
Morse felt sure that his flat would provide some sort of a clue, and if
not he would have to admit defeat, but only if nothing else
transpired before Friday.

Luckily Susan French was not at home so the two policemen had
a free reign to search Latimer's place without interference, although
Morse secretly wished she had been there for if truth be known he
fancied the lady in question, albeit she was old enough to be his
mother.

"What are we looking for?" asked Strange.

"I don't rightly know. Something to indicate that Latimer was
about to come into a great deal of money would help. I don't see
him being involved with either drugs, or jealous husbands, do you?"

"And of course from the *Ladybird Book of Detectives* they would
be the only motives for murder, right, Morse?"

"Well it is a start, and it has got you out of the station for a second day running."

"And no doubt for a second day running I will be missing my lunch at 12.30, and have to suffer whatever dried up leftovers there are when I get back."

It was a pretty non-descript flat comprising lounge, kitchen, bathroom and a single bedroom. Strange went off in the direction of the bathroom and kitchen. One part of the lounge had been given over to make an office, and it is here that Morse started his quest. There were papers a plenty with mainly bills, but all of them paid. In the desk drawer Morse found a chequebook for the National Westminster Bank, Clarendon Club branch in the High and, from inspection of the stubs, he was able to verify that Latimer wrote many cheques, but none for any significant amount, though he did note the absence of one name among the neatly written entries. He thought this curious, and no doubt it was for that reason that Morse quietly slipped the cheque book into the inside pocket of his jacket while Strange was out of the room.

"It is safe to say that he didn't have a girlfriend," Morse announced.

"I agree. There is no sign of female toiletries in the bathroom, and no feminine knick-knacks around the place. It is a bachelor pad alright, and not a home, make no mistake."

"More than that there are no personal love letters in the desk, and not a single photograph, save that one on the mantelpiece over there, which is obviously of his parents."

"Anything else, Morse?"

"He doesn't do much here in the evenings I warrant. There is no television, no radio, no records and hardly any books on the shelves."

"And he doesn't seem to eat either."

"Trust you to notice that, Strange."

"Give over. Look in the kitchen cupboards. All empty, and I mean empty. Not a single can of anything, and apart from that pint of milk going off in the fridge there isn't anything there either. In fact the only thing I can find are those two jars: one with tea, and the other biscuits ... and not even chocolate. Not much to go on is it?"

"On the contrary, I may have been wrong earlier for all this points in just one direction, and it gives me an idea ... and no I'm not going to tell you what it is just in case I'm wrong. Let me draw your attention, though, to the fact that there is not a drop of alcohol or a single cigarette in the place, and yet we know he enjoyed both from our search of the shop."

"I see what you mean. Just the bedroom to go then."

There was nothing of note in there either, just the usual things one would expect to find in a bedroom. However, there was a transistor radio on the bedside cabinet, and what was more it was tuned to Radio 3 – clearly, to Morse's obvious delight, they had similar tastes in music.

"Anything under the bed, Strange?"

"Well now, just look at these. A fine collection of magazines."

"So he likes a bit of pornography. That I didn't expect."

"Not exactly. They are all brochures from the travel agents."

"Now that is interesting. He was either planning to go somewhere soon or was a bit or a daydreamer."

Morse looked at the back cover of each and verified from the agent's rubber stamp that they had all come from the same shop – Thomas Cook's located right around the corner from his stamp shop.

"I think we have learnt enough about Mr. Hugo Latimer this morning. It is going to be a busy afternoon. I have three calls to make so I will drop you back at the station as I wouldn't want you to miss your precious lunch."

Chapter Eighteen

"Solvitur ambulando."

(Motto of the Royal Air Forces Escaping Society)

In contrast to Strange, at times like this, when there was detective work to be done all nourishment was of secondary importance to Morse. In fact, he could go for several days living only on liquid refreshment, taken only to support his brain. This was one of those instances, and so, once Strange had been deposited back at St. Aldate's, Morse made all haste to the High where for the second time that day he showed no regard for the traffic regulations, parking on the double yellow lines right outside No. 121, the city centre offices of the National Westminster Bank.

It was known as the Clarendon Club branch after the social club for Oxford businessmen, which originally met at the old Clarendon Hotel in Cornmarket. Just recently it had moved and now shared its address with the bank. Morse had never been inside but believed that there was a bar, reading room, snooker room and dining facilities for the exclusive use of the all-male membership. Morse wondered how long that would last in these days of women's liberation.

He presented himself at the counter and asked to see the manager.

"I am afraid he is at lunch and can't be disturbed," the assistant informed him. "He will not be back until after two-thirty, and will then be busy until after the bank closes. I could make an appointment for you to see Mr. Edwards for tomorrow morning."

"Must everything in this city revolve around lunch? This is a serious police matter. Never mind, I know where I will find him, but thank you for your help."

Morse had no time for either petty bureaucrats, or haughty bank managers, and he very much suspected that Mr. Edwards would fall into one of these categories. With some authority Morse marched into the adjacent Clarendon Club and asked in a forceful manner to see Mr. Edwards, who it was soon confirmed was indeed dining there, as he did most days. Having been directed he strode up to a table occupied by two diners – one around fifty, one much younger but both wearing the same old school tie as if it were a uniform, a practice that Morse hated.

"I am Detective Sergeant Morse from the Thames Valley Police, and I am looking for Mr. Edwards."

"Then you have found him," came the reply from the man of more mature years. "How can I help you, Sergeant Morse?"

"I need to look at the ledger for this gentleman," replied Morse taking Latimer's chequebook from his inside pocket and placing it in front of the bank manager who scrutinised it.

"That is confidential information that I am not allowed to divulge without an official request being made to head office ..."

"And this is a murder investigation, sir." Morse knew that he had overstepped the mark leaving out the word 'possible', but he thought that it would do the trick.

Both men stared at each other as if in a game of poker. Which one would break first? It seemed like an age had passed when finally Mr. Edwards broke the uneasy silence.

"Well, I am always happy to co-operate with the police. If you would like to wait outside until I have finished luncheon I will be with you presently."

"Now if you wouldn't mind, please, sir."

"Very well." He turned to his fellow diner. "Order some coffee, Adrian. I will return as quickly as this gentleman allows."

Within moments both men were in the spacious, though surprisingly smoky, office of Mr. Edwards back at the bank.

"As I am sure you are aware, and as your superior will shortly be aware, barging in and dragging me off from lunch just because you want some information is not the correct protocol. It might surprise you to learn that I do read the newspapers, and so know all about the Latimer murder, and was half expecting a visit from you. That is why I have his ledger right here on my desk for you to inspect."

Morse realised that Mr. Edwards was far from being the petty bureaucrat or haughty manager that he had expected initially, but was actually highly intelligent and the model of efficiency.

"I am sorry, sir. I am not used to dealing with persons who ..."

"Know what they are doing?"

"Yes, sir."

"Well there is a lot of it about in Oxford, and it annoys me just as much as it does you I am sure."

Both men understood each other and smiled.

"Let us say no more of your methods. What is it you are really wanting to know about Mr. Latimer's affairs, and I will see if I can help without betraying any confidences."

"Three things: was Mr. Latimer a wealthy man; was there any abnormal activity on his account; and when was the last time he made a payment to a Ms. Susan French?"

They sat in silence as the banker examined the ledger in some detail using his index finger to keep track of certain entries. After a few minutes Edwards closed the book, sat back in his chair and lit a cigarette – his tenth of the day if the number of cigarette ends in his ashtray were an accurate indication.

"In reply to your questions I can tell you that Mr. Latimer was not a wealthy man; he has never been overdrawn, but he has never kept more than a couple of hundred pounds in his account. There are no fluctuations on the account, and the last entry I can find concerning Ms. French is over a year ago. Does that help?"

"Yes … and no. It confirms one theory, but destroys another."

"Such is life I'm afraid. Now if you have no further questions I would like to return to my dining companion before they have to leave for London."

"Just one, I don't recognise your college tie and I thought I knew all the Oxford ones."

"That is because I didn't study at Oxford. I went to King's."

"Oh, the other place?"

"No, the *other* place … London. Almost acceptable, even for a bank manager these days I'm told."

Both men understood the joke and smiled broadly.

"Do come again, Sergeant Morse, but if you do maybe you could give me a little more notice, and in return you will find me so much more amenable."

Chapter Nineteen

"Is it possible to see England from Canada?"
I said, "No."
He said "But they look so close on the map."

(American customer enquiry at a travel agent)

Again Morse was lucky for there had been no additions to his car windscreen while he had been with Mr. Edwards. He decided that he would next try his luck at the travel agents in Cornmarket, for which St. Giles' would provide the most suitable parking. He was indeed fortunate for he found a space right outside the Eagle and Child, which he thought he may well visit later. A short walk found him inside the premises of Thomas Cook.

"Is there anything in particular, or are you just browsing," asked a rather attractive platinum blonde girl from behind the counter.

"Actually I am a policeman, and need to ask you some questions."

"Well we do get lots of policemen in here, and Costa Brava, that's in Spain you know," she added helpfully, "seems to be their favourite destination. Would it be for one week or two?"

"No, you misunderstand, Miss, I don't want to book a holiday, I just want some information for a case I am working on."

"Oh, well I can tell you that on most planes you can take two large cases. Does that help?"

Clearly he wasn't making himself clear so he thought he had better use the same tactic as he had employed at the bank.

"No, it is a *murder* case, and I need to ascertain if a Mr. Latimer has been in here recently."

"Oh, that poor man from the stamp shop. I read about it in the newspaper last night. Yes, he's been in here several times recently, and took a whole stack of our brochures away with him."

"We found them at his home, but I was wondering if you knew which destination he was considering?"

"Oh, that's easy ... all of them. He wanted to go around the world."

Now that was of interest. Evidently Latimer was expecting to come into some money soon, unless he really was just a daydreamer, though something told Morse that he wasn't the daydreaming type.

"Can you give me some more details please?"

The assistant turned her back on Morse and started to look along the shelf of lever arch files arranged on top of the filing cabinets that lined the sidewall of the shop. One was soon selected, and with minimal fuss she took out a booking form.

"Well he was not going until October, with the first leg of his trip being on the Q.E.2 from Southampton to New York. Would you like the full itinerary?"

"No, thank you. Has Mr. Latimer paid for this trip?"

"No, it is only an enquiry at this stage. There is a note here to that say he will be able to confirm by Thursday 1st April."

Another interesting fact for Morse to assimilate, especially considering the date he gave for his confirmation of the booking. Maybe Latimer was just a daydreamer after all. There was, however, still one final question to ask.

"And was Mr. Latimer going to be travelling alone?"

"No, the booking is in the name of Mr. and Mrs. Latimer."

Curiouser and curiouser thought Morse.

"Thank you for your help, Miss. I think you can safely cancel Mr. Latimer's booking, don't you?"

"Oh, no, sir, I couldn't do that. It says here that I have to keep it open until the 1st April."

"But he is dead."

"Oh, I know, but I would have to ask my manager first."

Morse decided to depart as quickly as possible lest some of his present interlocutor's sharpness might rub off on him.

Chapter Twenty

"A journalist's mission is to serve the public by seeking and reporting the facts as accurately as possible."

(New York University Journalism Handbook for Students – Ethics, Law and Good Practice)

Having ascertained two pieces of useful information Morse decided that it was time for a reward, so on leaving Thomas Cook's he made for St. Giles', not to return to his car, but for the Eagle and Child known by locals as the Bird and Baby – one of the most famous public houses in the city, and yet in spite of this still a place where a decent pint was served.

Morse particularly liked the small room to the rear of the building, where the Inklings were said to have met. If only he had been at St. John's College situated just the opposite side of the road during that glorious period between the 1930s and early 1960s when the likes of Lewis, Tolkien, Williams, Dyson and Coghill met to discuss their latest literary creations, life might have turned out very different for him. Although not to his particular literary taste what he wouldn't have given to have been present on that summer's day in June 1950 when C. S. Lewis distributed the proofs of *The Lion, the Witch and the Wardrobe* on the very spot where he was now seated with his pint of Morrell's best bitter. Such a pity that now the only evidence that any of them had ever been there were the faded cheaply framed photographs of the great men adorning the walls around the bar. Surely they deserved far better than that, Morse pondered.

Two pints were enough to provide the policeman with sufficient courage for his next task – confrontation with the press. A short walk back along Cornmarket, right into St. Michael's Street, past the Oxford Union building on the left, brought Morse to New Inn Hall Street, where the joint offices of the *Oxford Mail* and *Oxford Times* were to be found. Luckily Tim Coghlan was at his desk and not out on an assignment.

"Good to see you, old chap. Come to buy me a drink for the piece I did for you last night, though by the smell of things I detect you started without me?"

"You'll not get a drink out of me. You nearly cost me my job. I told you that it was just a body that had been found along Dead Man's Walk, and stressed that we didn't know whether there were any suspicious circumstances, and that at best it was a hit and run. So what do you do ... say that it's a bloody murder. You did it deliberately just to sell a few extra copies of your rag."

"And to get you a response from the public. Look, do you really think that you would have got any witnesses if I'd written that some old geyser died after falling off his bike? Do you really think it would have made the front page? No, you would have been damned lucky to get a postscript on page five next to the lost cats and dogs section?"

"What do you mean by 'got any witnesses'? Nobody has come forward, and I doubt if they will, even if they had seen anything."

"For your information, my dear fellow, my little piece has furnished you with no fewer than three witnesses I believe."

"And just where did you get that from?"

"From Strange. He telephoned me just after lunch, both to have a go at me for the same reason you have, tell me that I was likely to have a personal visit from you and to thank me, for it transpires that three people have rung Kidlington asking to speak with you personally about the case. It seems that you didn't want to be in the office today, or you've had to have bought the drinks at lunchtime."

"That maybe so, but you had no right to take such a liberty with what I told you, or rather with what I told you expressly not to say."

"Look, I've been a newspaper man all my life so don't try to tell me how to report a story to get the best out of it. I don't tell you how to be a detective, how much bitter to drink at lunch, when to go to the toilet or how many hands to use for that matter."

The two men glared at each other waiting to see who would break first. Unlike earlier at the bank it was Morse who broke the silence this time.

"Sorry. I actually wanted to come here to discuss something else."

"Apology accepted, old chap, now let's go and take that drink."

"Another time maybe, I need to drive back to Kidlington and see to those calls that have piled up in my absence, due to my press friend's acumen." Morse smiled.

"Quite right, so what other thing did you want to see me about?"

"I want to know if Latimer stood to gain any money from the Westgate development."

"Go on."

"You told me that with the delays to Westgate, property values in the vicinity are going down faster than the Titanic."

"Correct."

"You also said that your counsellor come director of the development company friend that you are investigating is buying up all the property at knock-down prices in readiness for phase two of the construction. If that takes place he will make a fortune."

"So how would that affect Latimer? His business was suffering just like all the others, and he would have stood to lose a substantial sum if he had sold out."

"Not necessarily. Suppose that he held out and was the last man standing. He would be a thorn in the side of the developers, and could cost them time and money."

"You mean that he could dictate a far higher price for his freehold?"

"In effect he could blackmail the developers."

"I see, and that in turn could be a motive for murder?"

"I never said that, but maybe it would be worth a little investigation by a journalist who was already suspicious? All I know is that he thought that he would be coming into some money soon."

"I will look into it and get back to you if I find anything. Then you will certainly owe me several drinks."

"That sounds like an equitable arrangement. I will look forward to it."

Chapter Twenty-One

"But shall wake soon and hope for letters,
And none will hear the postman's knock
Without a quickening of the heart.
For who can bear to feel himself forgotten?"

(W. H. Auden, *Night Mail*)

It was past five o'clock when Morse's pool car pulled into the parking bay back at Kidlington police station – just time for him to check his messages and complete his daily log, before heading out for what would surely be a disappointing evening in the company of philatelists.

The office was already devoid of life, but there were three new notes on his desk, each written in a different hand, and each with the details of a member of the public who had called in wanting to volunteer information on the Latimer case.

It was certainly too late now to follow up on these, so they would just have to wait until the morning. For the moment, though, Morse could live in hope that one of them may just have seen something of import that would help prove that this was no accidental death.

Paperwork completed in record time it was off to what in Saxon times was Cufa's Lea, but now known as Cowley, the home of Oxford's largest industry, the old Pressed Steel and Morris Motors works. This was most certainly the 'town' side of 'town and gown' Oxford.

Morse did not know the area well, and seldom came here unless on police business. However, he had read somewhere that St. James was an ancient church with its foundation in the mid-12th century, and that in the early 19th century the vicar had been one W. H. Coleridge, nephew to the poet who Morse ranked so highly in what was termed the Romantic Movement. Samuel Taylor Coleridge was of course a Cambridge man (and like Morse had never completed his degree), but was prone to bouts of deep depression which Morse mused may have been brought about by either his fenland surroundings, or from visiting his relations in Cowley. Just then while waiting at yet another set of red traffic lights he remembered the couplet from *Punch* magazine:

'See Coley, scarcely wise, and hardly just,
Over unburied Merritt raise a dust.'

This he recalled alluded to a former Victorian incumbent at St. James who refused to conduct a burial service for a 'notorious evil liver' by the name of Frederick Merritt. He locked the church in face of protests, but a large crowd, including not an insignificant number of navvies armed with picks, forced the door with the service eventually taking place with another priest presiding. Morse expected that his visit to St. James would be a little more sedate.

The church was easy to find, as was the adjacent building, which acted as an annexe for social events. Morse noted that the church itself was much the same as others in the area, save that its square church tower was not a tower at all, being no higher than the pitched roof of the main building. It was as if it had been chopped off at some time in the past, or more likely that there had never been enough money to complete the structure to the original design in the first place. All the parking spaces immediately outside the church had been taken, so it was several minutes more before Morse was to enter the hall. He was surprised to be greeted with the sight of around fifty middle-aged people, all men, sitting in rows, almost in silence. Nobody even glanced at the stranger who had just come among them.

At the front was a line of tables upon which were some specially constructed inverted v-shaped wooden frames about three feet high and four feet long. Each had horizontal rails such that they could display eight album pages over an upper and lower row. Morse quickly calculated that if all eight frames were used, then that would be a total of sixty-four pages, and given that the guest speaker might wish to talk about each page for a couple of minutes, then he was in for a very long evening of sheer boredom. Morse approached the person seated closest to him.

"I'm looking for Captain Boyd," he said.

"Ah, a new member are you, or maybe a guest? Well he is the gentleman over there in the blazer behind the desk."

Morse thanked the man and walked over to the person indicated.

"I'm Detective Sergeant Morse from the Thames Valley Police ..." he started in his usual manner.

"Ah, welcome to the club. Your colleague who telephoned yesterday said that somebody from the constabulary might attend tonight. I gather that you are probably here in an official capacity regarding Hugo Latimer."

"Indeed I am. I want to get some background information on him."

"I am more than happy to provide that, and I am sure that other members will be able to help as well, but could I ask that you wait until the interval to question me, as I need to get this meeting started, and I hate running late when I'm in the chair?"

Morse acceded to the request, and took a seat at the back of the room.

It was a well-organised affair with Captain Boyd giving a genuine welcome to everybody in the room, with an especial mention of Morse. Then the club secretary read the minutes of the previous meeting, to which there were no matters arising. This was followed by some announcements about exhibitions and the like that may be of interest to members. Next Captain Boyd rose and gave details of the death of the former chairman of the club, Hugo Latimer, asking all assembled to stand in silence for a minute as a mark of respect. With the club business attended to it was time for Captain Boyd to introduce that evening's speaker who, it transpired, had travelled all the way from Witham in Essex, to tell the eager audience about postal history.

Morse was pleasantly surprised as Ian Tickle was an excellent speaker who was able to keep the attention of all present with anecdotes to accompany each of his treasured album pages, which soon started to fill the display stands. He delivered his talk with a loud and clear voice as if he were a schoolteacher taking assembly in a far larger venue, the difference being that this audience were paying attention to his every word. Postal history it transpired related to anything to do with postal services prior to the introduction of the Penny Black in 1840.

Ian Tickle had been collecting such items for over twenty years and was able to display examples from all over the country demonstrating just how efficient, but also fragmented, the service was, for delivery in rural areas might necessitate several transfers of the mail between coaches and couriers. From the multiple markings on the letters (envelopes were not commercially available until 1845) it was possible to trace not only the route, but also the time taken, for mail to get from one part of the country to the other. Of particular interest were the markings when things had gone wrong, such as disruption due to bad weather, or even delays due to wars and military occupations. Hence every letter was like a jigsaw puzzle and told a story, but only if you were an expert postal detective such as Mr. Tickle. Ninety minutes passed before the break, and Morse was far from being disinterested. If all the meetings were this informative he would consider membership himself. In fact, the only things stopping him was the knowledge that the Chief Superintendent was a member – thankfully not present that evening – and that they only served tea and coffee during the break.

What he ascertained during the interval from a handful of members, including the chairman, was not what he had hoped to hear. It seemed that Latimer was 'well liked', 'a gentleman', 'always helpful', 'kindly', 'gave his time to the society freely', 'will be deeply missed', 'there will never be another' being among the platitudes. Again and again the members spoke of an honest person, whose world revolved stamp collecting and who was basically a decent chap living just above the breadline doing what he enjoyed most. So if the man had been murdered what could the motive be? Morse still had one last hope as he took the three approval books, that had been purloined from Latimer's safe, from his inside pocket and passed them to Captain Boyd once they were alone.

"Have you any idea why Latimer would keep such items locked in his safe? The same initials appear inside each booklet, maybe you recognise to which member they belong? It might be important."

The chairman, having given a cursory examination as he flicked through the pages, shook his head.

"No idea at all I'm afraid, but the person you would need to ask is Warren, our packet superintendent, who unfortunately isn't here this evening."

"And where might I be able to find Mr. Warren?"

"Actually it is Sylvia. We do have some lady members, you know. In fact, I was wrong for here she is now."

Captain Boyd gave a wave towards the door where a tall, smartly dressed woman of about Morse's age was standing. As she approached not a single person in the room took any notice of this Aphrodite with deep brown eyes in a mustard coloured tweed suit, and cream blouse with the top two buttons unfastened to reveal a little cleavage and the full extent of the string of pearls around her neck. Morse noticed though. It was the singular most interesting thing he had seen that evening, or any other evening that year for that matter.

"This is Detective Sergeant Morse from the Thames Valley Police, my dear. I don't know if you have heard about the death of Hugo, but this gentleman is looking into matters, and is curious about these approval booklets that he has found in Hugo's safe."

"Yes of course. I am dreadfully sorry for being late, but I couldn't get away, it is always hard at this time of year. Now then maybe you can get me a black coffee, David, while I try and help this poor gentleman with his enquiry. I am sure he has been very patient, and probably very bored, all evening. Postal history isn't everybody's cup of tea, even among philatelists."

Having practically dismissed Captain Boyd, she took Morse to one side of the room so they could not be overheard.

"You say your name is Morse ... no relation to Robert Morse, the actor and singer I suppose ... you look a little like him?"

"No, not as far as I know, Miss Warren."

"Pity, I rather like him, and please you can call me Sylvia, in fact anything but dear ... what should I call you?"

"Morse, everybody calls me just Morse."

"Well now looking at these booklets they certainly seem to be ours, but for one thing they are old stock. You see when we ran out of blanks a few years ago we reprinted, and changed the font slightly. I don't recognise the signature, but then I have only been around for a couple of years myself. If you can let me have them for a day or two I can look into it for you, and see if I can solve the mystery."

"Thank you, that would be most kind."

"By the way, I did read about Hugo's death in the *Oxford Mail*, but can't believe it was murder as he was such a sweet man without an enemy in the world. As I am sure you know he wasn't in the best of health, and a prime candidate for a coronary."

"I have to look into every possibility though, just in case."

"Of course. Well here is my address and number, why don't you come around on Saturday evening around seven and I should have the information you're seeking?"

Morse was quite taken aback. Had he just been propositioned, or was she just being nice to him. With a slight stammer he replied in the affirmative and took the piece of paper on which her contact details had been scrawled.

"Until Saturday then ... I will look forward to that," he replied just as Captain Boyd returned with a cup of coffee.

"I will look forward to that as well, Morse." She said with a glint in her eye.

Chapter Twenty-Two

"But, Mousie, thou art no thy lane
In proving foresight may be vain:
The best laid schemes o' mice an' men
Gang aft a-gley,
An' lea'e us nought but grief an' pain,
For promised joy."

(To a Mouse, Robert Burns)

After three early starts Morse decided that he was due a lie-in, and so it was not until nearly 9a.m. that he rose from his bed on the Friday morning. As he shaved, he reviewed the Latimer case, which on the face of it, even he had to concede was looking less like murder, despite the contradictions.

On the one hand he had learned that Hugo Latimer had never had much money, but on the other that he was booking a trip to go around the world. Everybody said he was a single gentleman, and the search of his flat supported this assertion, but then again he was expecting to go on his travels in female company, perhaps even a wife. Morse also pondered why there was nothing of value in his shop or home, and why Latimer kept some seemingly worthless stamp booklets in his safe. Maybe he had some scheme whereby he would get rich quick courtesy of the Westgate development. Morse would have to wait and see if press friend Coghlan could uncover anything in that regard.

Hugo Latimer was certainly an enigma, but one that he would solve given time. It all looked very bleak, but Morse was sure that there was one person who held the key to this investigation, and that person was Susan French who he would visit by day's end.

The thing most on Morse's mind presently, though, was the largest enigma of all, Sylvia Warren, and it was the thought of her, that he had taken to bed with him the previous evening. As he dressed he was still filled with mild erotic thoughts of what might transpire, or rather what he would like to transpire, on Saturday night if he were lucky. However, for now he needed to finalise his plan of action for the day ahead, after all McNutt and the Chief Superintendent had only given him until today to come up with something concrete in order to keep this investigation alive.

First he would contact the three witnesses who had come forward to see if they really had seen anything of note, then interview Susan French and finally call in on Coghlan. Yes, there was time enough to follow up on all the loose ends before he had to make that report, but only if he could avoid McNutt in the interim. It was best then that he stay clear of Kidlington and go to St. Aldate's where he could seek the assistance of Strange for a few hours. St. Aldate's had the added advantage that nobody would know that he was late for work.

At a little past 9.45 a.m. he entered the police station to be greeted by Strange manning the front desk.

"Thought that you would have been over at Dead Man's Walk along with the rest of the C.I.D. mob, Morse."

"Why?"

"Didn't you hear ... they've found another body there this morning, and this time there's no doubt ... it's murder!"

112

Chapter Twenty-Three

"Once is *happenstance*. Twice is coincidence. The third time it's *enemy* action."

(Chicago saying according to Auric Goldfinger)

Within minutes Morse was back at Dead Man's Walk where the scene was quite different from the last time he was there. For a start the place was buzzing with police all trying to look busy and important. However, only the two behind the police barrier came under that category. There was McNutt as senior officer, standing next to the bench thought responsible for the death of Hugo Latimer, and there was de Bryn, kneeling next to a body that lay prostrate upon that bench.

As Morse passed under the rope cordon the two men acknowledged him. McNutt was first to speak.

"Good of you to join the party, Morse. Didn't you get the message I left you, or maybe you were having a day off from the office, eh?"

"No, sir, I was still following up some leads on the Latimer death."

"Well you can leave that aside for the moment, Morse, as we have a definite murder here. I've done a quick examination of the body and he was hit from behind with a blunt instrument," said de Bryn saving Morse from any further embarrassment as to his lateness.

"But the question is whether the two deaths are linked?"

"Yes, of course it is, Morse, and that is the question you will be answering with a little hard work," came the sarcastic reply from McNutt

Morse approached a little closer. The body was that of a man in his late forties, and unlike Latimer was well dressed, clean-shaven and giving the appearance of a person of some status, if not affluence. He was wearing a three-piece suit of blue wool, a matching full-length overcoat with scarf and gloves, black well polished leather Oxford shoes, which from the markings on the sole had been purchased at Duckers – indicating that he was a man who could afford hand-made shoes. To complete the ensemble he had a white shirt – possibly of silk – and a bright red bow tie. That last piece of apparel sealed it for Morse – this had to be somebody that belonged to the academic world, for nobody else in Oxford wore bow ties as a matter of course these days.

"When did he die?" enquired Morse not expecting a helpful answer from de Bryn at this early stage of the investigation. He was wrong.

"It was a cold night, and he was well wrapped up. He probably met his end an hour or two before midnight I should say. There is no sign of beard growth so maybe several hours earlier. Rigor hasn't set in yet which isn't surprising given the temperature. If indoors I would expect rigor developing within five hours of death, but it takes far longer in the cold. I will have to do some calculations back at the laboratory before I'll commit."

"How on earth did nobody notice a dead body on a bench in the middle of Oxford for so long?"

"Well there is no blood, no signs of obvious injury, and as I said it was a cold night so there wouldn't have been many people walking along here after midnight, especially since they close the Grove Walk gate early evening. I guess that anybody passing would

114

just think it was some businessman who has had too much to drink sleeping it off."

"Can you say if the murder weapon was the same in each case?" asked Morse.

"Assuming that both are murder, man. We still have to establish that fact," interjected McNutt.

"Yes, and no."

"Please don't speak in riddles, de Bryn."

"I'm not. Yes, both were killed by a blunt object, but no, it may not have been the same object. The bruising on Latimer indicated something several inches wide, while this chap was killed with something rather less than an inch in width. Although both were hit from behind Latimer's bruising indicated a blow originating from the left of the neck, while with this one it clearly came from the right. Hence not likely to be the same person delivering the blow."

"Well that doesn't rule anything out. A hockey stick for instance has both a wide and a narrow edge if you turn it on its side, and there are people out there who can use both hands equally."

"Well now, that solves it … we only need look for an ambidextrous hockey player who goes out and practices at night in the freezing cold. Not very likely would you say, Morse?"

"That is a valid point though. Both deaths occurred during the evening. That might be significant," added McNutt.

De Bryn was next to make a contribution.

"A better point though would be to find something that links these two men together … and why Dead Man's Walk?"

"Have you managed to establish an identity yet?" asked Morse.

De Bryn produced a wallet and handed it over to McNutt.

"It seems that he's a professor in history at Lonsdale by the name of Tamati Cranmer."

"My God!" exclaimed Morse. "Then it's not just murder … we have a serial killer on our hands … and what is more I know who the next victim is going to be."

115

Chapter Twenty-Four

"We shall this day light such a candle, by God's grace, in England, as I trust shall never be put out."

(Hugo Latimer's last recorded words, 1555)

The two men walked at a brisk pace side by side. Neither wanted to break the silence as they passed along Grove Walk, Magpie Lane and Catte Street. At that time of morning the sun was not at its height, but still illuminated the Cotswold stone of the Radcliffe Camera in such a way as to give that cold winter's day some warmth. Having passed the Clarendon Building they turned left into Broad Street. At the west end of this aptly named thoroughfare, beside Balliol College, Morse crossed to the centre of the road and pointed to the ground.

"This is what it's all about, sir."

"Have you gone mad, man?" replied McNutt peering at a painted cross upon the road.

"All will become clear around the corner in St. Giles'."

A minute or so later the two policemen were standing on the steps of the Martyrs Memorial looking down the full length of that major route to the north, with the Randolph Hotel and the

117

Ashmolean Museum to their left, and St. John's College, Morse's *alma mater* to the right.

"Now do you understand, sir?"

"Are you saying that this case has got something to do with this war memorial."

"It's not a war memorial, sir, it's much older than that ... this is the Martyrs Memorial erected to commemorate the burning at the stake, at the spot in Broad Street we just passed, of the three Oxford Martyrs in 1555 and 1556. If you look at the inscription on the base I think you will see what I am getting at."

McNutt turned about and started to read with a growing concern.

'To the Glory of God, and in grateful commemoration of His servants, Thomas Cranmer, Nicholas Ridley, Hugh Latimer, Prelates of the Church of England, who near this spot yielded their bodies to be burned, bearing witness to the sacred truths which they had affirmed and maintained against the errors of the Church of Rome, and rejoicing that to them it was given not only to believe in Christ, but also to suffer for His sake; this monument was erected by public subscription in the year of our Lord God, MDCCCXLI.'

"My God, Morse, are you suggesting that we have some madman on the loose who is murdering innocent members of the public just because they have names similar to that of these clergymen?"

"I think that it very likely, sir."

"I need a drink. Come on," McNutt replied indicating the Randolph Hotel with a wave of his hand.

Inside that Oxford hotel the two men sat at a small window table peering out from Chapters Bar towards the Ashmolean Museum opposite. The waiter approached.

"I'll have a Glenfiddich ... and make it a large one please."

Morse was just about to order a pint when McNutt intervened.

"He'll have the same as me."

As the waiter disappeared McNutt contemplated the situation.

"It could still be coincidence," he started, "the names aren't exactly the same."

"Hugh for Hugo is pretty close, and Tamati I think you will find is the Maori equivalent of Thomas. I do believe that it will transpire that professor Cranmer hails from New Zealand originally."

The drinks arrived, along with the bill, which was placed on the table equidistant between them.

"Be so kind as to fetch me a copy of the local telephone directory will you?"

The waiter nodded and retreated.

"But why now over four hundred years later would somebody want to start some sort of revenge killing? It simply doesn't make sense. Is it some religious fanatic?"

"Well, sir, as somebody reminded me just recently it could be akin to the Agatha Christie novel the *ABC Murders* where there are a number of murders which seem to be linked to nothing more than the alphabet, but actually hidden among them is the real motive."

"Aye, you mean the best place to hide a murder is amongst other murders. You could have something there, Morse, but life generally isn't like a Poirot book."

McNutt finished off his malt before continuing.

"I doubt if there is any link between an old stamp dealer and an Oxford don, so maybe the real target is Ridley ... the murder yet to come," expounded McNutt. "There is a connection though ... both men were found at Dead Man's Walk, surely that can't be a coincidence?"

"Oh, I thought that you already knew the significance of that location. It was the general route taken in medieval times by funeral processions for those of the Jewish faith. They would walk from the synagogue at St. Aldate's along the outside of the city wall to the burial ground where the botanic gardens now stand. Over time it became known as Dead Man's Walk. Of course Latimer, Cranmer and Ridley weren't Jews so there may be a darker significance."

The waiter returned with the telephone directory.

"Same again, please, but not for him ... he's driving."

"Well now let's see just how many Ridleys there are in Oxford."

McNutt thumbed the pages, counting as he did so.

119

"My God, there's over a page of them, and a dozen no less with the initial N. If we have to provide protection for all that lot the overtime will be astronomical."

"Can't be worse than having to be on surveillance at the railway station," replied Morse under his breath, grateful that McNutt did not seem to hear him.

The waiter returned with McNutt's drink, and a second slip of paper that he deposited on top of the first.

"Right this is what we'll do. I'll return to Kidlington and see that the squad covers the Ridley angle, while you continue your enquiries into Latimer and whether there is a connection there between him and Cranmer, however unlikely, and, of course, with any of our Oxford Ridleys.

"Before that you need to get over to the *Oxford Mail*, and your press friend Coghlan. Tell him about Cranmer's death, but whatever you do make sure he doesn't expect that it may be a serial killer. Say that they are both accidents if you must. The one thing that we don't want to do is to start a panic among the public, especially the Jewish and Catholic communities."

McNutt took a gulp of whisky emptying his second glass. He then rose to his feet.

"I'm going to the toilet, while you settle the bill, Morse."

Typical thought the latter. He would be sure to remember for future reference this quaint police tradition whereby the junior officer always buys the drinks for the senior.

"I'll be off to the *Oxford Mail* then."

"Not until you've driven me back to Kidlington you won't. After all I am a chief inspector and you can't expect me to take the bus, or a taxi, and I can't drive after having had a drink ... that's what detective sergeants are for, eh!"

He saw the disapproving look on his sergeant's face as he left.

Morse examined the two pieces of paper on the table and, after some fumbling in his pocket, placed the exact money on top of them. The disapproving look was now on the waiter's face as he took the pile of coins, noting the lack of tip.

"Thank you, sir," he said, gruffly.

McNutt returned, and in an encouraging manner addressed his subordinate.

"Look, Morse, you work best alone, so I am letting you be a sort of roving detective who can follow his own nose. Just keep me informed. You've done some good work so far, but don't get carried away with too many fanciful ideas. If you solve this case by yourself there will be a promotion in it for you, man, and I shouldn't wonder if they might even rename this bar after you as well!"

Chapter Twenty-Five

"Nothing but silence
No spark of inspiration
No questions allowed
No dreams still within my reach.
No more options, a dead end."

(Caren E. Salas, *The End*)

All things considered it hadn't been a bad morning. Instead of being taken off the Latimer case he had been given a free reign to continue his investigations, and in his own way too. What is more he now had a new murder, an academic one at that, to get his teeth into, and the distinct possibility of a serial killer on the loose in Oxford. First though, irritatingly, he had to act as taxi driver and take McNutt back to Kidlington, before he could continue being a detective back in the city. At least he didn't have to stay for McNutt's lecture to his colleagues since he already knew exactly what he was going to be doing the rest of the day.

So having deposited McNutt at Kidlington it was back to the offices of the *Oxford Mail* in the city centre, where once again he found Coghlan, this time with his feet up on his desk, a paragon of inactivity. A slow news day thought Morse, as indeed Fridays tended to be, since most stories of note usually broke earlier in the

123

week, in order that they could be forgotten about over the ensuing weekend.

"Ah, Morse, come to buy me that drink have you?"

"Not exactly. I was wondering if you've had any time to look into Latimer for me."

"Yes, and it is bad news, old boy. Nothing going on there I'm afraid. Only a leasehold done annually in June, so he would have been out anyway very soon. *Ipso facto* no way he could be holding up the development for a king's ransom. Pity I thought you may have had something there."

"Never mind. Any luck with your councillor friend enquiries?"

"It is as you would say a 'ongoing' investigation, but I very much expect a successful outcome in a day or two," came the cagey reply from the investigative journalist.

"I had better be off, but I promise I will buy you that drink sometime in the not too distant future."

"Well I can tell from your breath that I have already missed out today ... and to think that you say us journalists are always on the bottle. Before you go, Morse, there were reports of a lot of police activity down Dead Man's Walk earlier. Know anything about it?"

"Yes, they found somebody there this morning. A tramp I believe who had been sleeping rough and died of hypothermia. I suspect in a day or two we will have their name if it is of any interest to you," Morse replied, thinking that perhaps he should be crossing his fingers behind his back just as he used to do when lying as a child.

"That would be much appreciated."

With that Morse was gone, glad that he had no more misinformation to impart. One line of enquiry had just been blown out of the water, but five others remained – the three witnesses who had come forward, Sylvia Warren and Susan French, who Morse determined would be his next port of call. First, though, he needed some nourishment given that he had not had anything solid in his stomach since the previous evening, and perhaps more importantly because he could now feel the whisky taking effect.

Chapter Twenty-Six

"Let us go then, you and I,
When the evening is spread out against the sky
Like a patient etherised upon a table;
Let us go, through certain half-deserted streets,"

(T. S. Eliot, *The Love Song of J. Alfred Prufrock*)

Even in winter, Oxford mid-afternoon is a wondrous sight. Looking down on what is essentially a valley from the vantage of Headington Hill Morse admired the Oxford skyline with the Radcliffe Camera, St. Mary's church and the Tom Tower being the three most prominent buildings among the dozen or so spires that formed the nucleus of the city centre. It was here that Morse decided to eat his lunch, a sandwich he had purchased on the way from a shop in the Covered Market. As he ate Morse reflected that Headington was now the site for the new Oxford Polytechnic, and he had no doubt that the powers that be had specifically chosen this elevated location so that their two thousand plus students could look down on those in the city, for perhaps the only time in their lives. Morse it had to be said, despite not coming from a privileged background, was a snob when it came to education.

As he approached Kennett Road he felt pretty certain that Susan French would be at home, even on a Friday afternoon when most women on payday would be out shopping. He was right and the doorbell was answered almost immediately. Ms. French led the way to the lounge where both were soon seated.

"Sergeant Morse, isn't it? Do you wish to search Mr. Latimer's flat again? Maybe a cup of tea?"

"No, actually it was you I needed to speak with Ms. French, or maybe I should say Mrs. Latimer?"

She looked down at the orange swirly patterned carpet before a tear could be seen emerging from her right eye.

"How on earth did you find that out," she said. "Nobody knows."

"Well the travel agent knows. You were going to accompany Hugo on his trip around the world were you not?"

She nodded as the other eye also produced a tear.

"It was pretty obvious really. When I was first here you said that Hugo liked to watch *Dixon of Dock Green* and yet there is no television upstairs *ergo* he must have watched it somewhere else, and your television is by far the closest. Add to that he had virtually no provisions in the cupboards, nothing in the bathroom either, the bed seems not to have been slept in recently, and so the only conclusion I could draw is that Hugo was spending most of his time elsewhere ... and where better than with his landlady, a landlady who from the bank records had received no rent for almost a year, and who was so distressed at the news of his death?"

"Well you're correct, we were lovers, and on Christmas day last he proposed to me. Hugo was basically a shy man who lived a lonely life devoted to his stamps. He had been my lodger for several years before he even invited me upstairs for a cup of tea. Slowly, very slowly, we became friends ... after that it took him over a year to invite me out on a date ... not much of a date it has to be said, it was to the local stamp club for a talk on surface printed issues of the late-19th century as I recall."

"Yes, I have visited the stamp club myself, and can see that it might not have been the most romantic of starts."

They smiled at each other.

"Oh, but it was ... Hugo was the one giving the talk, and he did so with such passion and authority that I felt honoured to be his guest for the evening. If they did degrees in philately he would surely be a professor. Then on that long walk home he took me on a detour to St. Clement's Road. He asked if I was hungry as there was a nice looking restaurant that he passed every day on his way to and from the shop. But would they still be open at that time of night? Of course they would for Hugo had enquired earlier, and had even made a reservation for two. It was only then over dessert that he told me of his feelings. Afterwards all the way home he held my hand as we walked the empty streets. Later he even gave up cigarettes and alcohol for me. He really was the most sweet and loving man you could hope to meet ..."

Clearly she had not visited his shop recently thought Morse.

"I noted though, even when I first called, that you don't wear a ring."

"No, I would if he had given me one, but poor Hugo didn't have enough money ... he only barely scraped a living out of his business you know."

"But he was expecting to come into some money soon, wasn't he ... otherwise how was he going to pay for your round the world travels?

"He told me that everything would work out just fine ... by the time we were to set sail for New York in October we would be married, and I would have both an engagement and a wedding ring. He knew that the shop was costing too much to run, so he had vowed to sell up, but still continue to deal from upstairs for a few select customers. He said he would sell his own collection if he had to in order to make sure that our dreams would come true, and now ..."

"You have no idea where this money was going to be coming from then?"

"No, I'm sorry I haven't a clue."

It was only then that the uncontrollable sobbing started. An awkward Morse acknowleged that evidently she had nothing more to impart that might be of use to him. He wasn't going to find a motive for Hugo's murder here, if indeed it was murder. All he had left now were the stamp booklets, which on the face of it had little perceived value. Morse made his excuses and left, leaving Ms. French alone to cry her eyes out, just as had done on his first visit a couple of days ago.

Chapter Twenty-Seven

"I can provide a witness who didn't see me at the scene of
the crime. That witness can also prove they didn't see
me anywhere else either, thus showing that I didn't
exist at that moment in time."

(Jarod Kintz, *99 Cents For Some Nonsense*)

Rather than make the journey back to Kidlington at rush hour,
Morse elected to end his Friday afternoon back at St. Aldate's, from
where he had started that morning. From here he would be able to
telephone the three witnesses who had come forward, and so be able
to ascertain whether he would have need to interview them at a later
date.

The first, rather unpromisingly, had given the name of John
Smith – surely a false name thought Morse as he dialled the number,
and waited for Mr. Smith to answer.

"Hello, who's that?" came an uneducated female voice located
somewhere within the Oxford dialling code area.

"My name is Morse, and I wish to speak with a Mr. John Smith."

"And where you from then?"

"The Thames Valley Police in Oxford. Mr. Smith telephoned us
in response to a call for information he saw in the *Oxford Mail* on
Wednesday."

"Hang on ... I'll get him for you."

Morse could hear the telephone receiver put down, followed by footsteps. There was around thirty seconds of silence before he could hear more footsteps, heavier this time, coming towards the receiver, which was eventually picked up.

"I phoned you lot two days ago ... took your bloody time to get back to me, didn't you? Don't you take murder seriously in Oxford?"

Morse didn't quite know how to respond so he ignored Mr. Smith's outburst.

"I believe you have some information relating to Dead Man's Walk."

"Yeah, I do, but how much is it worth?"

Morse knew the answer to this question as it had often been tried before.

"It is worth not being arrested for blackmail, or at best withholding evidence in a police investigation. I can send an officer around, and we can discuss the finer points at the police station if you would prefer, Mr. Smith?"

"Well if you put it like that I just want to say I saw somebody sitting there on the bench in Dead Man's Walk for over an hour. They were there when I went along Broad Walk going to St. Aldate's, and still there when I returned after six."

"Can you describe them? Were they alone? Did they have anything with them such as a bag?"

"Well they were wearing dark clothes, hat, gloves and scarf. They were reading the *Oxford Mail* so the face was obscured most of the time, but I am pretty sure that it was a woman, a young woman at that. They were certainly alone, and didn't have anything else with them. Seemed to me that they were waiting for somebody, a boyfriend perhaps."

Morse asked a couple of other questions, but nothing else of any importance was forthcoming. He thanked Mr. Smith for being so public spirited, with all the diplomacy he could muster, before ringing off. The next witness was a Mr. Brandon. Morse was lucky for he too was at home.

130

"Michael Brandon speaking, can I help you?"

"Yes, Mr. Brandon, I am Detective Sergeant Morse from the Thames Valley Police ..."

"Ah, you have called about me seeing somebody on Dead Man's Walk the other day."

"Yes, I wonder ..."

"It was man, in his twenties I should say. Saw him pacing up and down by the bench there at around six on my way home. Had a sport's bag at his feet, and a black umbrella in his hand. Waiting for somebody no doubt."

"Can you describe them in any more detail for me, please?"

"Tall, well over six foot, wearing a dark suit and coat. Clean-shaven. That's about all I noticed."

"Did they have a hat or anything like that?"

"No hat, or scarf, or gloves ... just the umbrella."

"Did they have a newspaper?"

"Not that I noticed."

Again Morse thanked the witness for his help before trying the third, and last, name on the list.

"Good afternoon. This is Oxford eight-nine-one-four-zero can I help you?"

"I would like to speak with a Mrs. Dorothy Evans."

"Speaking."

"My name is Detective Sergeant Morse from the Thames Valley Police. I believe that you were at Dead Man's Walk on Tuesday evening, and may have seen somebody there that we are keen to know more about."

"Yes, indeed. I cycle along there every evening. I remember Tuesday evening very well as it is the night I nearly came off my bike, when I went into a pothole just past the Grove Walk gate. I almost hit the fellow sitting on the bench reading the newspaper."

"Now can you tell me more about him please?"

"Well let me see, he was a short man, middle-aged and wearing dark clothes, with a rather distinctive scarf. I think that it was a Magdalen scarf, black with two white stripes."

"Did he have an umbrella, or a bag with him?"

131

"There was no umbrella, but there was a holdall with a hockey stick protruding from it, as he had to jolly well move it out of the way as I swerved towards him."

"Did he have a hat or gloves?"

"I didn't notice a hat, but there were definitely no gloves otherwise he couldn't have turned the pages of his newspaper."

"Anything else about him that you can tell me?"

"I do believe he had a beard, and it was *The Times* he was reading."

Again he thanked the citizen for their help before replacing the receiver. So what had he learnt from the three witnesses, all of whom seemed certain of their facts. Morse jotted down some notes.

The person of interest was a young female, or male, or perhaps a middle-age male. Whoever they were, they wore dark clothes, with or without a hat, scarf and gloves, though if they did wear a scarf there might be a connection with Magdalen College. They may, or may not, have had a sports bag, and if they did have one it might have contained a hockey stick. They may, or may not, have been carrying an umbrella. They may, or may not, have been reading the *Oxford Mail*, or even *The Times*. Finally they had a beard, while at the same time being clean-shaven.

Morse's conclusion was that the public should never be trusted when it comes to witness statements. On balance, though, Morse thought that Mrs. Evans's description to be the most reliable on account of it both fitting in with his hockey stick theory, and because she saw the person at closer quarters, not from Broad Walk. He would get her to come in to see if a photofit or artists' impression of the man concerned could be produced. It might help, but he doubted it.

As Morse left the police station for the weekend he crossed the road to Speedwell Street, and made for the new Magistrates' Courts outside of which he knew he could still obtain a copy of the *Oxford Mail* from the vendor who was always there until late. He purchased the paper noting that on page five there was mention of a tramp who had died of hypothermia the previous evening along Dead Man's

132

Walk. It was going to be a good weekend, on that Morse was determined.

Chapter Twenty-Eight

"Wild nights! Wild nights!
Were I with thee,
Wild night should be
Our luxury!"

(Emily Dickinson, *Wild Nights! Wild Nights!*)

There were great expectations for the Saturday night. Would it be the best of times, or the worst of times, pondered Morse, along with other Dickensian quotes that came to mind. Sylvia Warren had certainly made an impression upon him, as he was to spend most of the day preening himself, and he even made a trip to the barber's shop in Summertown. Late afternoon he showered and put on his best suit, along with a plain navy blue wool tie – a Christmas present from Wendy Spencer dating back to his student days. He noted from Ms. Warren's scrap of paper that she lived not that far from him in Chalfont Road, a respectable street running parallel to the Woodstock Road to the east, and the Oxford Canal to the west. Residences here were substantial having been built during the late Victorian period for the middle classes of leafy north Oxford. Many were semi-detached, and all had large gardens to the rear. Given the proximity, and the fact that he might well have a drink or two, he decided that he would walk the mile or so, despite the sub-zero temperature.

As he approached, he noted that the outside light had been left on and that the curtains in the downstairs bay window had been drawn, although the upstairs remained in darkness with the curtains open. He rang the bell and was kept waiting for what seemed an age.

"Ah, there you are, I thought that you weren't coming", smiled Sylvia Warren.

Morse looked at his watch. It was barely five past seven. As he entered two things struck him. First there was the sound of Brunnhilde's immolation from *Gotterdammerung* emanating from the lounge, and second that Ms. Warren was dressed in a rather attractive shirt and blouse combination. To be truthful it wasn't the design, or colour combination that struck Morse, but the fact that the skirt, unlike the other evening, ended some way above the knee, and that again both the top and second button of the blouse were undone. This was a very good sign, he thought.

Ms. Warren led the way, and as she opened the door to the lounge she made an apology.

"Oh, you must forgive me, but I simply adore opera. I suspect that your tastes are rather towards The Who, The Beatles, The Kinks and the like. I'm afraid that you wont find any of their so called music here, my record collection is limited strictly to opera and classical."

The evening was getting better all the time.

"You are mistaken Ms. Warren. I too adore opera, especially Wagner and, if I am not mistaken, this is the famous recording from the Bayreuth Festival of 1951 when it reopened for the first time since the war. I only wish I had been there to hear Heilige Braut as Brunnhilde lamenting the death of Siegfried and throwing herself, and her horse onto the flames of the funeral pyre."

"My, you are a cultured policeman."

"Opera is life ... there is beauty, there is ugliness, there is love and there is death ... all the important things are right there for those who wish to find them."

136

"Then we must go to the Royal Opera House together soon."

"That would be ..."

"Well that is settled then, but only if you don't keep calling me Ms. Warren. I think I told you last time we met that you can use my first name, but if you prefer to be formal it is Doctor Warren."

"You never said that you were a doctor."

"You never asked, you only assumed that I was not a professional."

"Now I understand."

"What?"

"As a doctor the calls upon your time are always greater in winter, and so that explains why you were late when we first met at the philatelic society. I should have picked up on that when you said that it was because of the time of year that you couldn't get away from work."

"I lied. I could have been on time, but postal history is not my scene, so I stayed around the corner at a perfectly nice little pub that sells a decent selection of malts. That is why I sent Captain Boyd to get me some black coffee, so that hopefully nobody would notice my breath."

Sylvia Warren continued.

"Talking of such things I haven't offered you a drink, Morse. I'm afraid I've no wine, not to my palate, but I do have some beer, not the fizzy stuff you understand, but a proper bitter, which has at least been blessed with the presence of hops. Failing that you may like to join me in a drop of Glenkinchie ... a present from a grateful patient ... it's not bad for a lowland distillery, though I prefer the more peaty varieties."

"The malt will be just fine," said Morse.

Sylvia Warren poured two large measures into cut glass tumblers. She assumed (correctly) that he preferred his whisky without dilution.

"Now then before we go any further let's get down to business. You asked me to investigate these stamp booklets."

"Have you managed to find anything out for me?"

"Yes, I think I have. I already told you that they were old stock from a few years ago, but there is more. I checked and there is no record of Hugo Latimer ever having submitted anything to the approval packet circuit."

"So why would he have produced these and yet never submitted them?"

"Well it is possible that he ran his own circuit, but then I would have expected him to print his own booklets, or at the very least use blank booklets rather than those of the philatelic society."

"But it was certainly circulated as stamps were purchased from them."

"Yes, but only by one person. As far as I could make out from their scrawl and I thought my writing was bad enough, the buyer was somebody with the initials 'TP'. I checked this too, and we did have a long-standing member by the name of Tim Plumridge. I got his application form for membership from the secretary, and the writing appears to match."

"You are marvellous."

"I know."

"But you used the past tense?"

"Yes, that is because he never renewed his membership this year, so he may well have moved out of the area, but I have written down the address we have on file for you to follow up ... no telephone number I'm afraid, and he's not in the phone book either. Also, according to the secretary, Mr. Plumridge hasn't been to a meeting for many a year ... nothing strange in that, though, for many members just enjoy reading the newsletter, and never attend anything unless it is of real interest to them."

"Anything else?"

"Yes, I was surprised by the contents of the approval books themselves. Have a look ..." she handed the booklets back to Morse, "you will see that there is no order to them. The stamps are not in sets, or by country, or under themes and the pricing is all wrong too ... far too high for such common items. The stamps here are not for the collector, but the sort you would send out to children at a penny each to start them off collecting. If they had been submitted to me

138

for inclusion in the club packet I can tell you that I would have rejected them without any hesitation."

"So why on earth would somebody like our Mr. Plumridge want to subscribe, let alone purchase, stamps from such a booklet?"

"Well, Morse, I have to leave something for you to investigate."

Morse smiled.

"Thank you, again. You have been a great help. Now then ... Sylvia ... tell me what got you involved in stamps?"

"It was my late father. He was the collector and ran the stamp packet before me. I just used to come along to the meetings as a little girl, a way of getting out of the house occasionally, and avoiding homework. I always liked horses so I started to collect horses on stamps ... you would be surprised just how many you can find from around the world. Then when my father died a couple of years ago they asked if I would continue, so I did, and I suppose I have never been brave enough to resign."

"Well I am very glad that you didn't."

"Why?"

"Otherwise I would never have met you ..." Morse suddenly realised that his automatic response revealed rather more about his feelings than perhaps a policeman should midway through a murder investigation. He blushed in embarrassment.

"Don't worry, I feel likewise. It isn't every day I meet somebody who likes both opera and malt."

She refilled the two empty glasses. Morse thought he had better change the subject.

"Do you practice here in Summertown?"

"No, I am not a G.P., I am at the J.R. and specialise in liver disease. Ironic really given the amount of whisky I drink."

Morse hesitated as he struggled to find an apt reply.

"I sing to you and I fear you as though you were judge, meter, implacable indicator, and if I can not surrender myself in shackles to austerity, if the surfeit of delicacies, or the hereditary wine of my country dared to disturb my health or the equilibrium of my poetry, from you, dark monarch, giver of syrups and of poisons, regulator of

139

salts, from you I hope for justice: I love life: Do not betray me! Work on!"

"Do not arrest my song ... I doubt if there are more than a handful of people in the world who know that piece of poetry by Pablo Neruda. You really are a most extraordinary man, Morse."

Morse blushed for the second time that evening.

"And do you live here in this large house all alone?" he said, hoping that there would be no mention of a Mr. Warren.

"Now then, that is not what you really want to know is it? What you're trying to find out is if I have a boyfriend or husband. Clearly I am not married, as I am sure you have already noticed that I wear no rings. Unfortunately it is the pretty young nurses on the wards who attract all the attentions of the patients. They never once consider that we doctors also have needs. We, of course, are expected to fall in love with other doctors, but if only they knew how boring most of them are, then they would understand just why I seek the company of handsome and cultured blue eyed policemen when they come along."

Morse gave a nervous cough before finishing off his whisky.

"Do I seem a little too forward to you?"

"Well it is not often I meet somebody like ..."

"Me? Well, have another whisky, the night is young, and life is too short, believe me, to beat around the bush don't you think?"

"I had better not otherwise I will be unable to drive home."

"Do you really want to go home tonight, Morse? I would much prefer that you stay and join me upstairs, where you can make love to me while Wagner plays below."

At that moment the record finished with the record player arm rising and returning to its rest position. Sylvia also rose, turned the record over, and replaced the arm at the start of the next track. Then seductively she walked across to Morse, offering him her hand, which was gladly taken. A visibly shaking Morse was led up the stairs to the master bedroom.

"I have a confession to make," said he. "I don't have to worry about driving home as I didn't come by car."

"I have a confession to make too. I already knew that. I saw you walking down the street from the bedroom window."

Chapter Twenty-Nine

"But all the same it's strange to me,
How very full the church can be
With people I don't see at all
Except at Harvest Festival."

(John Betjeman, *Diary of a Church Mouse*)

Sunday: a day of rest, a day at the end of the week, a day when good people go to church, but not for Morse, not for 'Pagan' Morse, not for Morse the atheist. For him it was just another day, albeit a day when he did not have to go to the office, a day when he could stay at home, or go to the pub, a day when he could read *The Sunday Times* from cover to cover at leisure, in fact a day when he could do whatever he damn well pleased. Happy thoughts, but not for him this day, as when on a murder investigation there was no concept of rest at weekends. Despite the most pleasurable interlude with Sylvia Warren the previous night, Morse left her bed and house by ten o'clock the Sunday morning, determined to interview Tim Plumridge, who he now felt sure held the key to certainly one death, and probably two, along Dead Man's Walk.

First he needed to go home if only to shave and change out of his best suit. Then it was off to the Boars Hill, a small hamlet just three

143

miles to the southwest of Oxford, but actually over the border and in Berkshire. Morse knew a nice public house in Boars Hill. He might be tempted to make a visit to The Fox on his way home, depending on what he was able to discover from Mr. Plumridge. Yes, a pint or two while doing *The Sunday Times* crossword sounded quite idyllic to him. It was what Sundays were for thought Morse as he drove along Yarn Way. He had no trouble in finding the Plumridge residence. It was a fine double-fronted detached house set back from the road, and approached by a not insignificant driveway. Planted next to the open gate was a 'For Sale' sign. Morse wondered how much a property like this would cost. Certainly out of his price range. Clearly Mr. Plumridge was a wealthy man.

The doorbell was answered by a young woman of no more than twenty-two years, wearing a tartan patterned skirt designed for somebody twice her age. She had short black hair, brown eyes and thin lips.

"I'm sorry, but we don't buy from hawkers," she said in a rather formal manner.

Why was it that everybody always thought that he was selling something?

"I am not a tradesman Miss, but a policeman from Thames Valley, and I am looking for a Mr. Tim Plumridge. My name is Morse."

"Oh, you had better come in then, and speak to father."

Morse was left in the large entrance hall with just an old oak table upon which was a vase, devoid of flowers at this time of year, to keep him company, while the young lady went in search of her father. The house was like a stately home, but built on a much smaller scale. Soon a man appeared, from what Morse took was the way to the kitchen, given that he was wearing a chef's apron.

"I believe you are looking for Tim Plumridge?"

"Are you he?"

"No, I am his son, Robert. I'm afraid that Tim passed away some six months ago, so I fear your journey is in vain."

That explained why he never renewed his philatelic society membership. It wasn't what Morse had expected to hear.

144

"I am sorry. I wanted to ask him some questions relating to his membership of the local stamp club."

"Why don't you come through to the sitting room and I will try to help you. I must apologise as we have only just returned from church, and I was busy helping my wife, Guna, with the Sunday lunch. Maybe I can get you some tea, or coffee?"

"That's most kind of you, but I can see that you are busy so I will try to keep my enquiry as short as possible."

Morse was led into a spacious room with no fewer than three settees of different fabrics, built-in bookcases along two walls and French windows leading out into the back garden along another. The final wall was rather overcrowded with framed family photographs spanning several generations.

"A beautiful house you have here, Mr. Plumridge, but I note that you have it up for sale."

"Yes, we are looking for somewhere smaller now that father is no longer with us, and Louise, my daughter, whom you met at the front door, has left home and lives in London now, so there are just the two of us. Actually the house belonged to my father, and so with the impending death duties we would need to sell up anyway."

"And tell me in what line of business was Mr. Plumridge?"

"The family money came from the manufacture of newsprint."

"Of course, Plumridge's paper. You supply most of the national newspapers don't you?"

"Not any longer I'm afraid. My father sold the company well over a decade ago when he retired. Where all the money went I don't really know. It just disappeared over the years until now this house is the only real family asset. In truth we have been living beyond our means for years."

"So you never joined the family business then?"

"Lord no, I'm not business minded in the least. I went off to college in Cambridge to read history at Queens'."

He pointed to a framed photograph of himself on the wall in which he was wearing a graduation gown.

"And what did you do after that?"

"For my sins I now teach history to the rich at Radley."

Morse understood the underlying tone of frustration for despite being a premier private boarding school founded in the mid-nineteenth century by the Reverend William Sewell, Radley College was not known for its academic excellence – more for whether you were a 'wet bob' (rowing) or a 'dry bob' (cricketing) person.

Just then Guna and Louise Plumridge entered, the former holding a large tray containing a pot of coffee and another of tea, along with cups, saucers, spoons, milk and even a plate of biscuits.

"I hope you don't mind," began Mrs. Plumridge, "but I was making some tea and coffee anyway so thought that you might like a cup."

Morse accepted graciously, especially the biscuits.

"What I really wanted to know about was Mr. Plumridge's membership of the stamp club."

It was Louise who replied.

"Well, I was the one who always helped granddad with his stamp collecting."

"So would you know anything about these?" Morse produced the stamp booklets from his inside coat pocket.

"Oh, yes. I remember these, they used to come in the post about once a month from the local stamp dealer."

"Such a nice man that Mr. Latimer, especially when Tim died," added Guna Plumridge.

"Mr. Plumridge must have had a fine collection built up over the years, but I am told that he very infrequently attended the stamp club."

"Well he used to when he was still able, but as he became more infirm he was content just to receive the booklets, and the newsletter, of course. You see he didn't go in much for displaying his stamps and entering competitions. He thought that was vulgar."

"I see, a private man, but tell me how do these booklets work?"

"Well, as I said, they would come in the post every month or so. We would look through them together, and might choose a few stamps for the collection, which we would sign for and then return the booklets in the post, along with a cheque for what we had taken."

146

"And did you buy a lot?"

"No, he set a strict spending limited of a few pounds per month, and before buying anything he would always take a photostat for his records."

"You have a photostat machine at home then?"

"Yes, there was one in granddad's study upstairs, left over from his business days," said Robert Plumridge.

"I would love to see his collection. Would that be …"

Louise Plumridge interrupted before Morse could finish.

"It was one of the first things that we had to sell after he died."

"And may I ask if it was worth much?"

Guna Plumridge was able to provide the answer to that question in some detail.

"That nice Mr. Latimer came and saw us all shortly after Tim passed away. He offered to buy back the whole collection. At first I thought that it might be a con, as you hear of these people who read the obituaries looking at who has just died, and going around to the relatives to buy their possessions cheaply. But this was different as, of course, we knew from the photostats exactly what was in the collection, and what Tim had paid for it. Mr. Latimer did point out that stamp collecting was a hobby and that therefore in most cases when people come to sell their collection that they should never expect to get back the money they put into their hobby. However, in Tim's case it seems that he had chosen wisely, and his stamps had held their value, even increased a little. In total adding up all the transactions it came to just under one thousand nine hundred pounds, and Mr. Latimer kindly made it up to a round two thousand pounds. That was a nice surprise for us all. I would like to have kept them for Louise, but we really need the money at present."

"That is a fair sum of money. How did he pay you?"

"In cash.

"I see. Would you by any chance have those photostats you mentioned?"

"Why on earth would you want them?" asked Robert Plumridge.

"Well I was hoping that I may be able to match up your father's stamps with those in the stamp shop."

"I'm sorry, but I disposed of them some months ago," replied Louise Plumridge in such haste that it left Morse in no doubt that the family were hiding something from him.

"Why don't you simply ask Mr. Latimer?" came a logical response from Guna Plumridge.

"I'm afraid I can't do that as Mr. Latimer is dead."

"Poor man, he didn't look that old," said Guna Plumridge with genuine warmth.

"No, he fell off his bicycle while cycling home earlier this week. I am just trying to tie up some loose ends to establish a clearer picture of his financial affairs."

Morse finished his tea and thought that he had better change the subject. He turned towards the daughter.

"London is a nice city, which part do you live in?"

"I have a flat in Pimlico close to where I work, but come home most weekends."

"A little bit of a change for you going from a village to a big city."

"Yes, it was at first but I really love it now. As you know London is just a lot of villages all joined together."

Morse spotted another graduation photograph on the wall.

"Is that you?" A rather stupid question given that father and daughter looked so similar, and both were seated in front of him.

"Yes, it seems an age ago now but was actually just last summer."

"And what did you read?"

"I followed in father's footsteps and read history."

"And did you follow those footsteps into teaching as well?"

"No, after so many years being surrounded by teenagers the last thing I wanted to do was to try and teach them something. I joined the civil service and work as one of the researchers in the Palace of Westminster. Most of my time is spent in the House of Commons library looking up things for MPs, so that they can look knowledgeable in front of other MPs."

"I suspect that in many ways teaching teenagers would be easier," joked Morse, and on that note he rose to leave having run out of not only biscuits to eat, but questions to ask. However, on his way to the front door Guna Plumridge took him to one side.

"Are you going to tell the Inland Revenue about the cash we received for the stamps? We all know it is wrong not to declare the money, but we would rather it be kept a secret. It will be a struggle for us to survive even with that money. If anybody needs to be blamed it is me for it was I who got Louise to destroy the photostats so that there is no record of Tim ever having had a stamp collection."

So that was the family secret that they were trying to hide. Morse had sympathy for them for it had always seemed unfair to him that you should not be able to pass on your possessions to whoever you wanted upon your death, without the State first taking most of them in tax.

"Please don't worry on that account, Mrs. Plumridge, my investigation pertains to the death of Mr. Latimer and not to yourself. You have been most candid with me in your answers, and I will leave it between you and the taxman how candid you are with him."

Morse rather thought that Mrs Plumridge was either going to burst into tears or kiss him. In the event she did neither. Morse departed for his appointment with a fox.

Chapter Thirty

"Sometimes, when words ring true,
I'm like a lone fox dancing
In the morning dew."

(Ruskin Bond, *Lone Fox Dancing*)

Alas no food, but then who needs food when there is best bitter on tap? Certainly Morse was content to sit by the inglenook fireplace caressing his beer, as carefully as if it were a valuable piece of artwork. After all it was beer that relaxed his body and mind, and in doing so let his thoughts take shape in that vast complex brain of his. What had he learnt that morning? Was it of any help in supporting his theory? Morse had to succumb to the inextricable truth that there was still no motive for the murder of Hugo Latimer, and yet he still felt sure that his death was not an accident.

The Plumridges seemed a rather decent group of people, all living in the family home, and rallying around to look after Tim Plumridge right up until his death – just as one would hope from those who go to church on Sunday. Louise, the daughter, was evidently fond of her granddad, as well as her father, given that she had followed in his footsteps and taken the same degree as him, and was now respectfully employed in London, while Mary was the typical stay-at-home wife whose only worry was being found out for not declaring a few pounds to the taxman. Then there was Robert, a frustrated history teacher at the local school, albeit a private one. There was no motive identifiable here for murder. Notwithstanding that, the mystery of the stamp booklets had been explained. A whole new set of questions now came to mind.

Morse knew from his visit to the bank that Hugo Latimer had nothing like the two thousand pounds he had paid to the Plumridges, so where had he obtained such a sum, and in cash too? Also it made little sense to him as to why Latimer would want to buy the collection back for more than he had sold it to Tim Plumridge in the first place. Maybe the stamps had risen in value by far more than he had revealed to the Plumridges, but surely not that much more? Then there was the nagging question as to where the collection was now. Had it been broken down and sold off over the intervening months? Again there were no signs of financial activity in Latimer's bank account to suggest that he had done so, and the search of his shop had revealed no such collection of any worth. Surely, if anything, he would have placed such an item in his safe, and not those worthless approval booklets. Whatever the answer might be to these questions Morse understood that, sizable as it was, two thousand pounds was unlikely to be a motive for murder, *ergo* Latimer's death was probably the decoy, and he must now divert his attentions to the late Professor Tamati Cranmer.

That he would do, but not before another pint, and certainly not before completing *The Sunday Times* crossword. This he solved in a respectable time of just under twenty minutes. Morse was pleased with himself. He then began to browse the rest of the newspaper, and in particular the arts section to ascertain what productions might be forthcoming at the Royal Opera House in London. Thoughts strayed to Sylvia Warren and to whether her tastes extended beyond Wagner to Mozart and the *Magic Flute*, which he noted would soon be in production there. The tickets would no doubt be expensive for

152

somebody on a Detective Sergeant's salary, but worth it he thought in view of the previous evening.

It was almost an hour before he saw it. There among the political pages was an article that provided ample motive for the murder that Morse believed was yet to come, and it was this that he would report to McNutt first thing Monday morning.

Chapter Thirty-One

Politician /pɒlɪˈtɪʃ(ə)n/ noun. 1. One who is actively involved or skilled in politics, especially one who holds a political office. 2. One who deceives or outmanoeuvres others for personal gain.

(*Free Dictionary* definition of a politician)

For the second time in a week Morse made a visit to Blackwell's bookshop on his way into work. This time it was not to purchase anything, but rather to reference the entry in *Who's Who* of the person who was now to be at the centre of his investigation. This time he was not quite so lucky for on his return to the car there was a parking ticket under the windscreen wiper. It was of little consequence to Morse as he knew that being on police business in a pool car any penalty would be revoked in due course.

On arrival at Kidlington he went straight to McNutt's office and told him about his visit to the Plumridges the previous day.

"Well, it seems like a dead end to me, Morse," came the considered opinion of his superior. "Apart from the couple of loose ends, to which I suspect there will be answers elsewhere, and nothing to do with murder, I think we can shelve that case for the moment, and concentrate our efforts on Cramner and Ridley."

"If it as we now believe sir, I think I have found the Ridley in question."

155

Morse carefully placed *The Sunday Times* newspaper article on McNutt's desk.

"Surely you must be joking, man!"

"Not in the least. It would be the logical choice, after all he is the most high profile Nicholas Ridley since 1555."

"But Morse, Nicholas Ridley the politician isn't the Minister of Parliament for Oxford is he, so why would he be connected with this case?"

"No, sir, he is the Minister of Parliament for Cirencester and Tewkesbury, but he does have two Oxford connections. I checked in *Who's Who* this morning. First he was educated at Balliol, and second despite being the representative for a constituency some sixty miles away, he does have a residence in Oxford, not far from Dead Man's Walk in fact ... that in itself seems significant to me."

"Hmm. I suppose it is possible, but what would be the motive?"

"He's been in parliament since 1959 so I very much doubt if he hasn't made an enemy of two during that time. In fact, just look at the newspaper article, and you will see that he is very much involved with the Selsdon Club, and they have very few friends."

"And just what exactly is the Selsdon Club?"

"There was a meeting last year at the Selsdon Park Hotel near Croydon where the then Shadow Cabinet put forward some extreme proposals which they say helped win the General Election. This informal group of Conservative Party radicals is dedicated to promote the case for free market policies. Their self-proclaimed leader is none other than Nicholas Ridley, and their politics are akin to those of Burke, Peel, Salisbury and Churchill ..."

"Enough, Morse. So enemies might include the entire Labour Party, the unions as well half the present government."

"More likely that it would be some disgruntled person who has been adversely affected by those policies. Maybe somebody who has lost their job, or seen a family member die in hospital for want of money being spent on their treatment."

"So in essence, Morse, you are telling me that the deaths of Latimer and Cranmer are merely unhappy preludes to the main event, which is to be the assassination of a high profile Member of

Parliament, which is being dressed up to look like a psychopath out for revenge for the deaths of the Oxford Martyrs in the sixteenth century?"

"It is possible, sir."

"Well, it is just possible, and we would look pretty damned foolish if we ignored it altogether. I will inform the diplomatic squad and they can take it from here. After all they have far more manpower than we do. They can certainly keep Ridley away from Dead Man's Walk if nothing else."

"What do you want me to do, sir?"

"Go over to Lonsdale and see if there is anything there we have missed regarding the Cranmer murder. If you are right, we will have two chances to get this person ... one when he makes an attempt on Ridley and the other from any clues left behind after the Cranmer killing. At long last things are starting to come together, and I feel we might now be one step ahead of the killer. Thank God it probably isn't a religious fanatic."

"I will see what I can find, sir."

"By the way, Morse, well done with your friend at the *Oxford Mail* ... I see that he bought your story about the tramp. You're learning."

Chapter Thirty-Two

"People who look down on other people
don't end up being looked up to."

(Robert Half)

As Morse approached from Radcliffe Square he could see that
the Londsdale flag – Oxford blue and white – was flying at half
mast. This was no doubt in remembrance of Tamati Cranmer. He
knew the way to the Master's residence, and so did not stop at the
Porter's Lodge, although he did give a cursory wave to those inside
as he passed. He proceeded straight to the first quadrangle of this
fifteenth century institute of learning, and from there he ascended
what was known as the Old Staircase to the first floor of the
wisteria-clad building where the Master's rooms are located. As he
entered the inner sanctum so he could feel the ever-increasing
hypocrisy of the place, made more sinister by the present incumbent,
Sir Michael Chipperfield. This evil necromancer was not known in
academic circles as the circus master for nothing.

The Master had absolute power over college affairs, the only
requirement for the job being that they should be sound of mind, be
in good health, not have taken Holy Orders and be without a

criminal record. Londsdale made no demand for any academic achievements. This was just as well, since Chipperfield had earned neither a doctorate, or professorship, save for the honorary titles awarded to him by various institutions. His whole career had been a success on the basis of not who he knew, but what he knew about who he knew. It is fair to say that Morse had little time or respect for him. He did not trust as far as he throw him, which wouldn't be that far even though Chipperfield was of slight build.

Although Morse was a St. John's man, he had visited the college on several occasions, having been invited on guest evenings to dine in the Great Hall. He entered the outer office to be greeted by Chipperfield's secretary, who verified by internal telephone that the Master was in college, and would see Morse directly.

"Ah, Morse, Oxford's finest, one of our own, well almost one of our own, such a pity that you gave up ... all over that woman Wendy Spencer, how disappointing ... and they tell me that you would have made a fine scholar given the right encouragement," came the greeting from the Master, who was busy gathering some papers on his large oak desk.

"You are, as usual, very well informed, though I doubt if I would ever have been in your league, Master."

"No, probably not, but our loss is Thames Valley's gain I suppose. No doubt you are here to enquire after our dear departed colleague, Cranmer?"

"You don't seem too upset about the loss."

"Fellows come and go, you learn that after a while, and just get down to deal with the paperwork."

"But not all of them are murdered though are they?"

"True, but the paperwork is much the same. Have to lower the college flag for a week as it was a case of dying *durante munere*, of course, but then back to business as normal. Hope that you noted that touch of compassion as you entered. Officially I am in a state of mourning. Madeira, Morse?"

"No, thank you, Master. I had forgotten your little tradition of not having sherry in college, but cannot remember why."

160

"We did serve that disgusting fortified wine from Spain right up until 1588 I believe, but thereafter those who produced it were none too popular in these quarters, so we switched to Madeira. Equally disgusting, but at least it's Portuguese."

"Of course, the Armada."

"Now then, do take a seat and tell me how I can help expedite your investigation," invited Chipperfield, having poured himself a large glass of the aforementioned spirit.

"You can start by telling me a little about the man."

"New Zealand by birth, came here in the 1950s, worked his way up through Tutor, Senior Tutor and then Fellow. His subject was ancient history, all good stuff I'm sure, but no commercial money in it for research, just the odd crumb here and there. Give me a scientist any day of the week, they're worth their weight in gold to the college. Not married, no current girlfriend. End of story *Deo volente*."

"Did you like him?"

"Like! I am the Master, I am not here to like people, Morse. He was affable enough, I suppose. He certainly liked women, though what they saw in him I can't imagine. Mind you he always dressed nicely, handmade suits and the like, suspect he spent most of his salary on clothes and women. Had to save him once or twice from scandal. Tried seducing at least two Fellows' wives with a 'come with me to Greece, or wherever, as my research assistant on an all expenses paid field trip'. Last one who took up the offer was on the next plane home when the poor cow found out that he had only booked one room with a double bed. Ha, served her right to be so stupid if you ask me. Thank God we don't let women study here yet, though mark my words it will only be a matter of time, and then we'll see the standards fall."

"By the sound of it you are not too disappointed to be shot of him, and yet you say you defended him when you could have had him dismissed for gross moral turpitude."

"Not necessarily, Morse. The statutes state that we must have a history Fellow. Even I can't override that one and put a scientist in his place. However, having a Fellow that is indebted to you is the

161

next best thing. For instance he worked the last few miserable years of his life for a pittance, and would have continued to do so for as long as I'm here."

"Anything else you can tell me about him?"

"No."

"Can I see his rooms?"

"You can, but it won't do you any good as they have already been cleared."

"Your mourning doesn't extend very far does it?"

"We can't just sit around and wait for things to happen. Somebody has to do something; colleges don't just run themselves, Morse. His room is a valuable asset and needs to be occupied as soon as possible. I did wait until I was given the all clear from your lot though just in case you think that there's anything suspicious in my actions."

"Did he have any hobbies?"

"Such as?"

"Train spotting, bird watching, stamp collecting ..."

"I am a philatelist, he was not."

"Then you must have visited Latimer's shop by the Westgate development?"

"I said that I was a philatelist, Morse, not a stamp collector. I doubt that he would ever cater for somebody who takes the subject seriously ... I buy my stamps direct from the London auction houses, not the dingy corner shop."

That was the second most interesting thing that Chipperfield had said in the space of their conversation Morse thought.

"Any reason why Cranmer would have been the other side of town along Dead Man's Walk on the evening of his death?"

"Not that I'm aware."

"Did he usually dine and spend his evenings in college?"

"He couldn't afford otherwise."

"Were you in college on the evening of his death?"

"I resent the possible implication, but I was here all evening."

"Did Cranmer have any religious beliefs?"

"None of which I know. I try to discourage that sort of thing. If he was religious, he certainly wasn't a Catholic as they are barred since ..."

"1588, I know," interrupted Morse. "Well, thank you for your help. I trust that you will not mind if I ask some questions around the college?"

"*Meus ut hospes sies.*"

"Please present my best regards to Lady Chipperfield."

"Would do, Morse, but she is away doing some brass rubbing in France with a couple of her friends at the moment. *Dominus vobiscum.*"

Back outside away from the choking atmosphere of the Master's lair Morse was to make just one further enquiry.

The Great Hall was small compared with many Oxford colleges, but like most comprised two long tables of oak plank with matching benches on either side for the students and a further smaller bench that served as top table perpendicular to these at the far end of the hall, with just one bench for the Fellows and guests. Next to this there was a notice board upon which was pinned the menus for the week. Morse was lucky in that underneath the menu for the current week, was the one for the previous seven days. With some stealth, though he was not entirely certain why he should act quite so furtively, Morse removed the older piece of paper, which he put in his inside jacket pocket.

Finally he sought out the butler, a curious title for the person who acts as headwaiter during college meals, but then this is Oxford as Morse was forever reminding himself. He ascertained from him the fact that he believed that neither Cranmer, nor the Master, for that matter, were present at dinner on the evening in question, though he could not say so with absolute conviction.

Chapter Thirty-Three

"Content the stomach and the stomach will content you."

(Thomas Walker)

Morse exited by the back door of Lonsdale, which was officially reserved for the use of Senior Fellows only, straight into the High where he crossed the road into Logic Lane. From here he proceeded via Merton Street and Grove Walk, but instead of turning left to the scenes of crime along Dead Man's Walk, he went straight on to cross Christ Church Meadow, emerging minutes later from the gate at the War Memorial Garden into the throng of St. Aldate's. Although he knew it by heart, he always paused to read the inscription from *Pilgrim's Progress* laid into the paving by those great wrought-iron structures; 'My sword I give to him that shall succeed me in my pilgrimage'.

At the bottom of Oxford's oldest street was the Thames but, more importantly for Morse, half way up was the Apollo pub where he intended to spend his lunch hour. However, first he needed to break his journey at Floyd's Row, and confirm his latest suspicion with de Bryn. Hopefully he was working at the mortuary today, and was not back at the William Dunn School of Pathology in South Parks Road. Morse was correct.

"Ah, there you are, Morse. Found any interesting hockey sticks lately?"

"Very droll, Max. Found any interesting stomach contents recently?"

"Such as?"

"I was hoping you could tell me if the final meal eaten by Cranmer corresponded to this concoction."

Morse produced the menu he had purloined from the Great Hall at Lonsdale, and pointed to the dinner menu for the night in question. Max fetched a red folder from under a bottle of whisky on his desk.

"For medicinal purposes only, Morse. Helps to calm the relatives down once they have seen their loved ones on the slab. What's worse I can't even claim for it. Now then ... let's see what the last supper was for our Professor Cranmer."

There was some shuffling of papers within the folder.

"Tomato soup, lamb chops with two veg. and cabinet pudding along with liberal quantities of wine and port," pronounced de Bryn.

Morse looked disappointed.

"Well he certainly didn't eat anything like that, Morse."

"I knew it. He ate outside of college that evening with somebody else, and I know with whom," said Morse.

"Would you like to know where they ate?"

"Don't tell me you found a receipt in his pocket?"

"No, not quite as finite, but given that his stomach contents were in the main composed of rice, chicken and a thick brown sauce I think that will give you a clue?"

"Indian or Chinese?"

"There were also traces of noodles and pork so without doubt it was a Chinese establishment."

"Thank you, Max. I will let you continue your medicinal work in peace."

"Promises, promises ... do feel free to close the door on your way out, old chap."

166

Chapter Thirty-Four

"It is a capital mistake to theorize before you have all the evidence. It biases the judgment."

(Sherlock Holmes, *A Study in Scarlet*)

At long last some of the threads were coming together for Morse. For no particular reason, save that he was passing anyway, he would call in at St. Aldate's and tell Strange of the latest developments, and see if he agreed with him as to the prime suspect. As expected Strange was on front desk duty with another officer whom Morse did not recognise.

"What brings you here, Morse?"

"Just passing. Thought that you might like to know how things are progressing."

"Indeed I would. You'll be alright holding the fort, won't you Roberts?"

The other officer nodded in assent. Inevitably Strange led the way to the canteen on the upper floor of the police station.

"Had lunch yet?"

"Yes, thank you, but do go ahead yourself," replied Morse lying knowing that his lunch, in liquid form, was awaiting him just up the road.

When both were seated Morse commenced.

"I have found somebody who is both a philatelist and with a link to Cranmer at Lonsdale."

"Well, who is it ... don't keep me in suspense."

"The Master of Lonsdale."

"Surely, you must be joking."

"No joke, Sir Michael Chipperfield I am sure was with Cranmer on the night of his death. He certainly didn't have much respect for his colleague."

"And the motive?"

"Not sure at the moment, but I will find one don't you fret. Nothing stays a secret for long in Oxford academic circles."

"And what about Latimer?"

"Again, I don't know. Chipperfield denied ever knowing Latimer in such a way that it belied the fact that he must have had dealings with him."

"You had better make absolutely sure of your facts, or you'll be for the high jump, matey. What about means and opportunity?"

"Lonsdale is not that far from Dead Man's Walk. Nobody would think anything of somebody entering or leaving the college carrying a sports bag. Also take into account that the Senior Fellows' door opens into the High and so adds a certain privacy as well. It probably explains why nobody has come forward reporting seeing anybody traipsing about with such a thing up the High. Don't forget too that Cranmer lectured in history so would certainly know of the Oxford Martyrs, as would Chipperfield. Best of all there is a witness."

"A witness. Have they identified him then?"

"Not yet, but I'm sure they will. Dorothy Evans, the lady who telephoned in following the call for witnesses in the *Oxford Mail*, gave a description that matches Chipperfield, and what is more she stated that he was wearing a college scarf."

"A Lonsdale College scarf?"

"Actually she thought it was a Magdalen College scarf, but she was wrong."

"How do you know that?"

"Well you know what happens at night?"

"What?"

"I thought you knew, Strange ... it gets dark! Magdalen scarves are black and white striped, whereas Lonsdale scarves are Oxford blue and white, and at night eyes have trouble distinguishing dark colours. Yes, it will be the vanity of Chipperfield that will be his downfall, mark my words."

"And where does the tramp fit into all this then?"

"Tramp ... what tramp?"

"The one who was killed in Dead Man's Walk."

"There was no tramp, Strange. That was just a story I concocted for the *Oxford Mail* because if they knew that the victims were named Latimer and Cranmer they might just have made a connection with the Oxford Martyrs and caused a general panic."

"But there bloody well was a tramp you know," came a rather unexpected reply from Strange.

"When?"

"Last November ... a tramp was found dead on one of the benches along Dead Man's Walk. Died of hypothermia just as reported in the paper."

"Good God, Strange. You're right. I remember now, and that must have been in my subconscious when I was trying to think of something to tell Coghlan."

A third death. He had better talk with de Bryn again directly. This changed everything thought Morse to himself. It certainly changed to zero his prospects of having a pint or two at the Apollo.

169

Chapter Thirty-Five

"A tramp, a gentleman, a poet, a dreamer, a lonely fellow,
always hopeful of romance and adventure."

(Charlie Chaplin)

"Twice in one day, Morse. I must have done something pretty bad in another life I guess."

"Tell me about the tramp that was found down Dead Man's Walk last November, Max."

A pained expression came over de Bryn's face as he tried to remember the person in question.

"Not a lot I can say really. He was a vagrant of around fifty years of age. Died of hypothermia. Nothing suspicious there given the temperatures we had leading up to Christmas."

"A name would help."

"No name, no next of kin ... at least nobody came forward."

"So what would have happened to him? A pauper's grave at the municipal cemetery, or perhaps the crematorium?"

"We don't call them pauper's graves any longer ... they are public health burials. I held onto the body just in case some one came to claim him, but after six weeks under the Public Health Act it is the local authority who has the duty of care to cremate, or bury, any person who has died where there appears to be no next of kin. In Oxford that means a burial just to be on the safe side."

"And just how closely did you examine him, Max?"

"I resent that, Morse. I always do a professional job as you well know ..."

"I know, I know, Max, and I am sorry to ask but might there have been something you missed, something that you weren't looking for given that it seemed all to clear as to how they died?"

"You mean like a ruddy great bruise to the back of the head made by a hockey stick I suppose."

"Yes, something like that ... you see if I am right this may be our missing body, Nicholas Ridley. It makes sense as our murderer, who presumably had done nothing like this before, needed to practice in advance of the main killings, and what better way than on some old tramp, who was probably close to death anyway and would not be missed."

"Well if you put it like that, yes it is just possible that something was missed. In fact a post-mortem would not have been carried out in such circumstances. It would have been a local doctor who would have signed the death certificate, and we would merely have stored him here. As far as I recall I was never asked to examine him."

"Thank you, Max. I would never think ..."

"I know, Morse ... well you had better get on to McNutt. He will be delighted I'm sure at what you are going to request."

Chapter Thirty-Six

Cul-de-sac /kuhl-duh-sak/ noun. 1. A street, lane etc., closed at one end; blind alley; dead-end street. 2. Any situation in which further progress is impossible. 3. The hemming in of a military force on all sides except behind. 4. *Anatomy*, a saclike cavity, tube, or the like, open only at one end, as the cecum.

(*Dictionary.com* definition of a cul-de-sac)

"An exhumation … do you know how much that would bloody well cost, Morse, not to mention the paperwork involved?" exclaimed McNutt who was evidently as pleased as de Bryn had suggested he would be.

"Yes, sir, I do but, given the circumstances, can we afford not to? If this tramp turns out to have been killed by a blow to the head rather than just hypothermia then we have a third victim, and therefore know that there is definitely a link between the other two. We would also know that it was premeditated murder, and not just the work of some religious crank. And if we could further establish that his name was Ridley then all the other Ridleys in Oxford can sleep safe and sound in their beds, and we would know that the killings are likely to cease. Think of the savings in overtime if nothing else." Morse thought that the last part of his argument might appeal the most to his Scottish superior.

173

"And if he is just a vagrant that happened to freeze to death in the wrong place?"

"Then it is just a dead-end, and we are no further advanced, but also not hampered either. It was you who taught me, sir, to follow my instincts and to pursue every lead, as eventually a lead will always find its way to the truth."

"You're right, man, on both accounts ... we cannot afford not to follow up, and I cannot afford to let you not follow your detective nose. Leave it with me and I will have the paperwork put in place."

"Thank you, sir. How long will it all take?"

"If we can find a sympathetic judge we should have a court order tomorrow, and the body soon afterwards. Meanwhile, what do you propose we do with Sir Michael Chipperfield?"

"There are two leads that I would like to follow up first, and neither can be done until this evening. However, I suggest we bring him in for questioning first thing tomorrow, and see if Dorothy Evans, the witness whom I telephoned, can formerly identify him."

"No, Morse we will not have him in for questioning, but merely seek for his assistance with our enquiries ... we don't want to go in there like a bull in a china shop do we now?"

"No, sir, God forbid that we would treat the Master of Lonsdale any differently from other suspects in a murder investigation."

"I don't want to antagonise the man, Morse, and I don't want him to take part in an identity parade either ... you will have to come up with something a little more subtle. Do you think this female witness is reliable?"

"I can be very subtle when called upon, and yes, sir, having spoken with Dorothy Evans she seems like somebody that is credible and not given over to flights of fancy."

"That remains to be seen on both counts, Morse. Meanwhile you had better go and type up your notes, just in case the Chief Superintendent wants to see them, as I am sure that he will be the first person Sir Michael will contact post-interview. I think that you had better make it an afternoon interview."

"Yes, sir ... we wouldn't want to spoil Sir Michael's lunch."

"I wasn't thinking of his lunch, Morse, more that if there were any follow up complaints directed at us then we wouldn't get to hear of them until the following day, which would give us enough time to defend our actions, or me to give you a boot up the backside. Does it also not occur to you that knowing he is to be interviewed in the afternoon might spoil Sir Michael's morning? Now on your way, Morse."

Back at his desk Morse was the model of efficiency and industry. He first telephoned Dorothy Evans, who, as suspected, was more than happy to help in any way she could. Morse arranged for a car to pick her up from home at two-thirty the following day. He also remembered to take a copy of Cranmer's photograph from his file since he would have need of that later. Although he wasn't particularly fast at typing, he did produce four foolscap sheets before five o'clock. Indeed he was just about to depart for central Oxford when the telephone rang.

"Morse," he said, delivering his standard salutation in a depressing monotone as if he were some bored teenager.

"Coghlan here, old boy. Don't sound so depressed. I have some good news for you."

"Oh, yes."

"Might like to have a look at tonight's paper. That dead tramp of yours was a little bit more interesting than you let on. Transpires that he wasn't a tramp at all. Did a bit of research, and think that you may have a serial killer on your hands. It's all to do with the Oxford Martyrs, you know."

My God, that was all Morse needed. He didn't want to admit to Coghlan that he had misled him the other day, and at the same time didn't want to alert the murderer that the link had been made with the Oxford Martyrs.

"Um, the Oxford Martyrs … I do hope that you are not about to publish something that might be sensationalist and backfire on you. If you say that there is some serial killer on the loose it's likely to panic the public. Maybe you should pass it by the Chief Superintendent's office first, as it might prejudice any ongoing investigation," suggested Morse helpfully, if not hopefully.

175

"Too late for that I'm afraid. First edition is already on the streets. Though it is good to know that you have spotted this angle of investigation as well. Can always count on you, Morse."

"What do you mean?"

"Well if you really had not thought of the link already then your first comment would have been to ask me more as to how the Oxford Martyrs fit into what looks like two murders, rather than try to warn me off publishing, wouldn't it now?"

It seemed there was nothing else that Morse could do for Coghlan had produced a *fait accompli*, and on that thought Morse had a favour to ask.

"Oh, while I have you on the telephone," Morse started, making it seem like an afterthought, "Sir Michael Chipperfield, Master of Londsdale, is coming over to give a talk at Kidlington next month. I have been tasked with adverting it here at the station. I don't suppose that you would have a photograph of him on file that I could use?"

"Our library has photos of all the college heads. I will have one made available for you, and left at the front desk if you would like?"

"Yes, I would be most grateful. No hurry."

"Don't worry, old chap it'll be there within the hour, and I won't even let on that he's a suspect … at least not until you tell me to. Agreed?"

Morse had never been a very good liar.

"Agreed."

Chapter Thirty-Seven

"At the time of evening when cars run sweetly,
Syringas blossom by Oxford gates.
In her evening velvet with a rose pinned neatly
By the distant bus-stop a don's wife waits …

Too much, too many! So fetch the doctor,
This dress has grown such a heavier load
Since Jack was only a Junior Proctor,
And rents were lower in Rawlinson Road."

(John Betjeman, *Oxford: Sudden Illness
at the Bus-stop*)

To the uninitiated Oxford – and Cambridge too for that matter
– may seem peculiar places, full of eccentric customs and traditions
of no relevance in the real world. Just ask any visitor, who has been
on a guided tour around one of the colleges, the distinction between
beddels, bulldogs, scouts and proctors, and likely as not they will be
at a loss for an answer.

Despite all these jobs seemingly being outdated for the 1970s
they do have the saving grace that each still provides a specific
function that actually works, and works very well. At the pinnacle of
the University tree are the proctors, those senior officers of the
establishment charged with enforcing University discipline and

sanctions. They are the ones to avoid since they are able to issue fines, for instance if caught cheating in examinations. These would be collected by the beddels who are in addition responsible for keeping the rolls of scholars with a licence to teach. The proctors are aided in their work by the Oxford University Police, better known as bulldogs, and distinguished by their bowler hats, which they wear as proudly as any police officer wears a uniform. Traditionally they were responsible for such matters as enforcing the wearing of gowns, and making sure that students observed the curfew hour. Although nothing to do with the Thames Valley Police, being a private constabulary, they have always had full powers of arrest within the precincts of the University, and to within four miles of any University building.

However, if one really wants to know what is going on behind closed doors in Oxford it is no good asking proctors, beddels or bulldogs. It is the scouts to whom you must turn. Scouts are the ones closest to the students and staff. They are at the very bottom of the heap: a college servant who is employed for domestic cleaning, and responsible for a set of rooms on a single stairway. But they are so much more than that to those they serve; they are the ones who keep their secrets, turn a blind eye to their indiscretions, clear up their little messes, and, in doing so, are also the ones generally most remembered in later years by returning alumni. They are lowly paid, but never grumble, since any lack of remuneration from their formal employer is counterbalanced by the tips they receive from those they serve so well.

For Morse this had one big disadvantage – it made the scouts fiercely loyal to those they serve, but not if that person was unpopular or unappreciative of their efforts, and it was this fact that Morse was relying on as he made his way back to central Oxford to seek out is own scout from his time at St. John's. As he drove, it did occur to him that Wood – no Christian names were ever used, though he believed that it was Kevin – might not remember him. No chance of that for scouts, as with the proverbial elephant, remembered everything and everyone.

St. Giles' was not too busy for that time of early evening, and so Morse had no trouble finding a parking space, almost outside the Bird and Baby, but this time that was not his destination. Instead he walked across the road to the Lamb and Flag where the scouts from St. John's gathered most evenings after work. In fact where else would they meet given that the public house in question took its name from the symbols on the heraldic badge of his *alma mater*? Although not as famous, and not known for any literary connections, the Lamb and Flag was, in fact, an older establishment having been on its site since 1695, a full five years before the Bird and Baby. It was also a larger pub, and not being on the tourist map was empty as Morse entered – empty that is apart for a conclave of six scouts from St. John's, just as Morse had hoped.

He approached the group, recognising Wood almost instantly as being the one in the centre with his back to the fireplace. It was most gratifying to Morse that Wood recognised him almost as quickly.

"Look there, gentlemen," he started, "if I am not mistaken I spy an old boy … Morse, isn't it, sir?"

"I am he … and you are unmistakably Mr. Wood … and I would be delighted to buy you a drink, old friend."

"That is very kind of you, sir, but we are all old friends here, so if it is your pleasure, it will be six pints of porter please, and whatever you are having yourself."

Morse hadn't expected that he would need to purchase more than one drink, but did so almost without flinching, and as he stood at the bar he could swear that in the reflection from the mirror behind the array of spirit bottles, that he could see Wood giving a sly wink and a smile to his colleagues. Seated with them, after having distributed the refreshments, he went through all the preliminaries of asking after their well being and that of their families, general chitchat, the fate of Oxford United so on and so forth. He did reveal in the course of his conversation that he had never left Oxford, and was now a policeman at Kidlington, before he turned to the topic he really wanted to talk about.

"You know I was at Lonsdale earlier with the Master who didn't seem at all happy with the world, and was particularly ill-tempered."

179

"Hardly surprising with his wife leaving him like that, and just before Christmas too," came a swift reply from one of the assembled scouts.

It was exactly what Morse had wanted to hear. At last a motive.

"That probably explains it. Did she go off with one of the other Fellows?" probed Morse.

"Well, you know us, sir, we are not prone to gossip, but in the case of Sir Michael I don't think that you will find that he has many friends around this table." The scout in question looked around at his colleagues all of whom nodded in unison. "Strictly between us then, I believe from one of the scouts at Lonsdale that it was with that Professor Cranmer, and who can blame her as it can't have been much fun with Sir Michael all those years." Laughter broke out among the group.

Quod erat demonstrandum thought Morse.

"I see in tonight's *Oxford Mail* that Cranmer was that body they found down Dead Man's Walk last week ... wouldn't surprise me if it was the Master just getting his revenge," postulated Wood.

"It's a thought at that," added Morse, playing down the connection, and pretending that he wasn't already several furlongs ahead of the field in this respect. "I am told that Sir Michael collects stamps."

"Quite right, sir," commented another scout who had remained silent until now. "Fine collection too. I remember that he showed it at the local stamp club a few years ago."

"So you must be a member of the Oxford and District Philatelic Society? What a coincidence, I was there at their last meeting, as a guest of one of the committee members, Sylvia Warren."

"Now I remember you, sir. Sat at the back and only stayed for the first half. A very lucky man, if I may be so bold, to know that attractive Dr. Warren. Mind you it would be a brave soul that would attempt to go out with her, what with her past record of men."

"Really, do tell me more?"

"No, sir, telling on despised members of college is one thing, but gossiping about a lady's virtue is quite something else."

180

Morse realised that he had gone too far, but quickly thought of a way to redeem himself.

"You misunderstand, I meant tell me more about the Master's stamp collection."

"Sorry, sir, the misunderstanding was mine alone. He collects college stamps."

"College stamps?"

"Yes, bit of a Cinderella subject really. You are probably already aware from your time with us that all the colleges have an internal messenger service, for delivering letters locally. Started in 1656 if I remember rightly, but wasn't until 1871 that the colleges started issuing their own stamps. First was Keble who had them printed at Spiers & Son in the High. Not all the colleges came out with their own stamps, but Merton, Exeter, Lincoln, Balliol, All Souls, Hertford and, naturally, us at St. John's certainly did. Over the years there were many different designs and printings, but it all came to an end in 1885 when the use of our own stamps had to stop as it was seen as an infringement of the Post Office's monopoly."

"You're wrong there, Mr. Jones," commented one of the other scouts. "Keble brought out a stamp just last year to celebrate its hundredth anniversary of the service."

"Quite right, Mr. Watson, trust you to remember that."

"So would such a collection be worth any money?"

"Oh, yes, sir. Some of them are very rare indeed ... rare enough to be in the Royal collection no less."

Wood decided it was time for him to add a little information himself. "I think most of us here know the story of Dr. James, our former President, who was interrupted by an undergraduate one evening in his room?"

They all nodded apart from Morse.

"Please go on."

"Well the undergraduate in question was more than a little surprised to see two men on their hands and knees engrossed in some activity. At first he probably thought that it was of a sexual nature, but in fact they were just sticking some stamps in an album,

181

and what is more the second person was quite familiar ... it was King George V."

They all chuckled. Morse decided to probe one last time.

"You know I've been looking for a hobby and collecting college stamps is something that would appeal to me ... I will have to pop along to Latimer's stamp shop, or ask the Master if he has any swaps."

"I wouldn't do either, sir," came the unexpected answer from Jones.

"And why not?"

"Well on the first account I don't think that Latimer will be able to help, him being dead and all, and on the second I am pretty certain that Sir Michael no longer has his collection as he disposed of it recently."

Double *quod erat demonstrandum* thought Morse. He had now established a link with Latimer for where else in Oxford might the Master of Lonsdale go to sell his collection privately, with no questions asked? Was this where Latimer was going to get his money from for his world travels, and if so where was that collection now? Was it hiding somewhere in the shop awaiting to be found, and if so why had Latimer not placed it in the safe instead of those worthless stamp booklets? Whatever the answer might be it must have been an unhappy transaction for the Master of Lonsdale, and one for which Sir Michael felt the need of compensation to the extent of taking the life of the stamp dealer. The irony of killing off persons with the name Latimer and Cranmer would certainly have appealed to Sir Michael's sense of history. The murderer had been revealed to Morse, and all he had to do now was to discover some evidence to prove it.

With no more to learn Morse made his excuses and was about to leave when Wood spoke.

"Thank you for looking us up, sir. I just hope that we have been useful in your investigation, and have pointed you in the right direction."

Clearly Wood had been in front of Morse all along and had, in fact, won this particular race.

"Indeed you have. Thank you, gentlemen, for all your help."

As he left the Lamb and Flag for the offices of the *Oxford Mail*, there was only one question that perplexed Morse – what was it about Sylvia Warren's past that might make him a brave man to go out with her?

Chapter Thirty-Eight

"He heaves his hoe in the rice-field, under the noonday sun,
Onto the soil of the rice-field, his streaming sweat beads run.
Ah do you or don't you know it? That bowl of rice we eat:
Each grain, each ev'ry granule, the fruit of his labour done."

(Li Shen, *Pity the Peasants (Ancient Air) II of Two*)

There it was for all to see in black and white on the display board in the window just to the left of the entrance of Newspaper House, the offices of the *Oxford Mail*: 'OXFORD RIPPER – TWO MURDERED' and underneath in smaller print 'INVESTIGATIVE JOURNALIST, TIM COGHLAN, REVEALS THE IDENTITY OF THE NEXT VICTIM – SEE PAGE 3'.

It was exactly what Morse had hoped to avoid, but it seemed that Coghlan had done his research, and had come to the same conclusion as Morse. Now that the populous of Oxford was in on the secret might there be a widespread panic? For certain the Kidlington switchboard would be jammed with calls from every crank in the parish. Each piece of information, though, would have to be followed up no matter how slight the chance of it being relevant to the case. It might just produce one or two decent leads, and if nothing else it would certainly annoy the Chief Superintendent when he saw the overtime sheets, although Morse suspected that his annoyance would in turn be taken out on him.

However, the article might be advantageous, as perhaps there was a chance that it would help unnerve Sir Michael prior to his questioning the following day.

Inside at the all-night reception desk Morse collected a copy of the newspaper, and also the file photograph of Sir Michael in full academic dress taken, Morse noted, in the Broad during the previous year's Encaenia procession. There was a cheeky hand-written note attached from Coghlan that simply read, 'Good hunting, Morse'.

A short walk brought him to Hythe Bridge Street, where in former times barges on the Oxford Canal would load and unload their wares. About half way along was the place he had come to visit – The Pearl Dragon, known to be the finest Chinese restaurant in Oxford, and the only one within walking distance of Lonsdale College. Morse had not eaten here before, indeed his palate was very unadventurous, and so this evening was going to be a culinary excursion into the unknown as far as he was concerned. This was surely where Cranmer had taken his final meal.

Having been shown to his window seat, a large menu was proffered. It was indeed extensive, and although it sometimes was lacking in clarity, and punctuation, he was able to choose one or two items of Chinese origin, and not resort to the English meals listed on the final page. He thought that he would steer clear of 'Fred's King Pawn with nuts' which he hoped was a typographical error, and instead decided upon the chicken and sweet corn soup, house special curry and rice with a portion of sweet and sour pork, and to finish some lychee. There was still the question of liquid refreshment. In this respect the menu was severely lacking, offering only a lager, or Double Diamond, the very worst, and certainly the weakest, pale ale imaginable. Morse settled for the Chinese tea in preference.

While waiting for his starter to arrive Morse summoned the manager over from behind the small bar.

"Everything alright, sir?"

"Yes, quite alright, but I want to ask if you have seen this gentleman here recently."

Morse showed the manager his warrant card along with the photograph of Professor Cranmer.

"Yes, he come here often, and always sit over there in corner."

"And was he here last Thursday night?"

"Yes, that is the day he usually come here."

"And at what time?"

"He always eat early when we open at five-thirty o'clock."

That would fit, thought Morse. After all if he was to meet his death along Dead Man's Walk shortly afterwards it would have to be early evening, before the gate at Merton Grove was locked, otherwise it would make no sense taking that route back to Lonsdale as it would involve a long detour via Rose Walk to reach the High.

"I see ... and was he with this person?"

Morse took out his recently acquired photograph of Sir Michael.

"No, it was not him."

The disappointment was evident on Morse's face.

"Are you quite sure? Don't be fooled by the academic dress, he would not have been wearing it on the night."

"Very sure. The person that he was with was a woman."

"A woman," repeated Morse. He certainly hadn't expected that.

"Yes, he often come here with different woman."

"Could you describe her?"

"Not really. She like all women, young and beautiful, all I notice. All customers look same unless regular, and she never been here before."

Morse thanked the manager and let him go about his business, which included bringing Morse his soup. The rest of his satisfactory meal followed at intervals, giving Morse ample time to read Coghlan's article in the newspaper. Both were much as he had expected: the former was a little too spicy for his liking, and the latter a little too sensationalist, especially with its slant towards it being some religious fanatic. Morse paid for his meal, but asked for a receipt, for surely he had been on police business this evening and was entitled to claim for the food on his expenses.

As he walked the streets back to his car at St. Giles' he pondered that the manager hadn't been much help ... or had he? If it wasn't Sir Michael in the restaurant with Cranmer, maybe it was Lady Chipperfield, prior to her brass-rubbing trip abroad? Could it be that on their way back to college after their meal that they went via Dead Man's Walk, where they were subsequently confronted by Sir Michael who was laying in wait for them? Was she an accomplice to the murder? He would need to track down Lady Chipperfield at the earliest opportunity, but not until he had interviewed her husband the following afternoon. The thought of bringing down the Master of Lonsdale was something that filled Morse with relish.

Chapter Thirty-Nine

"Ignorance more frequently begets confidence
than does knowledge."

(Charles Darwin)

What would surely be a remorseful day for Sir Michael dawned, but before the great showdown Morse needed to prepare, and also to rehearse, for the high drama that would unfold that afternoon. He therefore spent most of that Tuesday morning at Kidlington gathering his evidence, such as it was, before driving over to St. Aldate's, where he briefed Strange as to his part in the proceedings.

"So why exactly do you want me up a ladder in this dingy corridor changing the light bulbs?"

"Exactly because it is dingy ... it will recreate the lighting conditions along Dead Man's Walk at night time. There is no natural light along this corridor so if you remove all the ceiling lights, save the one at the very end to represent the moon, then that will be about right. Now if you pretend to be replacing one of the blown bulbs up the ladder when I come by with Sir Michael that will add some authenticity of the scene, plus we will have to stop to go around you."

"But why is all that so important?"

"Because in the interview room opposite the ladder will be our witness, Dorothy Evans, and I will mistakenly enter the room as we pass, and in so doing she will get the same fleeting glimpse of our murderer as she did the other evening."

"And you don't think that Sir Michael will see through this little charade?"

"Don't care if he does, there is nothing he can do about it as it is not a formal identification parade."

"And that is your great and subtle plan to trap him is it?"

"Well it's a plan ... and I do have one finishing touch to add which I will tell you about later. Meanwhile did you call his office this morning, and arrange for him to be here at two-thirty?"

"All done, Morse. His secretary didn't seem in the least bit surprised to get the call, and he didn't seem to be too bothered either. I just hope that you are not making a big mistake."

"He's the one who made the big mistake, mark my words."

At lunchtime Morse went off for a hair cut and a shave at Gerrard's hairdressing saloon, located in the basement of Shepherd and Woodward's. Of course he didn't need his hair cut – this having been done the previous Saturday – so it was just the lightest of trims for him that day, followed by a wet shave. He always enjoyed relaxing in the old fashioned barber's chair, and got tingles along the length of his spine when the razor was used on his neck. Not an electric razor, mind you, for Morse had no time for the modern hairdressers that were springing up all over town. Places where the skill of a barber, who through his experience built up over the years could render a perfect dry cut with just scissors and a comb, was replaced by some attractive girl who knew only how to use an electronic equivalent and make a cup of coffee. It was a small luxury that he treated himself to every couple of weeks, and always put him in good humour for the rest of the day. However, there was another reason for the visit, and that lay upstairs.

Arthur Shepherd was a tailor who had set up shop in Cornmarket Street in 1877, and his family business had remained there for fifty years until Arthur's son Ernest amalgamated it with that of another tailor, Wilton Woodward. Subsequently the shop relocated to the

High where it had been ever since. Today it is probably the largest supplier of academic gowns and robes in Oxford, making most of them in their own workrooms and embroidery shop. They also sell a range of academic scarves, ties, cufflinks and the like to students, as well as any passing tourist who wishes to pretend that they have an association with the University. It was the former that interested Morse, and having shown his warrant card to Peter Venables, son to Dennis who had bought out Ernest's share in the company just after the World War II, he agreed to lend him two college scarves (Lonsdale and Magdalen) for the afternoon.

Morse entered St. Aldate's station again just as the bell in Tom Tower was striking two. He had but thirty minutes left to prepare. He was pleased to note that Dorothy Evans had already arrived. She was a formidable woman, in her seventies, but still had the bearing of an old-fashioned schoolmistress. Most important of all, despite her advanced years, he could tell that her mental faculties were as sharp as ever. Morse introduced himself and led her along the corridor, which was almost completely dark, to the interview room beside the ladder obstructing the passageway. Once inside and seated in a position so that she was facing the door, Morse explained that at some time soon the door would be opened, and that she should note whether the person who would be standing there was the same as the one she saw along Dead Man's Walk. He further explained that she would need to sit in darkness to replicate the conditions of the other evening, but not to fear as one of the police constables would also be with her at all times, and would even bring her a cup of tea and biscuits, if any could be found.

The final set dressing was achieved as Morse draped the two scarves he had borrowed over the top of the ladder so that they trailed almost down to the floor. In order to do this he needed to affix them to the ladder with several drawing pins. It was perfect, for when opened the next time the door would reveal Sir Michael upon the threshold, with the scarves forming a backdrop. It was the best that could be done without actually asking Sir Michael to wear them.

191

At precisely two-thirty the Master of Lonsdale presented himself at the front desk at St. Aldate's.

"I thought that we would meet again soon, Morse"

"It is very good of you to come at such short notice, Sir Michael."

"Are you going to read me my rights and caution me? That's what they do on the television, I'm told."

"Lord no, Sir Michael. You are here simply to help us in our investigation involving the murder of your colleague. You may leave at any time you wish," replied Morse, who couldn't help but add, "at least for the present, anyway."

"I trust that you realise that time is money, and I have had to cancel an important meeting with a probable college benefactor to be here this afternoon."

"And what is the going rate for a Lonsdale Fellowship these days?"

"Anything from fifty thousand guineas upwards ... were you thinking of applying for one, Morse?"

"A little out of my league. However, as time is certainly money we had better get on with it, and find an interview room ... if you would like to follow me."

With that Morse ushered Sir Michael behind the front desk and led him along the corridor to where a man could be seen fiddling with a light fitting up the top of a ladder.

"Careful as you go, sir. The circuit's blown all the bulbs along here," said Strange with as much acting skill as he could muster.

"This room will do ... please go in, Sir Michael," instructed Morse.

Sir Michael entered.

"Oh, dear I am sorry, Sir Michael, that room seems to be occupied already," said Morse, who proceeded to the adjacent empty room.

Once seated, and the preliminaries of offering tea or coffee to Sir Michael had been observed, the questioning began in the presence of a female police officer who was on hand to record the interview. At first they were general in nature, which merely confirmed what was already known, and designed to put Sir Michael at his ease. Then things became more serious.

"So tell me, Sir Michael, when did you first suspect that your wife was having an affair with Professor Cranmer?"

For a moment, and only a moment, the Master of Lonsdale was taken aback. He had been caught off guard. First point to Morse.

"For around six months."

"And how did it affect you to know that Cranmer, the college Casanova, who had seduced various other women, now had his eye on Lady Chipperfield. I bet it filled you with rage."

"Not in the least ... you see Lady Chipperfield and I have what is termed these days as an *aperta nuptias*. We both turn a blind eye to each other's indiscretions. As long as she supports me in college life she can do what she pleases in private," he replied calmly.

"You didn't want revenge then?"

"I wouldn't say that ... but not the sort of *vindicta* you have in mind, Morse. I didn't plot to kill him, but I did have power over Cranmer to make sure that his college career did not progress as perhaps he would have liked. Then again you know that already, as I told you as much during our previous little *tête-à-tête*."

"On the night of Cranmer's murder neither of you were in college. In fact, it is known that Cranmer ate at the Pearl Dragon along with your wife shortly before his demise."

"Really, Morse. Are you quite sure of your facts? As far as I was aware Lady Chipperfield had already been in France for two days by then, but if you say otherwise I will have to believe you."

Morse was now the one who had been caught off-guard. He was annoyed with himself as he had not yet received confirmation as to when Lady Chipperfield had left on her travels.

"Even if your wife is not implicated, you certainly might have arranged to meet Cranmer that evening along Dead Man's Walk."

"Mere supposition, Morse. *Ubi est argumentum*? If you know anything about me at all you will know that brawling in public is not my thing."

"Can you tell me where you were that evening?"

193

"I could ... but I won't. Rest assured, though, that I do have an alibi should it be required in a court of law. For the present my whereabouts that evening must remain on a need to know basis, and you do not need to know."

Morse was losing this battle of wits, and so changed tact.

"Tell me about you stamp collection. I believe that it is unique and quite valuable."

"Indeed it is both of those ... but do get to the point and ask me what you really want to know."

"When we met last you told me that you were a philatelist, not a stamp collector, and had never visited Latimer's stamp shop."

"That is correct ..."

"So if not from him where do you buy your stamps?"

"From specialist dealers, and the London auction houses ... certainly not from those who purvey stamps to schoolboys."

"But you would consider him if you came to sell your stamps, and didn't want anybody to know of the transaction?"

"I would consider selling to anybody, but doubt if he would be able to afford to purchase such a collection as mine."

"But that is exactly what happened isn't it? I know that you disposed of your collection recently, and no doubt approached Latimer for a quick no-questions-asked sale. What went wrong that resulted in his premature death?"

"That is a most serious allegation, Morse. I think that you have been listening to too much college gossip, probably from the scouts, and have not done your research properly."

"*Me illuminare,*" replied Morse just to demonstrate that he was equally adapt in using the odd Latin phrase in his speech.

"Very well, Morse. You are wrong, and clearly do not believe me when I say that I have never had any dealings with Latimer. You are also wrong when you say that I have disposed of my collection recently."

"So where is it now then ... can you show it to me?"

"Absolutely, anybody may see it as from next month ... you see I did not dispose of it, but simply donated my collection to the

University archives where they are to put it on display at the Bodleian."

"That was very public spirited of you."

"Not really, the collection still belongs to me, and is simply on loan for a small annual payment. What is more, it will forever afterwards be known as the Chipperfield collection, will be insured and preserved in museum conditions, and all at the University's expense. Any other questions, or fanciful theories, that you wish to bring to my attention, Morse?"

Morse could see that he had been beaten on every front.

"No, you have been most generous with your time, Sir Michael."

Morse led Sir Michael back to the front entrance, wondering what sort of complaint might be forthcoming from his solicitor in due course. His question was answered as Sir Michael was about to leave the building.

"A word to the wise, Morse. If you want me to take part in an identity parade in future just ask, don't piss about trying to be subtle with your theatrics in the corridor. I am a reasonable man, and actually respect you … it is not often that I meet a policeman with some intelligence. Today you were wrong, but tomorrow you might be onto something, but only if you do your research properly in advance. That is what I tell my students, and that is my advice to you now. I trust you will not take it personally when I tell you that because of your lack of diligence you must be taught a lesson, and so do not be surprised if the Chief Constable wants to talk with you tomorrow. You were right about one thing though."

"And what was that?"

"You're not in my league. *Bonum meridianus.*"

With that he was gone.

It was as if Morse was some famous violin player standing on stage about to play when he discovers that all but one of his strings has been broken. He did though still have that one string at hand, and he prayed that it would remain intact.

"Sorry to have kept you waiting so long, Mrs. Evans. Were you able to make any positive identification?"

"It wasn't him."

The final string had just been broken – it would now be impossible for him to play even a single note.

"Are you quite sure? Did you get a good look at him?"

"There is nothing wrong with my eyes, young man. I tell you it wasn't him. Too tall and too old."

"Did you recognise the scarf."

"Yes, of course I recognised the scarf. I told you that it was a Magdalen scarf ... the one on the left."

"Not the one on the right?"

"No, that is a Lonsdale scarf."

"How can you tell in this light? They both look the same colour to me."

"Oh, they may be the same colour, but the stripes on the Magdalen one are a little wider. Have a look and you will see for yourself."

"How on earth did you know about the width of the stripes?"

"I worked at Shepherd and Woodward's behind the counter for nearly thirty years, so take it from me that I know one Oxford college scarf from another."

There was nothing for it but to see Dorothy Evans home, and go back to square one in his investigation. As it transpired the remorseful day had been Morse's and not Sir Michael's.

196

Chapter Forty

"The man who smiles when things go wrong has thought of
someone to blame it on."

(Robert Bloch)

What would Wednesday hold for him? Morse was pretty
certain that it wasn't going to be a golden day, not if Sir Michael
had kept his threat and made a formal complaint to the Chief
Constable. Complaints from arrogant, pretentious, egotistical, not to
mention Machiavellian, bureaucrats he could take in his stride, but it
was the feeling that he had been wrong in interpreting the clues
offered that made him so despondent.

Even now as he drove to Kidlington, Morse was convinced that
although Sir Michael had no motive for killing Latimer if what he
had said about loaning his stamp collection to the University
archives was true – and that could be easily checked, he did still
have both motive and means for murdering Cranmer. To his mind he
also had opportunity, at least until an alibi had been established.
After all, prevarication was not in Sir Michael's nature, so why did
he not want to reveal where he was on the evening in question?
Answer, because as yet no alibi existed. Yes, he would now be
desperately trying to establish one by calling in favours from God
knows where, or whom.

First, though, Morse would have to face the wrath of his superiors. If he was called to see the Chief Constable it probably meant the end of his career, whereas if it was just McNutt and the Chief Superintendent then he might just survive, as he had done before, and live to fight another day. Morse was pleasantly surprised to learn that it was just McNutt that wanted to see him as soon as he arrived.

"You're a blithering idiot, man, aren't you?" came the greeting from the dour Scotsman.

"If you say so, sir," replied a rather sheepish Morse.

"Is what you did yesterday your idea of subtle, Morse? Don't even try to justify your actions. The Chief Constable wants your desk clear by lunchtime, while the Chief Superintendent wants you suspended pending further investigation."

"And what do you want, sir?"

"A good question, Morse. I'm not entirely sure I have to confess. By rights, I should have your backside kicked all the way from here to St. Aldate's ... but given the circumstances, and having read the report you typed up for me, I can't help but think that if I were an ambitious young Detective Sergeant that I might not have done something similar. I still might kick your backside to Oxford just for all the extra paperwork you are causing following that newspaper article the night before last ... Oxford Ripper, indeed ... the phones haven't stopped ringing."

"So what are you going to do with me, sir?"

"I'm going to do exactly what I have been instructed ... I'm going to suspend you from duty for two days, but before that I want to know what your thoughts are on the case."

Morse relaxed a little as he realised that he had got off lightly all things considered. It was no doubt McNutt's intervention on his behalf that had saved his career again, and it was for that reason, more than any other, that Morse was forever respectful of his superior. He saw in McNutt the type of policeman that he would want to become, and looked to him to gently guide him in that direction. However, it wasn't a father and son, or even a master and student relationship. Morse saw himself more as a ship in a storm with McNutt at the helm trying to steer a steady path, but doing it in such a way that it would look like that the path chosen was the one that Morse had wanted to take all along. Morse guessed wrongly that it was similar to how one should manage a woman.

"Well don't just stand there gawking, man, you can thank me later down the pub for saving your bacon ... but tell me do you still think that Sir Michael is a suspect?"

"I was convinced that he was our man, but given the latest evidence I fear that he has nothing to do with the Latimer death. However, I still contend that he is at the bottom of the Cranmer murder ... it could be him, Lady Chipperfield, both of them in it together, somebody who owes Sir Michael a favour and has been leant upon ... somehow I just feel that he is involved right up to his master's neck."

"As it happens, I agree. The fact that he has made so much fuss about yesterday tells me that he has something to hide. Leave him to me for the moment, as you had better lay low for a while. I will have the alibis of Sir Michael and Lady Chipperfield checked, and pursue that side of the investigation myself."

"As much as I hate coincidences, I concede that there may after all be no link between the two deaths. The victim names might have been a large red herring, as could the fact that both bodies were found in the same location. In fact the death of Latimer might still be an accident, and not murder at all, in which case we still have Sir Michael for the other one."

"So you are now saying that we are possibly looking for more than one person?"

"Yes, and having said that I do have one other possible suspect for the Latimer killing that I would like to follow up on. Is there any news yet of the exhumation order, as that body may be crucial in determining whether we have a serial killer, or a coincidence?"

"The court order was granted late yesterday, and the body should be with de Bryn later on this morning. Why don't you go and visit him? I'm sure he will be glad to see you ... you know he has a high regard for your intuition."

199

"You forget, sir, I am suspended for two days ... here is my warrant card," replied Morse taking the item indicated out of his wallet.

"You're suspended when I tell you you're damned well suspended, Morse. The Chief Superintendent may have meant that I suspend you now, but it is up to me, and I have decided that you will be suspended for forty-eight hours starting in two days time at seventeen-hundred hours ..."

"You mean as from Friday evening?"

"Yes, I am suspending you on Saturday and Sunday ... you can hand in your warrant card on Friday evening, but keep the pool car keys if you wish ... in the meantime I will expect you to work harder than ever, stay out of trouble, and be back on duty first thing Monday morning. I trust my intentions are clear, Morse."

McNutt winked while Morse had an inward smile as he left the office.

Chapter Forty-One

"Every contact leaves a trace."

(Locard's Exchange Principle)

"Managed to find me then ... I thought that it wouldn't be long before you turned up," came the greeting from de Bryn – a distinct improvement from Mc Nutt's earlier that morning.

Indeed Morse had managed to track de Bryn down at his usual place of work – the Sir William Dunn School of Pathology, situated where South Parks Road joins St. Cross Road. Though not the most beautiful of Oxford buildings, and only constructed in 1927, largely as a result of persuading the trustees of the late William Dunn to part with a large sum of money, it was a functional and effective place. De Bryn's domain was on the second floor with an outlook across Oxford University Parks towards the Cherwell beyond.

"Have you had a chance to examine our friend?"

"I have, and you won't like the answer I'm afraid. There's no evidence of any foul play. He died from simple hypothermia, and even if he hadn't, his liver would have given up within months despite his age. He's over there, have a look for yourself," invited the pathologist.

"I'd rather not."

"Please yourself, there's no blood."

201

Morse went over, somewhat hesitantly, to the slab where lay the body of a young man in his twenties. He was surprised to see that the corpse was still recognisable as a human being, and had not decomposed to any great extent. He wore scruffy clothes, as one would expect of a vagrant. There was nothing remarkable except that for the second time in a week he noted a pair of, albeit well worn, Ducker's shoes. Was he the owner of them from some former time when he had been more affluent, or were they a charitable donation? Either way it was something that should be checked. Although Morse could never afford such an item himself, he was aware that Ducker always either put the name of the owner on the side of the shoes, or a ledger number – in this case there was a five digit number.

"Thank you, Max. Although you may think all this a waste of time, I might just be able to provide an identification. Have you got a photograph of the face from when he was first found?"

"I'll give you good odds that his name isn't Ridley," came the swift retort as de Bryn took a photograph from the unknown man's folder.

"In your words, Max, I couldn't possibly say," and with that Morse was gone.

Ten minutes later he was outside the shoe shop of Ducker & Son in Turl Street. Inside the premises appeared not to have changed since its inception in the late 19th century. It was the sort of establishment that Morse appreciated, and in which he felt eminently at home browsing the fine craftsmanship on display. He vowed that if only he had a spare hundred pounds he would certainly spend it on a pair of handmade Oxford shoes. He felt sure that he had read somewhere that Napoleon had once commented that one of the few advantages of being emperor was that he could have shoes specially made and broken in for him by some unfortunate person with similar sized feet. What a luxury that would be for a policeman, especially with all the walking his job involved. In fact, he further vowed that if ever he was made Chief Constable he would make sure that all officers on the beat were issued with Ducker's.

"Can I be of any assistance, sir," asked a smart gentleman of advancing years, probably the '& son' from the shop name.

Morse showed his badge, introduced himself and explained the problem.

"Well I can certainly take a look for you, Mr. Morse, if you would like to have a seat I will bring the ledger right away."

Morse, though, preferred to continue to examine the shoes on the racks, for it transpired that ready made shoes were also available at a discount, although not at a reduction that would bring them into his budget. A few minutes later Mr. Ducker junior returned with a huge leather bound folio, such as one might see chained to a bookcase at the Bodleian.

"Here we go .... yes, this particular pair were bought by a Mr. Ridler, a student at Christ Church some five years ago ... it says here that I made them myself. Is that any help?"

So close and yet so far, thought Morse. Just one letter off the jackpot, one lousy letter from enough score draws to win the pools. Surely it must be a typographical error?

"Are you quite certain that it was Ridler, and not Ridley?"

"Quite sure, sir. It is Joseph Ridler, and I have an address as well if that is any use to you. It seems that the shoes were a graduation present from his parents, and it was to them that the account was sent and subsequently settled."

"Would you remember if this was the gentleman in question?" Morse handed over the photograph.

"I never forget a face, sir. I daresay that it isn't the best photograph I've ever seen ... he doesn't look very well does he? However, it is unmistakably him."

Morse explained that the person concerned was deceased.

"When I said that he didn't look very well, sir, that was my little joke."

With that Morse took a note of the address and left for St. Aldate's. There he found Strange and reported his findings. Strange would take it from there and contact the parents for a formal identification, and re-burial, or perhaps cremation this time. In fact Morse wondered if that would set a precedent – being both buried and cremated. He also pondered that he had done some good that day with his detective skills, even though his own investigation and theories had themselves been as good as cremated. It very much looked as if he was looking at just one accidental death, and one unrelated murder. Sometimes Morse's imagination was just too vivid for his own good.

In his current state he required liquid refreshment. All that walking all over Oxford had made him thirsty, very thirsty. In fact so much so that he might even contemplate keeping the gnats employed and have a lager. However, he had no need to stoop that low when the Apollo was but a stone's throw away.

Morse stayed at this rather basic, somewhat rundown beer house belonging to Moorlands of Abingdon for longer than anticipated – in fact several pints longer. When he arrived home late evening he was surprised to find a note under his door. It read 'I would like to see those blue eyes of yours this evening, please, please ring me, it's been a hard day without you. SW xx'. Morse made his last vow of the day – that tomorrow he would telephone Sylvia Warren, and invite her away for the weekend, after all he knew he wasn't going to be working on either Saturday or Sunday. Suspension had its advantages and, on that thought Morse, collapsed into bed without undressing.

Chapter Forty-Two

"Neither a borrower nor a lender be,
For loan oft loses both itself and friend,
And borrowing dulls the edge of husbandry."

(Polonius, *Hamlet* Act 1, Scene 3)

The following morning Morse did something quite uncharacteristic, so uncharacteristic, in fact, that he had never done such a thing since he was a schoolboy – he showed his romantic side. First he visited the newsagents in Summertown and purchased a blank greetings card upon which he wrote a few words of apology to Sylvia Warren, followed by an invite to go away with him that weekend. Then he drove around to her house and slipped it through her letterbox in the sure knowledge that she would receive it that evening on her return from the JR. So much better than a telephone call, he thought.

His personal business completed he arrived at Kidlington around ten o'clock. Pleasantly there were no 'Monopoly' type instructions for him to go directly to McNutt, not to pass the coffee machine, not to collect two hundred pounds etc. So for the next two hours Morse settled himself at his desk, typed up his notes from the previous day, and made some telephone calls, the most important of which was to have Susan French brought in for questioning that afternoon. On hearing of this request, McNutt ventured out from his office.

"In God's name how can you think she's a suspect, Morse?"

"Well I do, sir. After all, she did conceal the fact that she was having an affair with Latimer. I think I can prove that she has motive, means and opportunity."

"That maybe, but surely you have forgotten that she is a woman, and your chief witness says that they only saw a man, a man wearing a college scarf, Morse."

"True enough, sir, but remember that there were three witnesses, one of whom says that it was a woman sitting on the bench. All three could be correct, for over the period of an hour why wouldn't there be three different people that happened to be on that bench for a time? Only one of them though is our murderer. I just chose to believe Mrs. Evans' account since as well as being the one who passed closest to the bench, she also seemed the most observant."

"Alright, Morse, but let's not have any theatrics this time. Treat her with respect and not as your only suspect, or we will both be out of a job come next week."

After lunch, taken at the Kidlington canteen, which was marginally better than the one at St. Aldate's, Morse drove the eight miles to St. Aldate's where Susan French was waiting for him in the very same interview room that had been used for Sir Michael. Morse was not a superstitious man, but none the less he hoped that this was not a bad omen. Also in attendance was a police constable to record the interview, though he noted that Ms. French had not brought a legal representative along.

"Thank you for coming, Ms. French. I hope that you have been offered refreshments, and have been cautioned since this is a formal interview."

"I have, but I don't understand ... am I a suspect?"

Morse chose to ignore her question. If he had answered truthfully he had the feeling that she might burst into tears, just as she had done on their previous encounters.

"You told me last time of your relationship with Mr. Latimer, and also that you knew that he was expecting to be coming into a significant sum of money soon ... at least enough for the two of you to travel in some style around the world."

"Yes, that is correct ..."

"We now know that he recently purchased a collection of stamps from a Mr. Plumridge, the sale of which we believe was going to be the source of that new found wealth."

"Hugo was a stamp dealer. He bought and sold collections all the time. I know nothing of his business activities."

"Ah, but you do, Ms. French. Wasn't it you who gave him the two thousand pounds in order for him to buy that collection?"

There was silence, followed by the not entirely unexpected sight of tears.

"It was a loan only. He said that I would be paid back in full directly he sold the stamps. It was an opportunity that he did not want to let go, as he said collections such as that only came about once in a blue moon."

"And where did you get such a large sum of money?"

"It was almost my entire savings in the Post Office."

"Isn't it also true that he never paid you back the money?"

"He would have done, I'm sure of that ..."

"Are you even sure that it was you he was going to take with him on his travels?"

This question visibly shocked Ms. French, who paused a while before answering.

"Yes, I am quite sure that there was nobody else in his life." The sobbing grew more audible at Morse's suggestion.

"The truth is that you found out that there was somebody else, and then you demanded your money back, but he refused to give it to you."

"No, no ... nothing like that."

"You knew his route home so you waited on the bench at Dead Man's Walk, which explains why he stopped and dismounted his bicycle ... you talked ... you argued ... and then when nobody was looking you hit him with a large instrument, such as a hockey stick, that you had taken with you."

"No, no ... I loved him ... I would never hurt him."

"You even hinted as much the first time we met when you said that it was you who killed him ... a slip of the tongue or possibly a confession ... either way you then changed your mind pretty quickly and went on about how you had given him your bicycle, and how the exercise must have been too much for his heart to take ... it was all very convincing."

"I tell you again, it was nothing like that ... I loved him too much. I would never hurt him."

Was Morse getting close to the truth? Was that last statement a partial confession for if it 'was nothing like that' what exactly was it like?

"You then took his wallet to make it look like a robbery, but you made one mistake."

"No, no ... none of this is true," she insisted between her tears.

"You also took his keys."

"Why would I want his keys? I don't understand what you are saying."

"Because you needed them. You thought, incorrectly as it happened, that the two thousand pounds was going to be in the safe at the shop."

"No, I never did any of this ... can you stop please, I can't take any more?"

"I will stop when you start telling me the truth ... you took those keys and made your way to the shop, but you didn't know that the safe needed a combination as well as a key. You tried to force the safe open but in vain. I observed the scratch marks around the combination dial where you tried your best to open it. Having failed, you returned to the scene of crime, intending to replace the wallet and keys, but by then it was too late as the police were already on hand, so you disposed of them in the rubbish bin on Merton Street. Finally you made your way home and waited patiently until I called the following morning at which point you played your part of the upset landlady to perfection."

There was no answer from Susan French who continued to sob into her handkerchief. Thankfully for her the door opened. It was Strange who gave Morse several pieces of paper on which were the particulars of four messages that had been left for him at Kidlington. The first informed him that the body of Joseph Ridler had now been identified by his parents, and so that strand to the investigation had now been closed. The next informed him that the alibis for both Sir Michael and Lady Chipperfield had been confirmed. Sir Michael it transpired had spent the night with his mistress (who was willing to make a statement if necessary) while Lady Chipperfield was, just as Sir Michael had stated, away in France doing her brass rubbing at the time of Cranmer's murder. It was a blow, but one comforted by the third message which was from Sylvia Warren. It seemed that she had been at home when Morse had visited earlier that day, and that she would be delighted to accompany him at the weekend. The last note was a reminder from Shepherd and Woodward that they would like their scarves returned.

"So Ms. French why don't you tell me all about it in your own words?" came a more reasonable question in a kinder tone from Morse.

It was a more confident Ms. French that now spoke in response.

"I have nothing to say ... none of what you accuse me of is true, and although I have nobody to vouch for me at the time of Hugo's death, I can tell you that I had nothing to do with it. In fact, I was at Bingo in Headington all afternoon. Does it seem reasonable to you that if I was contemplating murder that I would go and play bingo first? If I am not under arrest, I want to be taken home now, please."

Morse had to concede that the point she had just made was reasonable, and that his investigation was now crumbling.

"Yes, of course. Again thank you for coming, and I hope you understand that I had to ask you those questions in order to eliminate you from our investigation."

"Yes, I do understand, but you could have done in it a different way. Hugo was not some sort of a monster. He was a sweet and kind man ..."

With that the temporary assertiveness dissolved and Ms. French started to cry again. Why was it that everything time Morse spoke to Ms. French that it always ended in tears?

Chapter Forty-Three

bingo ('bɪŋgəʊ) *n, pl* –gos 1. A gambling game, usually played with several people, in which numbers selected at random are called out and the players cover the numbers on their individual cards. The first to cover a given arrangement of numbers is the winner. 2. A cry by the winner of a game of bingo 3. An expression of surprise at a sudden occurrence or the successful completion of something.

(Dictionary definition of bingo)

The futility of it all is what astonished Morse. It was worse even than train spotting. Why would anybody in their right mind want to spend an afternoon in an old, damp, dark, cold, ex-cinema crossing off numbers on a card in the full knowledge that the odds of winning anything were very much on the side of the house? Was this what passed for entertainment for the middle and old-aged? What was more in order to have the privilege of losing your money you had to become a member, as if you were joining some exclusive golf club. Morse just hoped that when he grew old he would never stoop to such depths and would always seek the company of a good book, fine music, and a bad woman, but not necessarily in that order.

He concluded that it was a place for those who were beyond redemption, beyond finding something meaningful to do in their latter years, and yet as he entered God's waiting room he noted that nearly every seat was occupied. Along the back wall was a bar, no doubt selling over-priced drinks and snacks. He made his way to the counter and having introduced himself asked to see the manager, who duly arrived, dressed in a bright red blazer similar to that worn by the bingo announcer on the stage, looking like a reject from some shabby holiday camp.

"Is there a complaint, officer?"

"No, I just want to verify if a Ms. Susan French is a member here, and if you know when her most recent visit might have been."

"I don't even have to go to the records to answer that one. She is one of our younger members, and comes every Tuesday and Saturday without fail."

"So she was definitely here Tuesday last week?"

"Yes, between four and seven ... if I am correct she even had a small win on that day."

"Is that all, officer?"

"For now, thank you."

"You are welcome to stay. Maybe I can offer you a drink."

"I don't suppose you stock any beer?"

"Only three ... there's a lager, an I.P.A. and a bitter."

"What's the bitter like?"

"I don't really know, all I can say is that we get it from Henley."

"Don't tell me that you keep Brakspear's bitter?" said Morse, surprised.

"Its got a bee on the label if that helps? Would you like to try a drop?"

"I certainly would," replied Morse, with enthusiasm.

"Would that be a half?"

The look of utter disgust at such a question was enough of an answer for the manager.

"Ah, a pint it is then."

Perhaps bingo halls weren't so bad after all. Morse considered that on balance maybe they were just above train spotting, for at least while being bored out of your skull you could get a decent pint, and furthermore did not have to brave the elements.

While this philosophical debate was going on in Morse's mind a peculiar thing happened, not strange in itself, but something that one only read about in novels of the cheap fiction variety. It was an argument – an event that happens countless times every day, but one that was to provide the detective with inspiration, and ultimately the way through the woods to resolve the deaths of both Hugo Latimer and Tamati Cranmer. It came in the form of an odious, little man who was slightly worse for wear. He entered the bingo hall looking for his wife.

"Thought I would find you here enjoying yourself spending the hard earned money I gives you each week for housekeeping," he said aggressively.

"Oh, and I'm not entitled to enjoy myself while you're out down the pub with your mates every night?" came the retort from a nondescript woman seated close to the bar.

"I work hard for my money, and I can spend it how I likes. I gives you that money, woman, to look after me, not to fritter it away down here ..."

"Precious little money at that ... and don't you think I don't know where you hide the money you get from all that overtime, and how you spend it on that fancy woman of yours you met at work."

"What fancy woman?"

"Don't you think I know you after fifteen bloody years of marriage, George?"

"Anyways you are making a scene ... you come home with me right now, woman."

"You're the one making the scene. Why don't you go home and wait for me instead. I'll be back at the usual time, and I'll make you dinner then, George. How the hell did I know you would be home so early from work, anyway? Your shift doesn't usually end until six."

"Well it does today, and there won't be anymore overtime either, cos I've just been made redundant ... that's why, and the least I could expect is my wife to be there for me, and show a bit of comfort at a time like this."

At that, the two looked at each other hard for a few seconds, before the wife rose, gave her husband a hug, and gathered her things as they went off home together.

Morse finished his beer, ordered another – he thought that two was the most he could possibly hope to get *gratis* out of the place – and then went home himself, the long way via the Drew Drop in Summertown, where he pondered his three-pint problem.

Chapter Forty-Four

"Three may keep a secret, if two of them are dead."

(Benjamin Franklin, *Poor Richard's Almanack*)

There was work to do that Friday morning, work in the form of a number of telephone calls to be made, the first of which ended thus:

"I will look into it for you, Mr. Morse, and see what I can dig up."

"That is very kind of you, Bursar ... you don't mind me calling on you tomorrow?"

"Well it is a weekend, but I will try to make myself available when you arrive. If, however, I am not in college for any reason I will leave my findings for you at the Porters' Lodge, or perhaps you would care to join me for lunch in the buttery?"

"Thank you for your help, especially at such short notice. I would be delighted to meet you for lunch, but hope that you will not mind that I will have somebody with me?"

"Not in the least."

"Until tomorrow then. Goodbye."

The next call ended in much the same way:

"I'm sure that I can find somebody with the requisite knowledge you seek. If, as you say, you will be visiting on Monday, why don't you join me for lunch at the Institute, and I will introduce you to our expert in corporate takeovers?"

215

"That sounds ideal. I will endeavour to be there by noon."

The third call was very similar.

"I will check the details immediately. I should have everything you need by lunchtime. In fact, why don't you drop by and be my guest for lunch, you know where I dine?"

"That is indeed most gracious of you. Shall we say twelve-thirty?"

"Excellent. I shall await you in the foyer. Good morning."

The day had started splendidly. Three, hopefully free, lunches obtained, and it was still not eleven o'clock. Only the final call, of a more personal nature, was different.

"I will look forward to welcoming you, and your wife, to our hotel this evening, Mr. Morris. I have booked you one double room with a view across the green for both Friday and Saturday evenings, and will reserve a table, and car parking space for you as well."

"Thank you, but the name is Morse, and it's not Mr. and ... are you still there?"

It never failed to surprise Morse how many people, especially those such as booking agents, who should know better, always got his rather simple, five letter, one syllable, surname wrong. If he had some foreign sounding name such as Layfollet, Lafarlett or LaFollett it would, likely as not, be spelt correctly. What annoyed him even more was on the occasions when they would argue, and tell him that he had spelt his name wrong, or that he should blame his parents – no he should only blame the person who was illiterate. Never mind, it was not the end of the world, although it might have been if McNutt had not liked what Morse was about to report to him.

"Ay, Morse, well it certainly makes a wee bit more sense than all your other fanciful theories to date. But, as far as I can see you only have circumstantial proof, and you will be needing firm evidence, man, if we want to stand a hope of a conviction."

"That is why I propose that we present this as a play in two acts. In that way we will find out if it is one or two persons involved, or maybe both of them acting together, sir."

"Yes, I take your point. If it is as you say, then one will try to protect the other, and hopefully give themselves away in doing so. It is actually a very clever plan, Morse. Well done ... a good piece of detective work. In view of what you say, you had better be suspended on Monday as well, and follow up in London. You will, of course be doing all this in your own time, and at your own expense."

"Yes, sir, I understand."

"But don't look so crest fallen ... you can keep your receipts as if you are successful, and this is the breakthrough we have been looking for I will let you claim for everything, including your dirty weekend away with Ms. Warren."

"Yes, sir, but how did you know about ..."

"This is my police station, Morse ... don't you think I know anything? I make it my business to know what my men are doing in and out of the station? Good luck to you, man, I am told she is a bonnie lass. Now be on your way, you got a busy day ahead of you, and a longish drive this evening."

Morse left feeling rather elated. It was as if he had just been given a private audience along with a blessing from Pope Paul VI himself. Lunch that day proved to be a fine affair as well. Mr. Edwards, manager of the Clarendon Club branch of the National Westminster Bank, was an excellent host.

"This is a little different from the last time we met," admitted Edwards. "Maybe we did not get off on the right foot then, so I hope that lunch at the club will repair any ill feeling."

"I did charge in like the proverbial bull in a china shop so it is I that should apologise for any ill feeling."

"Apology accepted. Now to business. Again I can't show you the records without formal authority, but I can answer any questions appertaining to them. Understood?"

"Understood. It occurred to me that I had been approaching this investigation from the wrong angle. I had been looking at the personal affairs of Hugo Latimer as a motive for his murder, while actually it is all tied in with his business activities. Would I be right in assuming that he also held a business account with you?"

"You would."

"Would I also be correct in saying that the business was profitable, but not what you would call a runaway success?"

"You would. It was barely profitable, making just about enough money to support somebody with modest needs."

"Would I also be right in saying that if you look back over the past six months or so, that a sum of two thousand pounds has never been paid into the account?"

There was a pause while Edwards consulted the ledger.

"Correct again."

"Now to the important part. I am going to suggest that once a month, until recently, probably towards the end of each month, that there was a payment into the account by cheque that is substantially larger than anything else that is paid in all month."

"That is pretty much correct, though the amount varies from month to month, from several hundred pounds to a few thousand pounds. It is these payments that basically keep the business going."

"And these larger figures are never for round amounts? I mean that they would not be for two hundred, three hundred, four hundred pounds but always an odd sum."

"Yes, that is true enough, but nothing unusual there I would say."

"Excellent. Now for example give me any one of those figures please."

"Well let me see ... one of the larger payments was for one thousand nine hundred and ninety-eight pounds."

"Then I am speculating that a few days earlier there was also a cheque paid in for just two pounds. Am I right?"

"You are ... I understand the underlying mathematics, but what does all this mean?"

"It means that somebody was keeping a secret. Look at the various payments and tell me if all the larger amounts were from the same account number."

"Yes, they were."

"And the smaller amounts I vouch were all from a different account number, but actually the same person each time."

"Again, yes they were, but not the same person as for the larger amounts."

"Oh, but I would be right in saying that the smaller amounts all came from this man?"

Morse took his notebook out and showed Edwards a name on one of the inside pages. Edwards nodded.

"And the name on the other account, the larger one ..."

"It belongs to a Mr. Pilgrimme, a Mr. Tud Pilgrimme."

"There you have it, a simple case of fraud, unless you think that Mr. Tud Pilgrimme exists, no doubt born in Norfolk and named after the local river?"

"There have been no suspicious activities on that account, I assure you."

"I know that you keep the cancelled cheques for a period of time, so I suggest that you gather together as many cheques as possible, along with all the statements, for both accounts, as they will be needed as evidence when this case gets to court."

"Yes, of course. I see it now ... it helps doing *The Times* crossword occasionally, or I would never have spotted the link in a million years. Shall we treat ourselves to some post-luncheon brandy to celebrate?"

"I'd rather have a whisky if it is all the same to you?"

"Whisky it is then ... waiter, two large malts, please."

Chapter Forty-Five

"The main difference between the two is simple ... the longer you remain in Oxford, the longer you want to remain in Oxford."

(Colin Dexter)

 T he concept of a parallel universe was one that was not entirely lost on Morse. Indeed from his knowledge of the childrens' television programme *Dr. Who*, broadcast on a Saturday evening immediately prior to *Dixon of Dock Green*, the latter according to Susan French being so loved by the late Hugo Latimer, he was aware of the various problems of attempting to travel through space and time. Surely the existence of Oxford and Cambridge were proof of such a parallel system, the former having occupied the centre of Morse's known universe for most of his adult life. Indeed Morse was immediately reminded of the old joke of how an Oxford academic changes a light bulb, the answer being that he simply holds the new bulb in place, and then just waits for the world to revolve around him.

It is certainly true that once someone has known either city, that they then instantly dislike the other, despite the fact that both have so much in common. Both cities are named after a river crossing, and arc known for their rowing and punting activities. Indeed both rivers change their name close to the city centre. Both are associated with the colour blue, and both have a Corpus

Christi, Jesus, Magdalen (though pronounced differently in each city), Pembroke, Queens', St. Catherine's, St. John's and Trinity colleges. Moreover each city can boast a Bridge of Sighs, and each makes the same mistake of basing it on the wrong Venetian structure. More annoyingly, both have railway stations some distance from the city centre, due to the then prevailing powers of the University. Both have magnificent college chapels designed by Sir George Gilbert Scott in the Gothic revival style – St. John's in Cambridge and Exeter in Oxford – and both have buildings by Sir Christopher Wren at Pembroke, Emmanuel and Trinity colleges in Cambridge and the Sheldonian and Christ Church in Oxford. However, most inexplicable of all was the fact that neither city was ever considered of any import by the Roman Empire.

Morse had never visited 'the other place' and so was looking forward to exploring the great unknown, not to mention the chance of a weekend away with Sylvia Warren. It transpired that she too had never been to Cambridge and was also excited by the prospect of visiting the area in the company of Morse.

His knowledge of the fenland city was limited to its great literary connections: Gray, Forster, Brooke, Byron, Tennyson, Russell, Kingsley, Wordsworth, Milton, Coleridge and most prominent of all, in Morse's mind at least, Housman.

The journey (roughly following the path of the now defunct Oxford to Cambridge railway) via Aylesbury, Bletchley, Milton Keynes (where the Open University had been established just two years previously – and which Morse thought would probably not last for another two) and Bedford was tedious, taking nearly three hours. It mattered not a jot as Morse was in the company of a woman he found both attractive and intellectual. He found it impossible to judge what it was about Sylvia he liked the most. All he knew was that with her he was at ease and happy for the first time in a very long while.

As the time passed there was never a silent moment in the car as the two lovers talked about their passion for music, places to which they had always wanted to travel, politics and family. Both had a fondness for everything Italian and wished to visit Florence in the

222

not too distant future. That could be easily arranged. As far as politics was concerned there was a difference in that Sylvia did not have the same socialist leanings as Morse, though each respected the other's views and were, in fact, far closer in their beliefs than their voting habits suggested.

Morse spoke at length about his father and the lonely years he spent at a Midlands Grammar School before his National Service down near Dorchester. Sylvia had had a different sort of upbringing being the product of one of the better private boarding schools in the country where she had excelled at everything academic. She had studied medicine in London where she had been the outstanding student of her class. She spoke too of her elder sister whom she had idolised from an early age. She had died in a car accident some six years ago after which Sylvia had undergone a deep depression. In return Morse confided how desolated he had felt at the death of his father, and also at that of his great-aunt Freda from Alnwick with whom he had spend many a school holiday.

Was there nothing to dislike about Sylvia Warren? She was a woman beyond compare, and on that thought some apt lines of Wordsworth came to mind.

> A perfect Woman, nobly plann'd,
> To warn, to comfort, and command;
> And yet a Spirit still, and bright
> With something of angelic light.

Morse just hoped that she felt the same way about him and did not notice, or care, about all his foibles. He vowed that he would make this weekend as romantic as possible, but then how could he possibly keep that promise with the knowledge that he had police work to carry out? He would have to tell her and hope that she would understand.

"I have a confession to make … there is a reason I chose Cambridge for this weekend."

"A police reason?"

"Yes, I am afraid so, but I promise that my enquiries will take virtually no time at all."

"You know, I would be almost disappointed in you if there had not been a reason connected with work for bringing me here. I forgive you, but only if you put your foot down and get us to the hotel before they stop serving dinner."

Morse had no trouble in finding the University Arms Hotel, but immense problems persuading the receptionist that he had made a reservation, albeit in the name of Mr. and Mrs Morris – something that Mrs Morris found slightly disturbing. It made her wonder if Morse was embarrassed to be associated with her, a point she was to bring up later over dinner, and one which very nearly led to their first argument.

For a hotel said to be the finest in Cambridge, it did not compare favourably to the Randolph back home. Granted it had a nice view across Parker's Piece, a flat and uninteresting piece of common land, roughly square and said to be the birthplace of Association Football. Although the Randolph has no open space close by it does at least look out on the Ashmolean, one of the finest museums in the world. The University Arms may be larger, and more imposing than its Oxford counterpart, with its copper-roofed towers, but that Friday evening it lacked any atmosphere. The meal could only be described, at best, as satisfactory, though Morse could happily report the following morning, that activities in the double bedroom post-dinner were far more so, and lasted into the early hours of Saturday.

Chapter Forty-Six

"Tennyson notes, with studious eye,
How Cambridge waters hurry by ..."

(Rupert Brooke, *The Old Vicarage, Grantchester*)

Breakfast consumed and *The Times* crossword completed it was time to see where so many writers and poets had been inspired. It was a dull non-descript day, but at least there was no wind, which tended to sweep in across the fenlands making it a bitterly cold place in winter. Although mild, there was no warmth either, and this Morse reckoned was in direct consequence of Cambridge, unlike Oxford, not being built with Cotswold stone, which even in the midst of days like this would always give off a reassuring glow to cheer any season. The main question of the morning was what to do before lunch. This was easily answered when Morse again remembered his Wordsworth.

> It was a dreary morning when the wheels
> Rolled over a wide plain o'erhung with clouds,
> And nothing cheered our way till first we saw
> The long-roofed chapel of King's College lift
> Turrets and pinnacles in answering files,
> Extended high above a dusky grove.

"Shall we make our way into town and have a look at King's College?"

"That sounds splendid, but just one thing before we go," replied Sylvia.

"And what is that?"

"I simply can't keep calling you Morse ... and as you won't tell me your first name from now on you will have to be my darling man."

Morse had no objection. In fact, the thought of being a 'darling man' gave him a certain buzz.

Walking hand in hand the two lovers made their way towards the city centre down St. Andrew's Street, past Downing College to Petty Cury.

"That's an unusual name. Do you have any ideas, my darling man?" she asked with such tenderness that it sent tingles up and down Morse's spine. It was then he remembered his schoolboy French. He had been good at French.

"I suspect that it is most likely a corruption from the French for *petit cury* meaning small cooks. Who knows it may have been an area known for its inns in the past times."

Sylvia was impressed with the sheer depth of knowledge that Morse seemed to possess on all things. Soon they were in the main market square.

"Not as fine as the covered market back in Oxford, or as impressive as Radcliffe Square," commented Morse as they walked across the plain square set out with market stalls such as one might find in any number of English market towns.

"But do remember that the Radcliffe Square was not liked when the Radcliffe Camera was added. People said that it was too large and out of place in Oxford."

"True, but then what do people know? Nikolaus Pevsner had it right when he said that it was certainly unparalleled at Cambridge."

"And he, I believe, lectured here in Cambridge for almost thirty years so he should know if anybody does."

It was Morse's turn to be impressed with the knowledge displayed by his companion.

Across the square, more formally known as Market Hill despite the fact that it was completely flat as far as the eye could see, was St. Mary's Passage running alongside Great St. Mary's Church. It was an imposing structure, but alas only a shadow of its namesake in Oxford. It was here though that Morse spied two things of interest. First was a Cambridge tradition he had heard about by the name of Auntie's Tea Shop, which he resolved they would visit for afternoon refreshments. The second was Ryder and Amies, the neighbouring establishment on the corner with King's Parade, founded in 1864 according to the writing above the shop window, and the equivalent of Shepherd and Woodward in Oxford. Morse had business to conduct here later. Sylvia Warren found a third point of interest at the base of the west tower of the church.

"Look over here. It says that this spot marks the datum point from which all distances from Cambridge are measured and that it was a William Warren, a Fellow of Trinity Hall, who in 1725 began to measure the one mile points along the roads from Cambridge at which were then set up the first milestones in Britain since Roman times."

"I wonder if he might have been a distant relation of yours?"

"Who knows … who cares, but will you look at that view. Isn't it grand?"

Indeed the vista along King's Parade was magnificent. To their right was Senate House, a neo-classical structure of Portland stone, from where Cambridge graduates receive their degrees. Nice as it was it failed to impress Morse who muttered something about Sir Christopher Wren and the Sheldonian. To the left though was the building that they had come to see. King's College was superlative in every aspect, and in every sense of the word.

"Listen. I think there's a service in progress."

She was correct. There was the faint sound of choral music floating across the morning air, lifting the spirits of anybody lucky enough to be present. It was without doubt a magical moment. They squeezed their hands together just a little tighter.

"Let's see if they will let us in," suggested Morse.

227

As with Oxford the colleges do not mind visitors if they look appreciative, and so Morse and Sylvia Warren were soon inside the great Gothic chapel gazing up at the largest fan-vaulted ceiling in the world, while savouring the efforts of the choristers. To both of them it was a heavenly experience as they sat there with their eyes closed just listening and holding hands for nigh on an hour.

Afterwards they wandered around the college grounds at leisure before making their way back along King's Parade, past Trinity to St. John's where again they were made welcome and allowed to enter via the Great Gate, above which the arms of the foundress Lady Margaret Beaufort were prominent.

"Such a pity that in these days of growing equality, and given that St. John's was founded by a woman, that it does not seek to be at the forefront of progress and admit women students," commented Sylvia as they passed between the crenulated towers of the entrance.

"I'm sure it will come very soon. Even the odious Master of Lonsdale I interviewed the other day recognises that it is inevitable."

She looked up and spotted that either side of the arms were supporters in the form of two stone creatures with what looked like an elephant's tail, an antelope's body and a goat's head.

"What strange type of mythical beast would they be?" she asked.

"They are yales, but no connection as far as I know with a certain academic institution in America."

They walked through no fewer than three quadrangles (more correctly courts in Cambridge parlance) before they came upon what they had come to see. To members of the college it was merely a way of crossing the River Cam from Third Court to New Court, but to everybody else it was the prettiest of bridges in the city. Even Morse had to admit that the Cambridge Bridge of Sighs with its neo-Gothic decoration and traceried openings was an icon that could seldom be equalled, and never surpassed. New Court itself was huge reflecting the growth of St. John's in the early part of nineteenth century. There were battlements, pinnacles and the ubiquitous fan-vaulting in abundance – no wonder it was known locally as the wedding cake. Even more impressive were the gardens that led off from the west side of the court. The wide borders and lawn were perfectly maintained, and despite the time of year there was even some colour present from the carefully selected shrubs that had been planted here.

"You can almost feel their presence can't you?"

"Who do you mean?"

"Wordsworth for a start ... he was a St. John's man, almost one of the Greats, but actually managed to get a pass. You know that this is the only place in the country where you can eat swan legally," stated Morse with some disgust.

"In fact I did. All along the river they had swan traps installed. Such a beautiful creature surely deserves a less barbaric death don't you think?"

"Indeed I do. Talking of which it is nearly time for our lunch appointment at Queens'. I hope that you will not be disappointed as I doubt if swan will be on the menu."

"Thank God for that."

They both laughed out loud at the thought.

On arrival at the Porters' Lodge the bursar was duly summoned and arrived promptly.

"Mr. Morse, I am Janice Whiting ... delighted to meet you, and your companion. I have made some enquiries and have some good news for you."

"Excellent ... it is most kind of you to see us at a weekend."

"As I said on the telephone, I am usually in College of a weekend so it is no trouble at all. Shall we go through to the buttery?"

"What a good idea ... it seems ages since breakfast, but do tell me after which queen is the college named?" queried Sylvia Warren.

"Margaret of Anjou, wife to Henry the sixth, he who founded King's College up the road," replied the bursar.

"How quaint ... if you are going to have anything that is a his and hers it might as well be colleges," commented Morse with a tone of sarcasm.

The Old Hall where lunch was served was rather smaller than expected for one of the largest colleges in Cambridge. It consisted of just two plank tables along with a top table, either side of which were chairs, not the more usual benches, providing barely enough room to move up the centre aisle. However, being a Saturday the place was almost deserted so there was no trouble in finding a seat. In fact the privacy was only broken by the stare coming from the three benefactors whose portraits hung on the wall behind the top table, and beneath the College motto *floreat domus*.

"You were correct, Mr. Morse, they were both here at the same time. You must understand though that it was just after the war when records were not kept in the same way as they are today. In fact, Mr. Plumridge was one of the first post-war intake of students, while Mr. Cranmer did not arrive until forty-seven on a post-doctoral scholarship from abroad. Hence they would only have overlapped in their time here for less than a year."

"But would they have known each other?"

"This is where my investigation has borne fruit." She passed Morse a large brown envelope, in which were several hand-written foolscap sheets. "I asked a couple of the long-standing Fellows and they remember Cranmer and Plumridge as being keen cricketers and hockey players. I checked the sporting records and, although neither obtained a blue, they did play cricket on the same team at least once. The Fellows are also of the opinion that they socialised outside of sport, and have both made signed statements to that effect for you."

Morse scanned the pages. It was much better than he had hoped, and provided the vital link that he sought. Tamati Cranmer had been at the college during the time Robert Plumridge was a student there, and what is more they had been friends.

Chapter Forty-Seven

"If you are cold, tea will warm you;
If you are too heated, it will cool you;
If you are depressed, it will cheer you;
If you are exhausted, it will calm you."

(William Gladstone)

After the elation at lunchtime the afternoon was not as euphoric, although no less productive. Morse wanted to visit Trinity College, the *alma mater* of Byron, Tennyson, Fitzgerald and, of course, Housman, and these were just the poets who had been there. To add to these were two kings, along with a future one, musicians such as Vaughan Williams, a couple of writers in the form of Thackeray and A. A. Milne, the philosopher Bertrand Russell, and not forgetting the fathers of both classical and nuclear physics, Sir Isaac Newton and Lord Rutherford. Morse pondered whether there was any other place on Earth that could boast having produced so much for humanity per square foot? Trinity had certainly produced more Nobel Prize winners than any other college in the world. Not bad for place that nearly didn't come into existence, and was only founded in 1546 as one of the very last acts of Henry VIII, the charter being signed just five weeks before his death.

For all its impressiveness, on the whole, it was a disappointment to Morse. It is often the way in life that when you come face to face with one of your heroes that they do not quite live up to your expectations. He had envisaged a more discreet and informal place of learning exuding character, not a purpose-built factory of achievement. It was the difference between seeing the old Morris Motors fledgling workshop at Longwall Street, and the later Pressed Steel production line at Cowley. Both impressive in their way, although (in Morse's opinion) only the former made real cars.

At the time these thoughts probably did not register that firmly in his brain, which was distracted by trying to solve the question foremost on his mind – now that he had a connection between Cranmer and Plumridge what could it be that led to murder? Was it sex, money or some other motive? Given that the world of academia was also a common link it was probably something to do with reputation and status, that common Oxford disease that was worth killing for time and time again. One had become a successful Lonsdale Fellow, with all its trappings, while the other had remained a school teacher, albeit at a good school. That must be it, thought Morse – at some time in the past something happened between these two men of learning which only now had come to the fore. Had Cranmer stolen Plumridge's research in order to gain his Fellowship? Could it be proven? Why wait so long to get revenge? Such were the thoughts passing through the detective's mind.

Normally in such circumstances he would retire to the nearest public house to work on the problem, but today was different – he was supposed to be relaxing, supposed to be a tourist, supposed to be with Sylvia Warren who he had almost forgotten was the person holding his right hand. So today, and for today only, he would seek the help and inspiration that a cup of tea from Auntie's Tea Shop could provide.

It was an establishment with atmosphere, and if Morse had thought about his earlier analogy, he could have made a comparison here with the Randolph. Both serve a good afternoon cream tea, but only one has character, while the other was built to impress. The staff, dressed in their black and white pinafores, which harked back to Victorian times, were both attentive and efficient. Morse was not one for scones and cakes, but could see that Sylvia Warren was very much enjoying her cream tea and that pleased him greatly.

Morse had one last thing to do that afternoon. He needed to purchase a Cambridge University scarf at Ryder Amies. Under normal circumstances this is something he would never consider doing for such items were just for tourists and poseurs were they not? He didn't even possess a St. John's scarf despite being entitled to wear one. However, following tea he went next door and bought a Queens' College green and white striped scarf.

Business done, Morse could once again relax and enjoy the company of Sylvia Warren, something he did back at the University Arms until the small hours of the morning (once again), and for that matter the following day as well. The visit to Cambridge had been a success on all fronts, but all too soon following a morning at the Fitzwilliam Museum, which Morse found inferior to the Ashmolean, and a visit to Grantchester to see if the church clock really did stand at ten to three, it was time to make the drive back to Oxford. As evening began to fall and they joined the A428 towards Bedford, Morse realised that for the first time since his own college days, and time spent with Wendy Spencer of bittersweet memory, his father had been correct in his assertion that he should be patient and wait. There was no denying the fact that he was in love with the person sitting next to him in the passenger seat of the loaned police car.

Chapter Forty-Eight

"You are now
In London, that great sea, whose ebb and flow
At once is deaf and loud, and on the shore
Vomits its wrecks, and still howls for more
Yet in its depths what treasures!"

(P. B. Shelley)

Morse was of the opinion that he had driven quite enough over the weekend, and so would make his sojourn to London by railway. While waiting for the next fast train to the capital that cold Monday morning he could not help but look around him for Dexter, the truant who had helped him so recently in the Jones case. He was not present, however, so Morse concluded, though probably wishful thinking, that maybe his talk with him had made an impact, and that he was today back at school learning how to become the crime writer that he had indicated he wanted to be.

There was plenty to occupy him on the hour-long journey, but once *The Times* crossword had been completed, Morse elected to simply stare out of the window and let his mind wander back to pleasant thoughts of Sylvia Warren and the weekend just past, and to plan the one yet to come for they had both agreed to be together again the following weekend. As a consequence he did not notice the passing of Reading or Slough, and it was only when the person nudged him as they rose to leave that he realised that they were already at Paddington. Although there was a direct route to Strand via the Bakerloo line to Embankment taking less than fifteen minutes, Morse had always felt uneasy about being underground, and consequently queued for the number twenty-three bus which would also take him from door-to-door, albeit in a time commensurate with that of his journey from Oxford to London. It did though have the advantage of passing some fine buildings as the double-decker made its sedate progress to Strand where Morse eventually alighted right outside number three-nine-nine, the offices of Stanley Gibbons.

Inside the home of stamp collecting, all was very modern and business-like with items for sale displayed under glass illuminated by bright spotlights. It certainly wasn't like Latimer's shop, and people here were certainly not encouraged to browse. In fact, no sooner had Morse entered the premises than a suited gentleman approached him, and enquired if he could be of assistance. Having introduced himself along with the nature of his enquiry, Morse was ushered to an upper floor where the 'specialist department' was situated. After some minutes a Mr. Jackson appeared. He listened intently to Morse's questions.

"Secrecy among stamp collectors is very common I'm afraid, Mr. Morse. We call it the open door syndrome."

"I don't quite understand."

"Let me explain. You see printed album pages for a country will have spaces outlined in black and sometimes a picture of all the stamps in a particular set. It is always possible to fill perhaps ninety percent of the album very cheaply, but there are usually one or two stamps per page that are more expensive. Their outline on the page looks very much like an open door which can only be closed by filling the gap and spending significant amounts of money. In truth we rely on the album manufacturers to include spaces for everything listed in our catalogues, however rare an item may be … it's how we make our money. The stamp in question may look exactly like the less expensive ones on the page, but differ by maybe the watermark, perforations, gum or plate number, you understand."

Morse nodded although in truth he only understood the concept, and had no idea what a plate number might be or why the perforations and gum might be different between stamps.

"It becomes an obsession with some collectors and, as with gambling, they don't want others to know just how much they spend on their hobby."

"So, for instance, would it be likely that some of these stamps might cost several hundreds of pounds ... a penny black for instance?"

Mr. Jackson smiled.

"Yes, and no. Yes, individual stamps can cost hundreds, if not thousands of pounds, and no not for almost all penny blacks. It is a common misconception that just because it was the first adhesive postage stamp that it must be valuable. There were something like sixty-eight million of them printed, and we pay around a pound a margin for them. Granted plate eleven, imprimaturs and the 'VR' official will set you back a tidy sum, but I can sell you a very decent example for under ten pounds."

Again Morse nodded without any conception what a margin, an imprimatur or 'VR' official might be.

"Now, say I had a decent collection worth something in the thousands what would be the best way to dispose of it?" said Morse.

"You could, of course, bring it to us, or any other stamp dealer, and we would make an offer on it. However, that is mainly for people who want a quick sale, and are in need of money. It would most likely give you the lowest return. If you knew the absolute worth, then maybe sale by private treaty would be best, especially if it is to be sold as a complete collection. However, my advice is always to put it in auction. The more valuable stamps I would have as separate lots and that way, by breaking it down, you would realise the highest possible value, but have to wait several months to get your money."

"And do you have any auctions around the first of April?"

"No, we don't as it happens. Our next auction is in the middle of February, and then nothing until June."

Morse looked crest fallen.

"Let me have a look though at the auction list."

He disappeared for a few minutes before returning with a sheet of paper.

"Robson Lowe have a specialised Great Britain sale on the thirty-first of March … does that help?"

"Indeed it does," and with that Morse thanked the philatelist, taking the sheet of paper on which the thoughtful Mr. Jackson had written down the relevant contact details and left for his lunch appointment in Belgravia.

Chapter Forty-Nine

"Why would I want to join an organisation that would encourage people like myself to become members?"

(Groucho Marx)

From a quick glance of the routes displayed at the bus stop on the opposite side of the road to Stanley Gibbons, Morse was comforted by the fact that there was a direct service (number nine) which would take him to Hyde Park Corner, just a couple of minutes walk away from Belgrave Square. What was more it ran every three to five minutes, and as if to prove the point he could see a number nine approaching from the direction of Aldwych. Transport in London really was a marvel he thought.

His destination was the Institute of Directors which was a grand building that made the Clarendon Club seem insignificant in comparison. Morse was shown every courtesy by his very distinguished host. He was given the obligatory tour, followed by a large pre-prandial sherry, a handsome three-course lunch with the best part of two bottles of wine, white with the starter, and red with the main course, coffee and brandy. The imposing dining room was decorated in a rich style with huge pictures showing British victories of the Napoleonic war adorning every space available. It was not until the brandy was served that the conversation turned to the purpose of the visit.

"Ah, here he is, Mr. Morse, our expert on mergers and takeovers. Let me introduce you to Sir Jon Byford."

A tall man in his mid-fifties, dressed in the usual pinstriped suit, white shirt and an old school tie was approaching the table.

"Detective Sergeant Morse of the Thames Valley Police."

"How do you do?"

"Sir Jon Byford"

"How do you do?"

"Now then I have looked into the takeover for you, and you are correct in that the company was definitely undervalued. The price to earnings ratio in the company accounts submitted to Companies House for the five years prior to the takeover clearly indicates this fact."

"So a separate non-disclosed payment may have been made?"

"Yes, that is how it usually works. For arguments sake let us say that a company originally worth eighty pounds is now worth a hundred pounds. I come to you and say that I will buy it for eighty pounds. That doesn't sound like a good proposition, until I tell you that I will also make a further payment of fifteen pounds in cash. This still doesn't sound like a good deal until you realise that since there is now no gain to declare from the sale and so there is also no tax liability either. On the other hand if sold for the true market value of one hundred pounds, the tax on the twenty pounds gain would be in excess of the five pounds difference. You see that sometimes accepting less is actually more," observed Sir Jon.

"But how would that work to the advantage of both parties?"

"Obviously the seller has a potential gain in that any money paid via a nominee avoids tax altogether. However, they have to be careful as to how they dispose of such a sum, otherwise the Inland Revenue will be onto them eventually."

"Yes, I can see that, but what about the buyer?"

"Granted it is a little more tricky for the buyer if they intend to sell the business on anytime soon since, for the purposes of accounting, the book value in our example would be only eighty pounds, when it should be the ninety-five pounds actually paid. If they subsequently sold the company for the one hundred pounds market value there will be a tax implication on the twenty pounds profit, rather than on just five pounds if it had been declared at the correct purchase price in the first place. The buyer did, of course, initially gain since the purchase price was five pounds lower than the true market value. The difference between the two can usually be lost in the accounting, since there is bound to be capital expenditure involved over a number of years. A good accountant can work wonders you know."

"And how might the buyer hide the second cash payment?"

"Simplicity itself ... they just put it down in the end of year accounts as a charitable cash donation ... untraceable."

"And by what amount do you think the company was actually undervalued?

"At a conservative estimate ... around a million."

"As much as that ... well that certainly is an amount worth concealing."

As he departed Morse thought that such a sum was also a very good motive for murder.

Chapter Fifty

"Accept certain inalienable truths
Prices will rise, politicians will philander, you, too, will get old
And when you do, you'll fantasise that when you were young
Prices were reasonable, politicians were noble
And children respected their elders."

(Lyrics to *Everybody's Free (to Wear Sunscreen)*, Baz
Luhrmann)

In consideration of the lunchtime intake of calories, both solid and liquid, Morse thought it best that he go on foot to his next meeting at Robson Lowe's in Pall Mall. It might be cold and dull, but still pleasant enough to walk back to Piccadilly, and then cut across Green Park, the most featureless of open spaces in London, to an exit in Cleveland Row, which took him to the corner of Pall Mall and St. James's Street.

That name registered somewhere in the prefrontal cortex of Morse's brain, and well it might for St. James's Street was the location of Justerini and Brooks, founded in 1749 and royal warrant holder for wines and spirits many times over. The history of the company was a romantic one, which appealed to Morse. It was an Italian by the name of Giacomo Justerini, who having fallen in love with an opera singer, Margerita Bellino, while in Bologna, followed her to London. He joined forces with an Englishman, George

Johnson, and together they established a wine merchants, appropriately named Johnson and Justerini, in the City of London. The love affair, alas, was unrequited and so did not last. Giacomo returned to his native land a decade later having sold his stake in the company to his partner, who in turn sold the whole business on in 1831 to a Mr. Alfred Brooks, who obviously liked the name of Justerini and kept it at the expense of Johnson's, renaming the concern as it is known today. Morse thought that the story would make the basis for a libretto, with perhaps some minor modifications, such as Giacomo committing suicide at the loss of his lover in the third act, probably drowning himself in a vat of fine wine (well if it was good enough a plot for Shakespeare, it would certainly be good enough for his opera).

Most importantly, though, was the fact that Justerini and Brooks were among the first companies to produce blended whiskies, the difference being that their blend included single malts in the mixture. Today that fine blend, J&B Rare, is an export product, available only outside of the country, or for direct sale at the company headquarters in St. James's Street. And so it was that Morse made a slight detour up the hill, and purchased a bottle to take home with him.

Around the corner in Pall Mall the offices of Robson Lowe were to be found on an upper floor almost opposite Marlborough House. It was here after he has shown his police credentials that Morse met a charming young lady by the name of Janet Owen. She certainly seemed knowledgeable on all things philatelic, but had the annoying tendency of calling everybody 'love'. Even more irritating was her habit of repeating everything up to three times, as if she were the main character out of Lewis Carroll's *The Hunting of the Snark*, making sure that whatever she said was true.

"Follow me please, just this way, here we go, love."

Morse followed, and soon the two were in the main auction room, where he outlined his problem before getting to the main question.

"So could you tell me if you know of a dealer by the name of Hugo Latimer?"

"Oh, yes, yes … yes, I know him well. Often comes here to buy the odd stamp or two, regular at our specialised Great Britain sales, in and out all the time, you know, love."

"Excellent, but I am more interested in whether he is currently selling any items in, for example, your sale at the end of March?"

"Yes, he is," came the reply, rather surprisingly without a repeat of 'yes' or a single 'love'. Morse was making progress.

"Can you tell me more?"

"Dear sweet man, lovely person, always a gentleman, came here before Christmas and told us he was retiring, selling up, closing the shop when the lease ran out, you understand. Hence if truth be known around half the lots in the March sale are his from stock, about fifty percent that is … almost two hundred lots."

"Could you identify for me which ones are his, and how much they are likely to fetch?"

"I can do better than that … much better, I can give you the auction catalogue and mark which lots are his. Then you can see for yourself the description, the S.G. Number and valuation. Why don't you have a nice cup of tea, love, while I do that for you? Good cup of tea will go down a treat … very refreshing a good cuppa."

Morse nodded and was soon sipping tea, while Ms. Owen was furiously putting ticks next to lot numbers in the said catalogue that she had brought back into the room, along with the tea and a plate of biscuits. Before Morse had time finish the last of the chocolate digestives he was handed the catalogue. He browsed through it with interest. The estimates certainly added up, and it would be interesting to see what the total realisation price might be, though Morse had a pretty shrewd idea.

"What are these numbers in bold at the end of the descriptions?" he asked.

"Didn't I say? Thought that I told you, must have forgotten to mention it, love … they refer to the photographic plates on the centre pages. You see every lot is photographed, so if you can't be at the auction you can still make a bid based on the description and the image."

The photographs were going to be very useful to Morse.

"I've been to Latimer's shop, and there are lots of other things there, less expensive things, so how would he dispose of those if he was selling up?"

"Well, we at Robson Lowe only deal with rare and valuable stamps. Most dealers you see make their bread and butter from low value sales ... packets of stamps and sets for under a pound, along with album accessories and the like. However, every dealer is usually lucky enough to have one of two customers who are serious collectors, or investors, who can spend hundreds on a single item. All those lots for March fall under that category, while all the other stuff would just be sold off as kiloware via smaller provincial auction houses, and in bulk, I dare say, to other dealers. Do you get it, love?"

"Indeed, I think I do, but I believe that Mr. Latimer also has a fine collection himself?

"Oh, yes he does, a very fine collection, one of the best I've seen in ages, got it in the back room if you want to see it?"

"That won't be necessary at this stage, but why do you have it here in the first place?"

"It's for our September sale ... can't flood the market with too many plums all at once, if you know what I mean?"

So that was why Latimer's personal collection could not be found, thought Morse. It seemed that his intentions towards Susan French were genuine, and that he was selling everything, even his own collection, to fund their new life together.

"Plums?"

"You see most dealers are also collectors, they collect plums ... that's what we in the trade call the best stamps in a collection. Dealers collect the plums over the years, and squirrel them away as a sort of insurance plan for old age, so that when they retire they sell off all the plums, and then live on the proceeds. Mind you most dealers never retire, and keep trading long after their shops have gone ... you know, a few high value, high profit customers, love."

That was everything Morse needed to know. The jigsaw puzzle was now complete, at least it would be after a few hours work that evening.

"That is all I need to know. You have been most helpful, but before I leave, would it be possible to make a telephone call to Oxford?"

"Of course it would, no problem there, just dial a nine first for an outside line. There you go," replied Ms. Owen pointing to the telephone next to the auctioneer's podium.

Morse did as instructed, desperately trying to remember the number for the main desk at St. Aldate's.

"Is that you, Strange?"

"Morse, where the devil are you, matey?"

"I'm in London, but I want you to do me a favour ... I now know why Latimer kept all those worthless stamp booklets in his safe, and I need you to go and get them for me right now ... clear the safe, take all of them, every single one, leave nothing behind. I will pick them up late this evening from the front desk."

What was more surprising than Strange not questioning him, or grumbling about the extra work he had just been given, was the fact that Morse realised that he too was now talking in triplicate – it seemed that Janet Owen's habits were catching, though thankfully he did not call Strange, love, though he saw the pun and smiled!

Chapter Fifty-One

"I see no good reason
Why Gunpowder Treason
Should ever be forgot."

(Nursery rhyme)

It was still mid-afternoon when Morse left Robson Lowe's so he decided to add an impromptu visit to his itinerary. This time there was no direct public transport route so Morse's only option was to walk or to hail a taxi. He elected for the latter and within minutes was at the main entrance to the Houses of Parliament.

His motive for coming here was not entirely clear. Although, it was the workplace of Louise Plumridge, she was not even a suspect in this case. In truth she was merely an excuse for Morse to see inside that great monument to the partnership of Barry and Pugin who had been jointly responsible for the rebuilding of the Palace of Westminster, as it is more correctly known, in 1837.

It was all a bit of a waste of time for it transpired that Jessica Plumridge was still on two weeks leave and not expected back until Thursday that week. However, he did manage to have a short conversation with somebody in the personnel office, and verified that since starting there Louise had been a hardworking employee. Her degree in history from Hughes Hall Cambridge had been put to good use in her work when compiling answers to Parliamentary

Questions. She was well liked and as far as it was known had no boyfriends. In fact, the vetting procedure found no evidence of her liking men at all – only that she was close to her parents and went to the family home most weekends. There was a revelation though – one of the references Louise had given on her application form was none other than that of Cranmer. On reflection was that much of a surprise? After all Cranmer, it was now known, had been a friend of her father so there was no good reason surely why he should not also act as an academic reference for his daughter? Even so the appearance of that name caused Morse to be uneasy.

It was already dark when he re-emerged from the sumptuous Gothic interior of the parliament building, so he took his second taxi of the day to Covent Garden. Here, on the far side of the market in Bow Street was to be found a temple to the arts, a building described as the most luxurious ever constructed in London when it opened in 1732. There was no doubt in Morse's mind, as he approached the box office, that the description of the Royal Opera House was still valid, although, as he was well aware, the epithet was for the original theatre, not the third re-incarnation of 1858, designed by Edward Middleton Barry, he of Palace of Westminster fame.

"Can I help you, sir?"

"Do you have any tickets available for the *Magic Flute* this Saturday please?"

"We have some left, sir."

"Then I would like two of your best remaining stall's tickets."

"I am sorry, sir, but we are all sold out in the stalls. I can offer you two seats in a box, though?"

"That would be perfect."

At least it was perfect until Morse was told the cost of his purchase. Morse could not help but recall that when the second theatre was opened in 1809, that the management raised the prices of seats to offset the cost of rebuilding – an increase from six to seven shillings for a box, but the increase was considered so excessive that it sparked off what became known as the Old Price Riots. These continued for over two months until the management eventually saw good sense and reverted to the original pricing.

He thought briefly about starting his own riot in protest, but satisfied himself that the cost, which equated to over a week's wages for a Detective Sergeant, was a small price to pay to be in the company of both Mozart and Sylvia Warren.

Chapter Fifty-Two

"Jigsaw, noun, 1.1 A mystery that can only be resolved by assembling various pieces of information: 'help the police put all the pieces of the jigsaw together'."

(Oxford Advanced Learner's Dictionary definition of jigsaw)

By the time he walked into St. Aldate's police station to collect the stamp booklets it was past ten o'clock in the evening, with Strange having long since departed for the comforts of home. Morse could have been there around three hours earlier if he had taken the Underground back to Paddington rather than the bus, and more poignantly if he had not also visited the Great Western Hotel at the station, where ladies of the night ply their trade to weary commuters. On this occasion, only the beer available from the Brunel Bar tempted him – four pints of temptation to be precise.

Back home he took a pair of scissors and proceeded to cut out the photographs of every stamp in the auction catalogue belonging to Latimer, being careful to write the S.G. Number and lot number on the back of each. He put these face down on the table in lines of ascending order by S.G. Number. Very soon Morse realised that with over two hundred lots to process that it was going to be a long affair, and to that end he decided to sample his earlier acquisition of J&B Rare. It was, indeed, very fine, perhaps the finest blended whisky he had ever tasted, certainly worth the price he had paid for the bottle.

By the early hours of Tuesday morning Morse's dining table resembled a model of Horse Guards Parade, with little squares of paper in straight lines as if representing the soldiers during the Trooping of the Colour ceremony.

Now all he had to do was to see if his theory matched the reality. He took a stamp booklet and turned the pages until he reached the first space where a stamp had been taken and signed for by Tim Plumridge. The writing below indicated that it was Stanley Gibbons number two hundred and thirty-six, and worth some three shillings. He ran his fingers along to the second row of cut outs on the table, and there to his relief was a photograph corresponding to number two hundred and thirty-six. It was an oblong stamp that fitted the gap in the booklet perfectly. He took some glue and pasted the cut out triumphantly into the space. All he had to do now was to check the valuation in the catalogue. It corresponded to lot number fifty-six – '1877 £1 brown-lilac Pl.1 (CD) Wmk. Shamrocks Sideways. A fine unmounted mint example of this very rare stamp. Seldom seen in this condition. Cat. £675. Est. £300-325'.

Eureka, he had solved the jigsaw puzzle.

Morse made a note of the estimate on a separate piece of paper and proceeded to the next purchase made by Tim Plumridge. Again there was a matching photograph on the dining table that he pasted into the space, and so this process continued until well past three o'clock in the morning, by which time a significant amount of whisky in the J&B Rare bottle had apparently evaporated, along with all the cut outs on the table, which had been found new homes in the now full stamp booklets.

His final action before bed was to add up all the estimates to obtain a total realisation price. This he had to do several times, just to make sure that his addition skills were correct at that time of day. Once his maths yielded the same total twice in a row Morse was able to satisfy himself that had Latimer lived he would have been in line to receive in excess of two hundred thousand pounds at the end of March, which even with the auctioneers' fees deducted was still a substantial sum, and would more than cover the expense of a round the world cruise for two.

Chapter Fifty-Three

"O, what a tangled web we weave
when first we practise to deceive!"

(Walter Scott, *Marmion*)

At times Morse could show remarkable feats of energy and could even go without sleep for up to seventy-two hours with relative ease. This was just one such occasion, as he knew now for certain that the final stages of this double-murder case were fast approaching. Morse's excitement had risen in tandem with his adrenalin levels, so it should come as no surprise then, to learn, that despite him working until nigh on four o'clock, that he was one of the first to arrive at Kidlington later that morning.

A scrap of paper on his desk greeted him. It was a telephone message taken while he had been away in London. It was from the manager of the National Westminster Bank and read: 'Pilgrimme account dormant – balance almost £300,000 – Edwards'. It was exactly as he had hoped, and meant that there was now enough evidence to make an arrest, subject to the approval by McNutt, whose booming voice Morse could now hear as his superior entered the office. He was talking with somebody from administration about finding a placement for a new recruit by the name of Lewis, but on noticing Morse he soon turned his attention to him.

"Ah, the Prodigal Son returns from the wilderness I see," announced McNutt.

"London could hardly be described as a wilderness, sir ..."

"I meant Cambridge, man ... my office ... five minutes ... and get me a tea on the way."

McNutt was obviously in good humour, excellent humour for the dour Scotsman, and Morse hoped that he could improve his temperament even further with his findings. Just as a barrister might do in court, he outlined his case for the arrest of Robert Plumridge on the suspicion of murder of Hugo Latimer, and waited for a response from his superior. It came quicker than expected.

"Aye, I do believe you have cracked it, man, but tell me again just concentrating on motive, means and opportunity."

"Well it all started when Tim Plumridge sold his paper business some years ago. I ascertained from the Institute of Directors that it was undervalued by around a million pounds. In fact, this was to avoid tax, with the difference being split between the buyer and seller. Plumridge received the sum of half a million pounds into a separate bank account ..."

"This is the account in the name of Tud Pilgrimme."

"Correct ... a rather obvious anagram of Tim Plumridge. Over the years Plumridge tried to dispose of the money by investing in rare stamps, using the ghost account to pay for them in the main."

"And this is where those stamp booklets come in, you say."

"Yes, it all had to be done in secrecy, with the rest of the family knowing nothing about it. Hence he arranged with Hugo Latimer to send what were, in essence, worthless stamp booklets, but with the odd expensive item among the chaff. The trick was that to avoid any suspicion, they used a rather simple schoolboy code to identify the better items. If for example a stamp was worth a hundred pounds it was priced at a shilling in the booklet, and if a thousand pounds it was given the value of a pound. Plumridge would pay this amount from his personal account, and then send a further cheque from the Pilgrimme account a few days later for the balance."

"And just how long did this wee scheme go on for do you think?"

"For many years, right up until his unexpected death six months ago. The booklets were sent out once a month, and just in case the taxman made enquiries, Latimer kept all the returned booklets in his safe as evidence. After all he had nothing to hide since both cheques did go through his business legitimately."

"And just how much did you say we are talking about?"

"In total around two hundred thousand pounds. There is still three hundred thousand pounds in the Pilgrimme bank account."

"Now you say it all went wrong when Plumridge died."

"Indeed. It was then that Latimer became greedy, most likely driven on by his need for money for the new love of his life, Susan French. He approached the Plumridges and offered to buy back the stamps, in the knowledge that they were in need of money and required a no questions asked transaction. Rather brazenly he even told them that as a hobby they should not expect to get back the same amount as had been paid, but then having set the expectation low, said that on reflection Plumridge had been a wise investor and that his stamps had risen a little in value. Hence he was able to offer them two thousand pounds, a figure that they gladly accepted, especially Mrs. Plumridge who was glad of the cash, which naturally she did not declare for death duties as part of the deceased estate."

McNutt nodded.

"And, of course, as you explained they had no reason to doubt Latimer, since he had the original books as proof, and could show them just how much had been paid originally. Actually he had no need to do this since the Plumridges kept photostats of the booklets themselves, and, of course, they could always verify what had been spent from the cheque stubs belonging to Tim Plumridge's personal bank account."

"Exactly, the risk of being exposed was negligible, but then somehow it all went wrong for Latimer. I suspect that Robert Plumridge found the Pilgrimme cheque book, and worked out that Latimer had cheated them out of in excess of two hundred thousand pounds, and that at a time when the family home was up for sale to pay for the inheritance tax bill."

"Fine, you have established the motive, but not the means or opportunity."

"This is where I need to do a little more work, sir. As de Bryn confirmed death may not have been by a fall, but could equally have been from a blunt object such as a hockey stick, and from my visit to Cambridge I confirmed that Plumridge was both a cricket and a hockey player while he was there."

"A little tenuous to say the least, Morse. I was a hockey player in my time I'll have you know ... I trust that I am not to be a suspect?"

"I believe that if we search the Plumridge home we will find the murder weapon, and if we're lucky forensics might just be able to help tie it in with Latimer."

"Perhaps ... and opportunity?"

"Well he would certainly have time to get from where he works at Radley College to Oxford, and carrying a sport's bag with a hockey stick protruding would raise no suspicion. I suspect that he may have already confronted Latimer in his shop without success, and so mistakenly thought that the stamps in question were in the safe. He could easily find Latimer's home address from the telephone directory, just as I did, and could also work out his most logical route home, along with the best place to intercept him."

"Are you saying that he didn't necessarily mean to murder him?"

"I'm pretty sure that was not his intention. I think that he simply wanted to confront him again, maybe knock him out for a while, get his keys, return to his shop and retrieve the stamps from the safe. The fact that he took Latimer's wallet as well makes me think that maybe Latimer did not recognise his assailant, and so Plumridge tried to make it look like a simple mugging. However, as we know the safe requires a combination as well as a key. That was a miscalculation. I did note scratch marks on the safe as if somebody had tried to force the door open. By the time Plumridge returned it was too late for the police were already on the scene and, of course, Latimer was dead. Evidently he had hit Latimer too hard and killed him. That was another miscalculation, so he simply disposed of the keys and wallet in the nearest bin. His third, and final, mistake."

"Proof, man ... you will need hard proof, and I doubt if he will confess to murder upon your evidence thus far."

"Don't forget we also have a witness, and I very much suspect she will be able to place Plumridge at Dead Man's Walk just before the murder."

"Fine, just suppose we can get Plumridge for manslaughter, possibly murder, what's the connection with Cranmer, or are you still convinced that it is the Master of Lonsdale?"

"That was my mistake, and I confess that my dislike for Sir Michael as a person might have clouded my judgement in that respect. However, the point is that Plumridge was friends with Cranmer while they were at Cambridge. It just has to be more than coincidence that they were both there at the same time, and that both deaths took place within days at the same spot. I have no idea what may be behind that murder, but think that under questioning all will be revealed. Even if he is not the guilty party, he is involved and will lead us to the murderer I am quite certain ... it may turn out to be an arrest in two acts as I postulated previously."

"Enough. Like you, I also hate coincidences. I'll get you a search warrant for the Plumridge house. Meanwhile you had better get over to Radley and make an arrest. Take Strange with you to assist if you think Plumridge will put up any resistance. Do an initial interview this afternoon to see if he confesses, and if not set up an identification parade with your witness for tomorrow morning. A night in the cells might help concentrate his mind."

"Thank you, sir"

"No, don't thank me, man. You have done a fair job, but a good solicitor will run rings around us ... we still have a ways to go to make this case watertight."

Chapter Fifty-Four

"And some shall picture pounding ball
On turf of sodden field,
And some the fight on fiery pitch
When grit refused to yield;
And some shall think of desk and pen,
And organ-voices heard again,
And laughter ringing merrily
Adown the aisles of memory."

(H. L. Elvin, *The School Song*)

It was like a miniature Eton College. There were grounds stretching as far as the eye could see for sport, some eight hundred acres designed by Capability Brown no less, an infirmary, cloisters, an imposing chapel, dining hall, and a large mansion, Radley Hall, at the centre. Morse approached from Radley village itself, driving up a wide tree-lined avenue to where a number of cars were parked at the top. He ignored these and continued on to the main building further up on the left, where he pulled up as close as he could to, what appeared to be, the administration block. However, before he could ascertain if he was correct a senior member of staff informed him, in no uncertain terms, that he would need to move his vehicle. Morse did as he was instructed with good grace, before enquiring where the headmaster could be found.

"You're not a parent then?"

"How would you know if I am, or not?"

"Any parent would know that Radley College has no headmaster, but a warden. From your attire I suspect that you are a policeman."

Morse wondered what it was about his dress that had given him away. He hated the air of privilege and pretentiousness in equal measure, which always had the effect of making him even more formal and pretentious than his interlocutor.

"I am Detective Sergeant Morse of the Thames Valley Police, and, if it is not too much trouble, I would like to see the warden, or what passes for a headmaster in these parts."

"Follow me if you would be so kind," came the reply, as if from some retainer left over from the previous century.

Morse was led into the building, along several corridors adorned with various plaques commemorating sporting achievements, and finally into the outer office of the warden, where an elderly lady greeted him in an altogether more respectful manner. Following introductions and stating the purpose of his visit, there was no further delay, and Morse was sent straight in to see the warden. For some unknown reason he hesitated, as if he were a pupil having been sent down to receive 'six of the best'. He had no need to be apprehensive, though, as the warden was a charming man, if not a little out of touch with reality and somewhat eccentric.

"Can't all this wait until the end of the day? I mean to say, Plumridge has three periods to teach this afternoon ... it really is most inconvenient you wanting to arrest him now."

"I am afraid that the business of murder is rather inconvenient for all concerned, especially the victims."

"Oh well, if you must, I will have my secretary fetch him from where ever he is at present, and get somebody to cover his periods. Any idea how long he may be away from the school?"

"That rather depends on the jury I suspect."

"I rather doubt that Mr. Morse. I have known Plumridge for some years, and I can tell you that you won't find a straighter bat in England, and when your investigations reveal the same I will be expecting him back here, where he belongs, as quickly as possible."

At this point Miss Codling was dispatched to find the history teacher.

"When is this murder supposed to have happened?"

"Murders plural, warden. The first took place early evening on Tuesday the week before last, and the second was late on the Thursday evening of the same week."

"Taken your time in coming here haven't you?"

"It wasn't quite as straightforward as a game of cricket ... even then you can play a test match for five days and it will still end in a draw."

The warden acknowledged the analogy with a nod of his head.

"Quite so, I suspect you know what you are doing, though I will vouch that you have the wrong man, and I will gladly be a character witness for him if it comes to it."

A surprised Robert Plumridge entered.

"Mr. Morse, what brings you here ... some more questions about philately?"

"I'm afraid not. I am here to arrest you on suspicion of the murder of Hugo Latimer and ..." but before he could finish Plumridge had turned ashen and fainted on the carpet at the foot of the warden.

This was new thought Morse.

"Oh, come, man, on your feet ... worse things happen at sea! Now do you understand, Mr. Morse, just how much you are upsetting the smooth running of the school?"

It was then that Morse wished that he had brought Strange along for the ride, rather than send him off to help search the Plumridge residence. He would surely know the correct procedure in such circumstances, and would probably find it amusing to boot. As it was there was little Morse could do but wait for Plumridge to regain consciousness. Luckily the school nurse was soon on hand to administer some first aid in the form of smelling salts and a cup of tea, the cure for almost every ailment at boarding schools up and down the country. Thirty minutes later and Plumridge on trust and without handcuffs was in Morse's car driving back to Oxford in silence, but not before Plumridge had made arrangements for a solicitor to attend him at the police station.

Unfortunately silence is how it remained for the rest of the day with Plumridge, in the presence of his solicitor, refusing to answer anything but the most basic of questions. Morse tried probing by saying, for example, that there was a witness who could identify him at the scene of crime, but the only response to such questioning was a firm 'no comment'. It wasn't going to be as easy as he had envisaged. He would need to resort to 'plan B', and have Plumridge detained overnight in a cell. Maybe McNutt was correct and it would loosen his tongue, or at least make him more cooperative. There was more bad news to come in a call from Strange.

"Sorry, Morse. I've had the whole house searched and no sign of either a college scarf, or hockey stick, I'm afraid. Closest thing to a blunt instrument was an old cricket bat in the shed, which I'll send over to de Bryn just in case. Oh, and you had better watch out, the mother and daughter were nigh on hysterical ... it wouldn't surprise me if you get a visit from one, or both, of them very soon."

"What about the other items I asked you to try and find?"

"I've got those alright ... the photographs, and we discovered the cheque book in the name of Pilgrimme taped under the top drawer of the desk in the study."

"That's something at least. Let me have them by the morning when I will be continuing the interview with Plumridge. I'm sure something else will turn up by then."

In truth Morse was far from certain that anything would, as he had put it, 'turn up', but not everybody was so downbeat. Somebody had leaked the arrest to the *Oxford Mail*, as was evident from the mid-afternoon headline which proclaimed, 'OXFORD RIPPER ARREST'. No names were mentioned in the ensuing article. Under normal circumstances Morse would be have been furious at the paper not waiting for an official press release, but on this occasion he smiled as he rather thought that it might even be productive.

Chapter Fifty-Five

"O my God, hear me cry;
Or let me die!"

(Henry Vaughan, *Anguish*)

Six feet by ten feet isn't very big. Although in English prison terms the cells at St. Aldate's were generously proportioned, being a dozen square feet larger than most. It was not the size of the room that depressed Robert Plumridge so much, but the lack of windows and natural light. There was a basin and stainless steel toilet in one corner, a metal bed with a mattress no thicker than four inches pushed against the far wall, and a table and chair along one side. That was it – a liveable space, with three meals provided each day, much the same as his student accommodation had been at Cambridge. The only difference was that here he was not free to leave as he pleased. It was in these stark surroundings that Plumridge was to contemplate his future overnight. Despite the comforting words of his solicitor, his prospects appeared bleak to him and even the dawn of a new day did not improve his outlook. It was in this context that Plumridge asked to speak with Morse alone, without his solicitor present.

"So you wish to make a statement?"

"More of a confession … I am the person responsible for the deaths of Hugo Latimer and Tamati Cranmer."

"Go on," instructed Morse as if his statement was of little interest to him.

"It is as you indicated yesterday. I discovered, more by chance than anything else, that my father had been using a secret account to invest in rare stamps ... rare stamps that Latimer bought back from us by deception for a fraction of their real value. I had always been suspicious of why there was not more money following the sale of the family business, and now I knew that it had all been a tax dodge, which my father didn't wish the rest of the family to know about."

"So what exactly did you do about it?"

"I kept it secret from the rest of the family, and confronted Latimer in his shop. He just laughed at me, saying that he had bought them fair and square, and that they would be staying in his safe under lock and key until they were sold on. I knew that time was short so I came up with a plan to steal them back. I waited for Latimer to shut up shop that night, and followed him home ... it wasn't hard as although he was on a bicycle he was so slow that I could easily keep up on foot. I estimated that Dead Man's Walk was the best location to stop him ... close to his shop, and yet despite being in the city quite a lonely spot with a wall all along one side and railings along the other so, unless there was another walking along the path, we would not be seen. When I didn't have a late period at school I would come down to Oxford and stake out that spot. On the third occasion there was no one around, or at least that is what I thought, until you told me of your witness."

"How did you intend to stop him? It couldn't be easy as, despite his slowness, he was on a bicycle, and you were on foot."

"I thought of that and took along my old cricket bat with which to threaten him. I concealed it under my coat, but hoped that he would stop when he saw me and that I meant business, return with me to the shop, and hand over the stamps."

"But it didn't work out that way did it?"

"No, when he recognised me, he pedalled faster to escape, so I hit him with the bat as he passed. I didn't think that I had struck him that hard, and had no intention of killing him. I only wanted his shop keys. He fell off his bicycle ..."

"You killed him none the less."

"I didn't think so ... he was unconscious, but still breathing when I took the keys from him."

"And that is all you took?"

"Yes, I didn't need anything else. I rushed back to the shop and try as I might I couldn't get the safe open as it also had a combination lock. Realising that I had failed, I rushed back to Dead Man's Walk with the intention of replacing the keys in his pocket, in the hope that when he regained consciousness that he might not remember who hit him."

"But when you got back the police were already there?"

"Correct."

"So what did you do with the keys?"

"I panicked and threw them away in the nearest bin I could find ... and then I went home."

"What about Cranmer? I know that you were acquainted with each other while at Cambridge, and by all accounts became friends ... what went wrong?"

"Again you are correct in that we were friends right up until a few months ago when I discovered that he was having an affair with my wife."

So that was it, thought Morse, but why had that motive not crossed his mind before, given that Cranmer was such a womaniser, as Michael Chipperfield had been all to quick to confirm during their meeting. Perhaps it was because Mrs Plumridge had seemed like a stereotypical church going, God-fearing person who would never do that sort of thing. Maybe it was true what people say, that the ones you least suspect were indeed the more interesting characters in life who needed watching.

"Why wait until now though to get your revenge?" he asked, after a pause.

"Well I reckoned that sooner or later the police would make the connection between Hugo Latimer and my father, and would come calling, so I wanted to avert suspicion. Being a history teacher, the names Latimer and Cranmer were not exactly unknown to me, so I decided that now was the perfect time for revenge. If lucky, the

269

police would go off on the wrong track and maybe think that there was a maniac on the loose in the footsteps of the Oxford Martyrs."

"The newspapers certainly took that angle."

"But not the police ... I should have known when you first called at the house that it was likely that you would investigate my past associations, however distant."

"How did you kill Cranmer?"

"Exactly the same way as Latimer, and in the identical spot so that again you would all think that it was some madman. I simply called him up and asked if we could meet for a drink. We did and later I led the way back along Broad Walk, conveniently forgetting that the exit at Grove Walk would be locked at that hour, and so we would need to divert along Dead Man's Walk, where earlier in the day I had secreted my cricket bat next to a tree. I was relieved to see it still there as we passed. From my experience with Latimer I knew that it could kill, and so I did the same thing again, only a little harder given that Cranmer was considerably younger and fitter."

"And he didn't struggle, try to run away or even notice you retrieving such an object."

"He had been drinking, Mr Morse. I had not, though he wouldn't have noticed given the amount he had consumed. His reactions were slow, and he was in no state to run away, or do anything else for that matter."

"I see. Is there anything else that you would like to add?"

"No, that is enough to convict me don't you think?" he observed grimly.

"If that is your story I will send an officer in who will help you put it all in writing, after which there will be an identity parade and following that you will be formally charged. Is that clear?"

"Yes. Thank you. It is a great weight off my conscience."

Chapter Fifty-Six

"Untruthful! My nephew Algernon? Impossible! He is an Oxonian."

(Lady Bracknell in Oscar Wilde's
The Importance of Being Ernest)

"**N**o, sir."

"What the hell do you mean by that, man?" boomed McNutt who had recently arrived at St. Aldate's. "You've got your man ... he's in the next room dictating his confession to Strange isn't he? On the strength of it I have stood down most of the team."

"Yes, sir, but he is not our murderer," stated Morse with some conviction.

"And why not?"

"Too many inconsistencies in his statement, sir. For a start he knew nothing about the wallet being taken from Latimer. Then there is his description of Latimer ... all wrong."

"What do you mean?"

"Well, from every account Latimer was a quiet, placid man who wouldn't have gloated or laughed at Plumridge when confronted."

"That's just speculation on your part, Morse."

"Maybe, but he wouldn't have indicated that the stamps were in the safe, when they were already at the auction house in London, would he now, sir?"

McNutt pursed his lips.

"You may have a point there ... anything else?"

"I am pretty sure he has the murder weapon wrong as well, and I simply can't believe that Mrs Plumridge would be having an affair with Cranmer."

"Is that it? You're basing his innocence on your belief that the wife is incapable of having an affair. It is like the vicar saying that there is good in every one ... clearly any vicar who says that has not met the people we come into contact with every day. If you stay in the force as long as I have, Morse, then you will pretty much not be surprised if you hear of Mother Teresa having an affair with the Pope!"

"No, it's more than that, sir. He has also got his facts wrong with respect to Cranmer ... he says that they went drinking together on the night in question, but de Bryn found no excessive amounts of alcohol in his bloodstream. However, he did find the remains of a Chinese meal in the stomach contents. Plumridge made no mention of having had a meal with Cranmer."

"So how does he know all the other details about the murders, those details that were never in the newspapers?"

"Elementary, because the murderer told him, but only told him the basic outline of events, and not the finer details."

"So Sherlock, you mean he is covering for the murderer?"

"Precisely ... when I asked him if he was going to confess to being the murderer, he didn't say 'yes' but answered by stating that he 'was responsible' for the deaths. He later told me that his statement was 'a weight off his mind' ... and that is simply because he is indirectly responsible and in his mind is doing the honourable thing."

"Which is?"

"What he has always done ... protecting his family."

"What now?"

"Well I did warn that it may be an arrest in two acts, and that we have merely reached the interval ..."

"Enough of your similes ..."

"Actually it's a metaphor, sir."

Before the conversation became any more heated, the telephone rang. McNutt answered it and listened intently, saying little except a 'thank you' at the end.

"That was de Bryn. He confirms that the cricket bat retrieved yesterday is definitely not the murder weapon ... too thick."

"Much as I thought, sir."

"So do we charge him, or let him go?"

Before Morse could answer, the telephone rang again. This time it was not for McNutt, but for him. It was Tomlinson, the Warden of Radley College, who seemed quite agitated.

"Is that Detective Sergeant Morse?"

"Yes," came the stilted, though grammatically correct, reply.

"Listen, I told you yesterday that you had the wrong fellow, and, on reflection, I can prove it to you."

"Please continue."

"You said that the first murder took place early on Tuesday evening the week before last. Is that correct?"

"It is."

"Well then, it certainly couldn't be Plumridge, as he was here until nearly nine o'clock that evening."

"And would there be any witnesses who could verify that for me?"

"Quite a few, actually ... all the parents of form three who spoke to him at the parent's evening that night."

"I see, that is most helpful, Warden, though I wish you had remembered this at the time."

"Well I have now, so I will expect Plumridge back here this afternoon."

"I'm afraid that might not be possible, as he is still helping us with our enquiries, though I fully expect that he will be there tomorrow morning."

"Well, I jolly well hope so, or there will be serious repercussions. It might interest you to know that the Chief Constable's son attends the school."

At that point the telephone was disconnected from the Radley end. McNutt had overheard most of the conversation.

"We have no choice now ... you arrested the wrong man, Morse, and we will have to release him immediately ... why on earth did you say that he wouldn't be free until tomorrow morning?"

"Because I need this day, sir, and besides there is still the identity parade at eleven."

"Surely you are not going to go ahead with that now? It will be a waste of time."

"Quite the opposite, I feel it will be quite instructive, sir. Plumridge doesn't know that we are aware that he is innocent, and nor does the rest of the family."

"And so what's your point?"

"My point is that just as Robert Plumridge has covered for his family, so now I think that they will try and cover for him, and in doing so will make a mistake. I'm counting on it. I'm close, very close to a solution I assure you, sir."

"Oh, you had better be for all our sakes, especially yours, Morse ... your whole future career as a detective may very well hang in the balance."

Chapter Fifty-Seven

"There is nothing more deceptive than an obvious fact."

(Sherlock Holmes, *The Boscombe Valley Mystery*)

It is a trait of the older generation that they are more reliable and punctual than those younger than themselves. Maybe it is out of respect for their fellow humans, or perhaps because being that much closer to death themselves that they all too aware of how precious time has become. Whatever it may be, Dorothy Evans was no exception to this observation, and arrived nearly thirty minutes earlier than expected for the identity parade. The formalities observed she was ushered along the corridor to see Morse, while preparations were made to find some willing suspicious looking members of the public.

"Do sit down, Mrs Evans. I am glad that you are early as I wanted to show you something."

Out of a plastic bag Morse produced the scarf that he had purchased the previous weekend.

"I know that I have shown you scarves before, but I just wanted to check that this was the correct one, as I may well have been confused the other day."

"Of course it is, Mr. Morse. I told that that it was a Magdalen College scarf I saw ... black with two white stripes, just like this one."

"The only problem is Mrs Evans, that this is not a Magdalen scarf at all, but a Queens' scarf. You omitted to tell me that you are colour blind didn't you?"

"That may be so, but I still recognise that scarf. I may be colour blind, but I can still count, and Queen's scarves have two extra white stripes in them, being dark blue on white ... nothing like this one. Remember, I worked at Shepherd and Woodward for a good many years, and must have sold hundreds of them during that period."

"However, if you look closely this one isn't from Shepherd and Woodward, but has a Ryder & Amies label, and is from Cambridge. What is more it is dark green on white."

"I'm most dreadfully sorry, Mr. Morse ... I never thought that it might be a Cambridge scarf, after all we are in Oxford, and so I assumed that any one wearing a college scarf would automatically be from Oxford. It never occurred to me that they may be from that other place."

"For what it's worth, Mrs Evans, it never occurred to me either until just recently. At least we have the right identification now ... and talking of identification, they should be ready for us in the yard out back."

As they walked Morse explained the correct procedure. She was to go up and down the line, taking her time, and should she recognise any one, she should not point them out there and then, but tell the officer in charge afterwards.

Strange had surpassed himself this time, picking such a similar group of men that any one of them might be mistaken for the other. However, Morse had faith in Mrs Evans and wondered if there would be any reaction when she saw Robert Plumridge, who was standing in the fourth position.

She walked up the line quite quickly, before returning at a slower pace and hesitating for a moment in front of number four. It was exactly what Morse had hoped would happen. She then went straight over to Strange, and whispered something to him. The volunteers were thanked for their time and dismissed while

Plumridge was led back to his cell. Morse went over and joined Mrs Evans.

"It was none of them I'm afraid, though the man in position four does bear a passing resemblance to the person I saw, but he's far too tall. I'm so sorry I haven't been much help."

"On the contrary, you have been the greatest of help, Mrs Evans … more than you realise at this stage I assure you.

Once Mrs Evans had been escorted away to the reception area to await her taxi home, McNutt appeared.

"Well it's a complete balls-up, Morse. I will have to release him now, as there are no grounds on which to hold him a moment longer."

"But Plumridge doesn't know that does he, sir? As far as he is concerned the witness stopped in front of him, and most likely identified him. If we can hold him just a little longer I am sure it will pay dividends."

McNutt rolled his eyes and pursed his lips, exhaling a large sigh.

"Very well, Morse. I'll have him kept here until early evening, and then release him without charge, but you had better be right."

At that moment Strange returned holding a piece of paper in his hand. It was a telephone message for Morse that had just been received. Coghlan at the *Oxford Mail* had apparently come up with something important, and wanted Morse to call round as soon as possible. However, before he pursued that line of enquiry, Morse had one final trick up his sleeve that morning.

"Have you got those photographs I asked you to get from the Plumridge residence?"

"Yes, they're at the front desk, Morse."

"Excellent."

With some haste the two men made their way there where Morse picked out one of the images in question. He then went around the counter to join Mrs Evans, who was sitting waiting for her transport to arrive.

"I have one last thing to show you, Mrs Evans. Now maybe you might …" but before he could finish his sentence Mrs Evans pointed to one of the figures in the family group.

"That's the person … no doubt about it, with a scarf half covering their face that is definitely them."

At last the break through he had been hoping. He had been right all along. The feeling of relief, mixed with elation, on Morse's face said it all. He still had more proof to find, of course, but at least he now knew without a shadow of a doubt the identity of the murderer.

Chapter Fifty-Eight

"I'll get back to my important work now,
And you'll no doubt try to stop my crime …"

(Extract from the *Dear Boss* letter supposedly written
by Jack the Ripper)

It didn't take that long for Morse to walk the half a mile to New Inn Hall Street where he discovered Coghlan was to be found busy at his work.

"Ah, got my message then, old boy. Thought that you would be around here in double quick time."

"So you've got something for me that might be important?"

"You bet I have, but first you have got to promise me something."

"And what might that be?"

"Well if, and when, you make a proper arrest I want your word that you will give me an exclusive for the paper."

"And just why should I agree to this demand?"

"Because you owe it to me for God's sake, Morse. Do you have any idea of the grief I have had already from the head honchos here asking me where I got the information from about your little arrest yesterday, and how much I have had to protect your identity from them, old boy? Hmm, you might like to know your Chief Constable was onto my boss this morning as well."

"Sorry about that, but I assure you that it was necessary. You can have your exclusive, and we'll have a drink together as well when this is all over," promised Morse.

"It had better be a very large drink ... no, on second thoughts it had better be a night out at the very least."

"It's a deal. Now what do you have for me that is so earth shattering?"

Coghlan took a postcard out of his drawer and flicked it across the desk to Morse.

"This came this morning. You will see that it was posted with a first class stamp from Didcot, and addressed simply to the *Oxford Mail*, but it is the reverse side that will interest you the most."

Morse picked it up as if it were some rare piece of porcelain to be handled with the upmost care. It read:

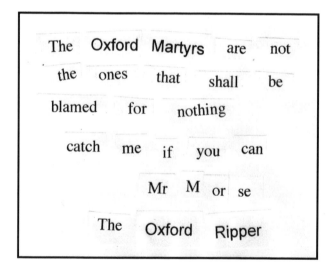

"You're right, it is interesting. It is also a mistake."

"A mistake ... what do you mean, a mistake?"

"The person who sent this wants us to think that they live in, or around, Didcot, but they don't."

"And what makes you say that?"

"Well look at how hurriedly, and clumsily it has all been put together. It is an all too obvious attempt to divert attention, and intended to lead us down the path of thinking that it is some maniac akin to Jack the Ripper. It was you who first put into print the idea that the killings of Latimer and Cranmer were connected with the Oxford Martyrs. You even identified the next victim to be Nicholas Ridley, causing widespread panic among those in the vicinity with that name, and, I might add, a lot of extra overtime for my colleagues."

"So it isn't genuine then?"

"Oh, its genuine alright, and copied from the original Jack the Ripper case of 1888. As any student of history will tell you Jack the Ripper taunted the police with his so-called 'Dear Boss' letter he supposedly sent to the newspaper. There was also the Goulston Street graffito, attributed to Jack the Ripper, that was removed by the police in case it stirred up anti-Semitic feelings. If memory serves me correctly it read something like 'The Juwes are the men that will not be blamed for nothing'. I think the parallel is clear."

"But what makes this postcard a mistake?"

"Well you are a newspaper man, do you not see anything odd?"

"Not really. It has obviously been put together by cutting out words from the newspaper."

"More than one newspaper though. Most of it is clearly in Times font from *The Times* itself, but look at the recurrence of the word 'Oxford' and also 'Martyrs' and 'Ripper'. These are unusual words that would be hard to find in any edition of *The Times*. Hence you will observe that they are in a different typeface ... in fact, they are in the font used by your newspaper."

"I hadn't noticed that ... and of course 'Oxford' will appear multiple times in any edition, and it was I who have included words such as 'Martyrs' and 'Ripper' recently. However, I still do not understand why it is a mistake using words taken from two common newspapers."

"Because the *Oxford Mail* is not circulated in the Didcot area as far as I am aware. Therefore it must have originated from the environs of Oxford, and just posted elsewhere to mislead us ... and I know why it had to be Didcot. The person in question was in a hurry, and does not drive a car."

"Anything more?"

"Only that it indicates the innocence of the person we currently have in the cells. Have a look at the postmark more carefully."

"It carries yesterday's date."

"Not only that but, as it was sent first class, the date stamp also gives the time that the mail was sorted ... a time just after your newspaper had hit the streets, and some hours after the arrest had been made, so clearly it could have not been written by our suspect, but somebody attempting to prove their innocence."

"They're a clever sod. I'll give them that."

"Not really ... I suppose you noticed my name there?"

"Yes, and again as it is not a common name, they made it up from letters taken from three separate words."

"That's not what I meant. You see but you do not observe?"

"Observe what, exactly?"

"My name was never mentioned in any of your articles, so how come that this Oxford Ripper knows to address his missive to me personally? That was their biggest mistake. This postcard has to have come from somebody who is known to me already in this investigation ... and I know exactly who sent it, and I bet you anything that a similar postcard will arrive for me in tomorrow's post as well."

"Make it ten pounds and you're on, old boy."

Chapter Fifty-Nine

"It is small reason you should kepe a dog, and barke your selfe."

(Brian Melbancke, *Philotimus: the Warre Betwixt Nature and Fortune*)

In order to prove his point Morse first needed to visit the Post Office in St. Aldate's – a magnificent building dating from 1879 that illustrated just how important the postal service had become since its inception not four decades earlier. Here he purchased a single first class stamp, something Morse seldom did since he was firmly of the opinion that any second class mail he sent was undoubtedly worth the wait on the part of the recipient. He also bought a postcard with a photograph of St. Giles' from an adjacent gift shop.

On his return to the police station he set to work creating his own version of a 'Dear Boss' missive using that morning's newspaper, which by this time of day had been discarded with the crossword not even attempted in the rubbish bin to the right of the front counter. Time was short so he did not worry too much about the quality of his workmanship, but was pleased with the result nonetheless. It would certainly shock Coghlan the following day when it was due to arrive on his desk, if all went according to plan.

Without further delay he made for the railway station where, as luck would have it, there was only one window open from which to purchase tickets, and, naturally, a long line of people wishing to travel. He contemplated using his warrant card to jump the queue, but decided against abusing his authority, not on moral grounds so much but more because he had noted the departures board along with the fact that he had just missed a train, and that the next was not for another forty minutes. Eventually he reached the front of the queue.

"A cheap day return to Didcot, please."

"First or second class?" came a reply with all the enthusiasm of a tortoise about to enter hibernation.

"Second."

"That'll be nine shillings."

Morse handed over a ten-shilling note, surprised that it was not more expensive.

"And can I have a receipt, please?"

"Just keep your ticket as the receipt, love ... next."

The fact that tickets could be kept at journey's end if desired was just what Morse wanted to hear. He proceeded onto the platform where the waiting time for the next Didcot train was now less than thirty minutes. It was only while waiting that Morse remembered that he hadn't taken any form of sustenance that day. As a consequence he decided to visit the station buffet, where he purchased two sausage rolls along with a plastic cup of coffee to consume on the train. He noted that the person who served him was probably a not too distant relation to the woman in the ticket office – at least both displayed a similar level of enthusiasm for their respective jobs. Back on the platform somebody tapped him on the shoulder from behind, nearly causing him to spill his drink.

"'Ello Mr Detective. Back here again ... are you on another case?"

Morse looked around to see the beaming face of Dexter, the trainspotting truant. He was almost glad to see him.

"Still not at school then, I see."

"Well I tried what you told me ... I really did, but the teachers are idiots you know, and besides it's much more fun here I can tell you. I've started writing though, and have even used that book you gave me ... honest I have. Do you need any help from me today then?"

Morse smiled at his illiterate friend as an idea struck him.

"In fact, I do. I remember you saying that you wished that you lived in Didcot, where the variety of trains for you to spot is much greater ... correct?"

"Yeah, that's right."

"Well it's your lucky day ... I have here a return ticket to Didcot, and all you have to do to earn it is to promise to put this card in the post box at the station ... there's bound to be one there somewhere. You can return when you want, as far as I'm concerned. However, I need you to drop off the used train ticket at the police station in St. Aldate's before you go home."

"Alright, it's a deal."

He took the postcard along with the train ticket that Morse proffered. A look of concern came across his face.

"Er, Mister, I've seen this sort of thing before in the newspaper ... you're not that Oxford Ripper are you?"

"No, but I am the man who, with your help, is going to catch him."

"Oh, it's a sort of trap then is it? Hmm ... that could be something for me to put in my book ... think I'll call my story Dead Man's Walk ... not a bad title is it?"

"Very good ... just be sure to drop off the train ticket tonight as I will need."

"For your expenses I suspect. Yes, I can see why ... wasted your money didn't you?"

"How do you mean?"

"Well you only need a child ticket for me ... bet you wished you'd seen me here before you bought it, would have saved you a few shillings?"

Morse smiled. He had found something of a rarity for Oxford – somebody who was both intelligent, and with common sense. He left the station knowing that he now had time on his hands. He was still thirsty, very thirsty, and the solution to that problem lay inside the Albion public house in nearby Hollybush Row. It was a strange place whose name was either derived from that of a ship, or from the old Gaelic name for Britain. The sign outside, inexplicably, depicted a Roman soldier against the backdrop of what looked like the white cliffs of Dover. To Morse it would have made more sense if it had been a Cavalier, given that formerly during the Civil War there was a guardhouse that stood on the site. He would, at some point in the not too distant future, write to Morrells and ask them about their pub sign, but for now he was content to warm himself in front of the coal burning fire beside the central bar, while caressing a pint of Old Don. It was gone seven o'clock or, to put it another way, three pints later, that Morse emerged back into Hollybush Row, and made his way to the Pearl Dragon for his second Chinese meal in a week.

This time he chose something different from the menu, and while he waited for his meal to arrive he called the manager over.

"Good to see you again, sir."

"And you."

"You must like the Chinese food here?"

"Yes, it's growing on me," came the guarded reply. "I have another photograph for you to look at, if you would be so kind?"

"Of course, sir … anything to help police."

Morse presented him with the same family group picture that he had shown Dorothy Evans earlier in the day. The reaction was similar.

"Ah, much better, sir, that is the person from other night no question."

Without hesitation the manager had identified exactly the same person as had Evans.

At that moment Morse's food arrived. After a long day he could now relax and enjoy the 'haute cuisine' that lay before him – a prawn omelette with chips and peas from the selection of English meals offered on the back page of the menu.

Chapter Sixty

"Constantly choosing the lesser of two evils
is still choosing evil."

(Jerry Garcia)

There was little Morse could do that Thursday morning until after he had seen McNutt, and he was at some important briefing with the Chief Constable and not due back at Kidlington until after lunch. It was valuable time, wasted time, but there was nothing he could do about it – he simply had to wait.

The highlight of the morning was a call from an excitable Coghlan to inform him that, just as predicted, another 'Dear Boss' postcard had arrived at the *Oxford Mail* offices.

"Do you want to come over and see it?"

"Not really ... but can you tell me if the postmark is the same as the previous one?"

"Oh, yes, exactly ... well it has a different date of course, but exactly the same in every other respect. However, the address is written by hand and not cut out from a newspaper ... I'm sure that forensics may be able to turn up something from the handwriting. Do you want me to read you what it says?"

"I suspect it will be in just one font this time, and say something along the lines of 'Dear boss ... I hear that you have caught me but I am still free ... catch me if you can Mr. Morse ...' and be without a signature this time."

"That's brilliant, old boy ... how on earth did you know the text, not to mention that it would be in just one font, and not say that it was from the Oxford Ripper?"

"Because Coghlan, *old boy*, when I wrote it I only had *The Times* to hand and could not find the words 'Oxford' or 'Ripper' in yesterday's edition, and couldn't be bothered to cut out any more words for the address, and so wrote that part by hand."

"You bastard!"

"Now, now ... no need to swear. I'll come around for my winnings later, when I get a chance."

Getting the better of Coghlan put him in a cheerful disposition. It also confirmed another part of his theory.

Eventually McNutt did make an appearance and listened intently to Morse's progress report.

"I see that you made good use of the extra time I gave you."

"I hope so, sir."

"It seems that you have it watertight ... so we'd better go and make an arrest, hadn't we?"

"Before we do that, sir, I would like to go over and speak with Mrs Plumridge, and forewarn her ... if you know what I mean?"

"Morse, sometimes I think you're too soft for this sort of work, especially where women are concerned. May I remind you that this is a murder case ... why on earth do you want to go and forewarn her, man? It's not as if its going to make a blind bit of difference to her in the long run."

"But it will to me, sir. After wrongfully arresting her husband the day before yesterday, not to mention holding him in the cells overnight, I think we owe it to her."

"Well, I suppose it won't do any harm to wait a couple of hours ... not exactly going to flee the country is she? I will have the warrant, and all the other paperwork, made up in the meantime. If I give you until three o'clock will that be long enough for you to do your good Samaritan bit?"

"Thank you, sir."

The drive over to Boars Hill was pleasant enough, though Morse was in no mood to appreciate the scenery. He did not relish the prospect that was before him and, if truth be known, he had a great deal of sympathy with the Plumridge family and the situation in which they now found themselves – decent people forced into evil by circumstance. It was Guna Plumridge who opened the door.

"Mr. Morse ... I was quite expecting another visit from you sooner or later. You are welcome to come inside, although I am afraid that my husband is back at Radley, and I am here all alone."

"In fact, it was you that I have come to see."

"Well here I am ... are you going to arrest me?

"That rather depends on the outcome of our conversation."

"You had better come in then ... you know the way."

This was a far more formal and assured Guna Plumridge than the one who had on the previous occasion asked, almost begged Morse to keep secret the sale of stamps to Hugo Latimer. No tea or biscuits were offered this time.

"So how can I help you, Mr. Morse?"

"Perhaps you can clarify something for me ... yesterday when we interviewed your husband he told me that you had been having an affair with Professor Cranmer ..."

"Indeed."

"And have you been having a relationship with him?"

"It is true that is what my husband told you but, no, I have never been unfaithful, Mr. Morse ... I assure you on that point."

That statement rather restored Morse's faith in his own abilities of character assessment.

"But, your daughter, Louise, has, hasn't she?"

"Yes."

"And your husband was just trying to divert attention away from Louise in the knowledge that she was responsible for Cranmer's murder?"

"Yes, of course he was ... wouldn't you, Mr. Morse?"

"Alas I have no family as such, and so can only say that I do believe that I might act in a similar manner should such a circumstance arise."

Guna Plumridge began to realise that underneath Morse was a kind and sensitive man, who was only trying to do his job in the most sympathetic way possible. However, he was about to deliver a bombshell.

"Has Louise recovered from her abortion?"

"What would you know of that, Mr. Morse?"

"I know from the Palace of Westminster where she works that she has been on leave the last two weeks, and only returned to work yesterday. January is a rather strange month in which to take a holiday in this country, and to spend it at home even stranger ... weather not exactly sunny, and no sign of any family illness or other calamity to require her presence here, so I deduced that she was here because it was Louise who needed her family, and especially her mother at this time."

"Of course, you are correct, Mr. Morse. Will you promise me to be as discreet as possible with what I am about to tell you." Guna Plumridge was close to tears.

"I will do my very best, as far as my duty allows."

"That is all I ask. My husband does not know everything, and it would break him if he did. You see Louise has been having an affair with Professor Cranmer for several years. When she told me at Christmas that she was pregnant with his child it put us in a quandary ... as Christians we would not want to destroy any human life, but given that Cranmer wanted nothing to do with the child, and he further put pressure on Louise to have the abortion saying that a baby would destroy her career ... we reluctantly agreed to the termination being carried out privately."

"That is all I needed to know. I do not wish to distress you further, Mrs Plumridge."

"I assume that you will be arresting Louise then?"

Morse glanced at the clock on the mantelpiece.

"As I speak she is being arrested in London, and will be brought to Oxford for questioning."

It was only now that Guna Plumridge broke down in a flood of tears.

"Thank you for letting me know, Mr. Morse ... it was good of you to come and tell me personally. If anything it is a relief that it is all finally over."

"At least you will not have to sell your beautiful house now."

"Do you really think I would want to live here a moment longer?"

"No, or course not, but you should know that the Pilgrimme account used by Tim Plumridge to invest in stamps still has three hundred thousand pounds in it. I suspect that even with whatever back tax and death duties might be payable, that there will be enough remaining for you not to have to move from the family home if you wish. A good solicitor may even be able to make a claim against the Latimer estate for fraudulently obtaining those stamps so far below market value."

"Mr. Morse … I don't care about this house, or those ruddy stamps … I just want my darling daughter with me, and not in some wretched prison. Now please be good enough and leave."

Morse left in silence, and made his way back to Kidlington where he was to learn that due to the lateness of the hour Louise Plumridge would be detained in a cell overnight in London, before being brought up to Oxford first thing in the morning. He also learnt that a search by the Metropolitan Police had been conducted at Louise Plumridge's Pimlico flat, and that a hockey stick along with a Queens' College Cambridge scarf had been recovered.

Chapter Sixty-One

"Love looks forward, hate looks back,
anxiety has eyes all over its head."

(Mignon McLaughlin)

Given her Christian background, Morse expected Louise Plumridge to be contrite, but the person who faced him across the table in interview room number two on Friday morning was far from showing any remorse. She had already written down a preliminary statement overnight, which Morse now read with interest.

"So when did you first become aware that Hugo Latimer had not been honest when he bought your grandfather's stamps back for a mere two thousand pounds?"

"It was just after Christmas when I was clearing out granddad's desk that I accidentally came across the cheque book in the name of Tud Pilgrimme. I noted that payments were made monthly to Hugo Latimer, and after comparison with the stamp booklet photostats that I had made, it was immediately apparent to me exactly what had been going on. I calculated that we had been fiddled out of around two hundred thousand pounds, and I intended to get it back for the family."

"And how did you go about it?"

"I replaced the cheque book and told nobody that I had found it. I thought of going to a solicitor, but knew that they would only say that under contract law Latimer had made an offer which we had accepted, and that would be the end of the matter. Funny really, you hear the phrase of *caveat emptor* but never the reverse."

"*Caveat venditor*."

"Anyway that is when I decided to take it up personally with Latimer."

"In your statement it says that you went to the shop and confronted him, but to no avail. How did he seem when you left him?"

"He was shaken, and asked to be given time ... he promised to make amends and see that I got the money our family deserved. I waited a couple of weeks and heard nothing from him, so I decided that I needed to show him that I was serious and had not forgotten about him."

"So you followed him home one night in order to ascertain the best place to accost and threaten him."

"Yes, and that place was Dead Man's Walk."

"But it all went wrong, and you killed him didn't you?"

"Again ... yes. It is as I put in my statement ... I took my old hockey stick with me and waited beside the bench in Dead Man's Walk for him to pass on his bicycle. He saw me, but did not seem to recognise me."

"What makes you say that he didn't recognise you?"

"Because I was in a long black coat and had a scarf half across my face, so I would have been surprised if he had recognised me after our one encounter."

"Somebody else recognised you from your scarf."

"Yes, that was a stupid mistake. I took father's old college scarf from when he was at Queens' in Cambridge, and thought that to most all college scarves look pretty much the same."

"And it was now that you hit him."

"No, no ... I never hit him. I simply thrust my hockey stick between the spokes of the front wheel of his bicycle. This made the bicycle wobble ... he became unsteady and went into a pothole which sent him flying. The next thing I knew was that he had hit his head on the arm of the bench and was lying on the ground unconscious. I swear that I thought I had just knocked him out ... I had no idea that he would die, otherwise I would have called for help."

So de Bryn had been correct all along and the bench was the cause of death, thought Morse.

"Why did you remove the keys and wallet?"

"I looked around and there was nobody about so on the spur of the moment I took the wallet to make it look like a hit and run. The keys I needed as it suddenly occurred to me that maybe I could get to his shop, get the stamps, and return to replace the keys before he recovered."

"You went to the shop then?"

"Yes, but having got inside without any difficulty I couldn't get into the safe as it needs a key and combination. I had the key and try as I might with my penknife I couldn't prise the combination dial off. After a few minutes I left before anybody who might be passing saw me and had me arrested as a burglar."

"I noted the scratch marks on the safe. You say on page three that by the time you got back to Dead Man's Walk the police were already there."

"It was only then that I realised that Hugo Latimer was dead ... I panicked and threw the keys and wallet away in the nearest bin I could find. I didn't think that they would be recovered."

"And all this you later confided in your parents."

"Only father."

"That would explain why he only had half the story when he confessed to the murder on your behalf."

"Manslaughter, surely."

"That rather depends on the judge and jury. It might interest you to know that the stamps were not in the shop, but were already at a London auction house awaiting their sale. It is possible, probable even, knowing the character of Latimer, that following the sale in a couple of months time, he was going to keep his promise and rectify the situation."

"And how was I to know that, Mr. Morse? As far as I was concerned he was just a conman who had been fleecing our family for years. If you look at it like that he was a greedy man who got what he deserved."

Up until that moment Morse had built up a modicum of sympathy for Louise Plumridge's actions, but now he could see a darker side to this young lady – one which was to get even darker as he continued to read the pages in front of him.

"Tell me about how you came to know Tamati Cranmer?"

"He was a friend of my father's ... they were at Cambridge together reading history, though I guess you know that already.

Morse nodded.

"He went on to become an academic of some note, while my father, arguably the cleverer of the two, was left to teach the rich kids at Radley."

"But how did you come into contact with him?"

"It was shortly after I expressed an interest to follow in father's footsteps and read history as well. You were at college here weren't you, Mr. Morse?"

"Yes, I was at St. John's for a while ... what of it?"

"Didn't you notice that there was something missing there?"

"Like what?"

"Women, Mr. Morse ... the female of the species. We might be just as clever as the male, but not in the eyes of the supreme masters and keepers of education around here, the Universities of Oxford and Cambridge. We are not allowed into their little ivory towers, though that is all beginning to change for the better."

"That isn't quite right ... there are colleges in both Oxford and Cambridge just for women, and I know that you went to one of them ... I remarked on your graduation photograph when I visited your home for the first time."

"Oh, yes, Mr. Morse, I went to Hughes Hall, Cambridge."

"I don't see the problem then."

"Hughes Hall for your information may be an all female establishment set up in 1885, but it is only for graduates or mature women. I was rejected by all the colleges at first, and it was only because father had Cranmer pull some strings and use his influence that I got in at all. Women students are not generally welcome at either Oxford or Cambridge I assure you."

"I begin to understand now ... and that is when you started having an affair with him."

"You understand nothing, Mr. Morse ... that is when he started to rape me systematically over a period of years. His reward he said for getting me a Cambridge education. He also insisted on acting as a reference when I applied for my position at the Palace of Westminster. I don't tell my parents everything you know."

"Except when you became pregnant by him; you confided in your mother didn't you?"

"Yes, the last thing I wanted, though, was his child ... I'd rather have died, so it was I who insisted on the abortion."

"And when did you decide to murder Cranmer?"

"I wanted him to suffer, Mr. Morse ... I wanted revenge for how he had treated me ... and all the others that he preyed on over the years. The idea came to me when I realised that Latimer and Cranmer were the surnames names of two of the three Oxford Martyrs."

"Very clever ... you wanted to disguise his murder as being the work of some kind of maniac with a vendetta against the Oxford Martyrs?"

"Well it almost worked ... at least that is the angle that the newspaper took."

"As I read it, you lured Cranmer to the Chinese restaurant following your abortion ..."

"As far as he was concerned, all was well and I had simply done as he wanted, and now he could continue raping me at will. Well, I had something different in mind. Earlier that evening I secreted my hockey stick beside the bench in Dead Man's Walk. I led Cranmer there after dinner. He thought that I was slightly drunk and up for sex ... right up to the point where I hit him as hard as I could with my hockey stick. It was easier than I had expected."

"What made you send the 'Dear Boss' postcard from Didcot station?

"When you arrested my father I could see that you were getting close, so I needed to divert your attention back to pursuing a religious maniac. Hence I created that postcard that I sent the *Oxford Mail* in haste, and posted it at the station, breaking my train journey on my way back to London. I knew that at the very least you would have to release my father, since you already had him in custody at the time of posting, and hopefully would start looking for suspects away from Oxford. By the way, how did you know that I posted it at the station?"

"Two reasons. First it seemed logical so I tried it out for myself and observed the same postmark as on your missive ... and second there was your used train ticket to London that was found in your wallet when you were arrested yesterday. They don't collect the tickets on this line, and you were foolish not to throw it away."

"And how is my train ticket incriminating?"

"You are probably not aware that each ticket inspector carries a unique clipper, and so from the punch marks made on a ticket every journey can be traced."

Morse produced Louise's ticket from his pocket. "You will observe that your ticket has been punched twice ... once with a 'V' when you got on at Oxford, and later with a 'S' indicating that you broke your journey at Didcot. It is an exact match to this one."

Morse now produced his own ticket from Wednesday – the one Dexter had delivered back to Morse as instructed. He placed both tickets side by side on the table for Louise to view.

"That's very clever, Mr. Morse. You a train spotter in your spare time?"

"No, but I am good friends with one. It is surprising what you can learn from such people, and a good book on the subject." Morse paused to reflect. "Anything else you would like to add?"

"No."

"And that is it ... no regrets?"

"No regrets, Mr. Morse ... both men deserved what they got."

Chapter Sixty-Two

"I don't like novels that end happily. They depress me so much."

(Cecily in Oscar Wilde's
The Importance of Being Ernest)

"Cheer up, Morse ... you've just solved a double murder," said McNutt enthusiastically. It was praise indeed, and yet as his superior had noted Morse was melancholy. "Look she's evil and deserves what she gets ... two murders, or one murder and a manslaughter at best," he continued.

"You know, that is exactly what she said about Latimer and Cranmer ... that they deserved what they got, and in some ways I agree with her. If she is evil, then it is men like Cranmer that made her so."

"That's not our concern ... she broke the law and you have done your duty ... it's up to the courts now. Look on the bright side, it's a feather in your cap, and if this doesn't lead to you becoming Detective Inspector Morse I would be very surprised."

"Well I can certainly do with the extra salary, sir."

"That's more like it, man. Maybe you will even spend some of it on a half decent car ... you can't keep borrowing pool cars for the rest of your life."

"Well I do have my eye on a Jaguar, or maybe just get the Lancia repaired ... I can't make up my mind at present, but guess that if promoted I could do either."

"For Christ's sake don't keep that foreign excuse of a car ... get the Jaguar, it'll suit you to a T."

"I think I will wait and see if I get that promotion first."

"You are looking a bit off colour, man. I think you need to go and see a doctor."

"I'm tired, but otherwise fine, sir."

"You don't get my drift do you, man. I mean that you should go and see a doctor this afternoon ... Dr. Sylvia Warren would be my choice, either that or you can hang around here and buy everybody a drink at lunchtime."

"Ah, I see what you mean, sir. Thank you. I do believe the first option sounds the more attractive to me, but I'm sure she won't be at home yet. However, I do need to go and see Susan French and inform her of the latest news."

"Well go and do that then, but for God's sake get yourself out of the office, and enjoy yourself this weekend ... you deserve it."

Morse did not wait to be told a second time, and within minutes he was making his way back to the Headington area of Oxford. He hoped that Susan French would be at home – she was, and opened the door without delay. However, the expression on her face showed that she was far from pleased to see the detective standing there.

"You had better come in. I hope that you haven't come here to accuse me again."

"No, quite the opposite. I have good news in that we have the person who killed Mr. Latimer. I can't give you an identity, but can tell you that they have made a full confession."

"Thank you ... it helps a little, but won't bring Hugo back to me will it?"

"There's also a good chance that you will get the money you lent him as well. The stamps he purchased that loan are due to be sold off at auction within the next couple of months."

"I don't care about the money, Mr. Morse."

"I'm sure you don't, but in the years to come it will be useful to you ... I meant to ask, did Hugo leave a will?"

"Yes, we had made a joint one several months ago ... he left everything to me."

Morse then outlined the story about how the two thousand pounds she had lent Latimer was used to buy back the collection of stamps worth many times that value.

"I knew that Hugo had done something like that for it haunted him ever since Christmas. He said that once the collection was sold that he was going to give all the money back, save for ten percent which he reckoned was fair to keep as commission."

"Yes, I somehow thought that he was going to do something along those lines. It will be up to you now, what you do with the proceeds of the sale."

"I will do as he intended. He was a good man, Mr. Morse, but like most of us tempted by greed, but in the end he saw the error of his ways. He even told me that to make it up to me he was going to sell his own collection, so we would still have enough money to go around the world."

Morse left her not exactly happy, but not in tears either. It was approaching three o'clock and already darkness was falling. He had ample time to drive home and change into his best suit, before picking up Sylvia Warren at six o'clock as they had arranged. If perhaps he was an hour or two early it wouldn't matter – there was a chance that she would be at home, or if not there was a perfectly good public house in which to spend the time. He was on her doorstep shortly after four o'clock, and could see that there was a light on upstairs. Morse rang the doorbell in anticipation, and with some vigour, several times. In his pocket were the two tickets for the *Magic Flute* that he had purchased in London for the following night. He couldn't wait to see the surprise on her face when he gave them to her later that evening over dinner.

Rather sheepishly Sylvia Warren opened the door a fraction. She was dressed only in a long white towelling dressing gown as if she had just come out of the shower, or bath.

"It's you ... but you're not supposed to be here until six."

"Well I'm early ... I can come in can't I?"

"I'd rather you didn't ... please go and come back at six, and ask me no questions I beg of you."

Morse was shocked and confused. Just then another voice, a voice he recognised, came from a man in a matching towelling dressing gown, standing at the top of the stairs on the landing.

"Ah, Morse ... come to check on my alibi for the other night I see ... well you have rather caught me *in flagrante delicto*, with more than my trousers down, I'm afraid. Do you know Dr. Warren, or would you like me to introduce you formally?"

"Not well enough, I'm afraid, Sir Michael, but then do you ever know somebody entirely?" questioned Morse philosophically, to the master of Lonsdale College.

"I'm sorry, Morse ... I really am ... you're a lovely man, really you are." Sylvia Warren looked at Morse with tears in each eye.

"But not lovely enough I gather."

"I tried to warn you ... I have needs Morse, more than most ... I need a man that I don't have to leave notes for begging him to come around, and then wait up all night for him just in case, only to receive a card the next day by way of an apology ... and what is more I need a man who is not afraid to be with me, and doesn't feel that he has to book hotel rooms under false names."

Morse did not know how to react. In the end he did nothing but just stood there, stunned.

Then just to add to his distress she added, "I hope you know that I was falling in love with you ... please remember that if nothing else. Come back at six o'clock and let me explain ... please say that you will come back at six o'clock and forgive me," she pleaded.

"It is I who must apologise, for I only came around to say that I can't make it tonight as I have to go to Shepherd and Woodward to return some items, and then because of the investigation will be working all weekend, and so couldn't see you anyway. I too am very sorry, and hope that you will forgive me ..." and at that point he broke off the conversation and turned away, before his voice cracked to reveal his true feelings.

For the next two hours he wandered aimlessly around Oxford. Not quite without purpose for he did remember to return the scarves he had borrowed to the University outfitters. As the bells at Carfax

Tower struck six o'clock he found himself outside the offices of the *Oxford Mail,* just as Coghlan was leaving for the evening.

"My sources tell me that you got your man, or should I say woman, old boy. Congratulations."

"I see you got yours as well," said Morse pointing at that evening's edition of the newspaper on display in the glass cabinet beside the entrance." The headline read 'COUNCILLOR RESIGNS IN PROPERTY SCANDAL'.

"Don't worry you'll be on the front page on Monday, and before I forget here's the money I owe you. I guess that's why you're here."

He took the notes out of his wallet and placed them with all due ceremony in Morse's hand.

"Now then when are you going to give me that exclusive interview and night out? We're just off now to celebrate the resignation of our councillor friend ... fancy coming?"

"Not tonight if it is also the same to you. However, I will take you out ... in London tomorrow. You can get your exclusive as we travel down on the train ... there's also a boy called Dexter I want you to meet ... you might consider taking him on as an apprentice in a year or two ... he may be what you would call a rough diamond, but he's very sharp and would make a good reporter. He wants to be a writer one day."

"Just give me a clue to how you solved it?"

"Alright ... like Sherlock Holmes I hate coincidences ... so I simply kept looking for a link between the two victims until I found one."

"Is that it? Oh, well, I will see you tomorrow then, old boy."

"By the way you will need evening dress."

"Evening dress ... must be a posh place you're taking me to."

"I just hope you like Mozart?"

If you are interested in **Colin Dexter** and **Inspector Morse,**
Lewis or **Endeavour** then you should join

The Inspector Morse Society

Membership includes:
Endeavour **Newsletter – Special Society Publications**
Meetings – Member Promotions – Free Gifts

For further details send an A5 S.A.E. with 2 x 1st class stamps to:
The Inspector Morse Society, Endeavour House,
170 Woodland Road, Sawston, Cambridge, U.K., CB22 3DX.

Join online at www.inspector-morse.com